ONE TO LEAVE

By Tia Louise

Cover design by Steven Novak
Novak Illustration

To Mr. TL, my only cowboy.

To all my faithful readers,
and to Ilona and Candice for your love and support.

Contents

Prologue 7

Chapter 1: Homecoming 13

Chapter 2: Leaving 29

Chapter 3: Big Sky Country 43

Chapter 4: Where the Wind Blows 37

Chapter 5: New Best Friend 57

Chapter 6: Chinook 67

Chapter 7: Massage Therapy 105

Chapter 8: The Cabin 121

Chapter 9: Layers Deep 149

Chapter 10: Change of Plans 163

Chapter 11: House Guests 173

Chapter 12: Worst Case Scenario 187

Chapter 13: Aftermath 197

Chapter 14: Closure 209

Chapter 15: Fire in the Desert 223

Epilogue: A wedding 243

Acknowledgments 273

About the Author 275

Exclusive Sneak Peek: *One to Protect* 277

Exclusive Sneak Peek: *One to Keep* 289

PROLOGUE

Years ago, behind enemy lines.

The gun felt right in my hand. Heavy and tight. My back pressed against the dusty wall of the stone shelter where we waited, watching.

We were pulling out. It was our last day in the camp, our last day in country. Conflict hadn't ended, but we were handing over the fight to the local military. Still, we were Marines. First in, last out. Our final job was to provide support, watch for any sign of ambush, before we made our way to the airfield.

The majority of our men had gone ahead with the convoy, but I stayed back with our CO. He was a good leader, and we'd been together since the beginning. While I sat on the gritty floor, he stood by the square window staring out at the miles of tan desert. I was pretty sure I knew where his mind was.

Bending my outstretched leg, I rested an arm on top of my knee. "Thinking about home?"

Derek blinked once and looked down before turning steel blue eyes on me. "Eighteen months is a long time with only a week at Christmas."

"Women make you soft, soldier."

His mouth tightened, and I had to laugh at his reaction. I was pretty happy to be headed home myself, even if I didn't have a girl waiting on me.

"You're the only shithead I'd let get away with a crack like that."

Calling each other "soldier" was an ongoing joke between us.

"It's because I'm your best man. You'd have lost an arm without me."

He exhaled a laugh, and I put the butt of my rifle on the floor, wrapping the shoulder strap around my wrist.

"Keep talking, fucknut." His elbow bent, and he pinched his top lip. "I'll be waiting to laugh when a sweet pair of baby blues knocks you on your ass."

"Not happening." Using my gun, I pushed myself to standing. "I'm more of a hazel guy."

Derek's arm dropped, and he smirked. If I was happy, he was three times as glad to be pulling out. Only I'd be back. Being stateside was just a break for me.

I walked over to stand by the window. "This is my life, and it's no kind of life to share."

"Are you questioning my loyalty, Corporal Knight?"

"Not at all, Lieutenant Alexander. You're a great Marine. But guys like you do your time and retire. Go home, get married, have kids."

"You're a lifer."

"Damn straight." I straightened my back to stretch my tired muscles. "Only way I can give one hundred and ten percent is not to have somebody waiting on me."

A shadow moved around the corner of the bungalow across from us, catching my eye.

"My dad was a lifer, and he had a family."

"Mine too. And we both know how shitty it was growing up with them leaving, Moms crying."

Long nights, sitting against the wall staring into darkness, we'd shared just about everything to pass the time, to keep from going insane from the monotony combined with the stress of knowing at any time we could be blown up or shot. We were walking targets, and we'd been lucky.

"You're right," he exhaled, looking away again, out at the sea of beige. "I'm proud of my service, but when the time comes, I'll walk away."

"You've got another road ahead of you." I didn't think any less of him. Some guys in this outfit didn't have the right stuff, the right attitude or the honor, but that could never be said of this guy. "I'm glad we served together."

"Now who's getting soft?" His deep laugh was the last sound I heard before the staccato *clank!* of a grenade dropped into the space with us.

We had seconds, if that long. No time to speak, only time to act. Reaching down, I grabbed it, and threw it as fast and hard as I could. It was just out the window when the *BLAST!* threw us both against the opposite wall.

My back had been curved from the throw, and I hit a bare space. I was winded, but not hurt. Derek was out cold. White smoke filled the room. Our luck had run out, and we were under attack.

Shots fired outside as I made my way through the blindness to where his dark body was slumped on the stone floor.

"*Fuck!*" I shouted. He was as big as me and twice as heavy, but I'd be damned if I left him. With a deep grunt, I hauled him onto my shoulders.

His voice was a groan in my ear. "Stuart. Go on. Go."

"You're not dying today, soldier," I shouted back.

Months of working out and not much else between the explosions and the darkness had me strong as a damn mule. I went up the short flight of steps to the exit. I had no idea what I'd be stepping into when I went through that door, but they knew we were in here. We couldn't stay.

I held Derek steady on my back as I peered into the smoke and dust filling the air. Two bodies in robes right ahead of us. Not Americans. We couldn't do anything for them, but I would do something for us.

A convoy had been preparing to transport the last of us two houses down. If I could make it that far, it was possible we'd be safe. I couldn't see a damned thing as I made a break for it. My thighs burned with the exertion and the extra weight, and my lungs seized from the smoke. Derek was a fucking dead weight on my back, but I barely noticed with the adrenaline pumping in my veins. I was born for this.

Blinking hard, I could just make out the hulking shapes of the armored trucks waiting to take us away.

"We're almost there," I shouted, even though I was pretty sure he was out again.

Taking the first step, I dug in with my heel, trying to gain speed with traction. Combat boots, thirty-seven pounds of weaponry, ordnance, spying shit, and my commanding officer. I ran as fast as I could to the symbol of safety. I was just there when my feet went out from under me. My ears rang with the noise of the explosion, and pain shot like fire through the lower half of my body. I flew forward and landed on my chest in the dirt.

I couldn't stop shaking. It wasn't fear—it was adrenaline combined with the effort I'd been pushing to get us to safety faster. My brain tilted on its side. The trucks were near, but they couldn't see us in all the smoke and confusion. Bodies were running all around us. I needed to get up, but I was dazed.

God dammit! I was made for this. I tried to force myself to get up, but my body didn't respond. I was above myself looking down. Derek lay on my back exposed, unprotected. *What the fuck was happening to me?* I fought against this pansy-assed flake-out. I had to get back down there. I had to carry my brother to safety. I was stronger than this.

Somebody had to see us, but the whole place was in confusion. Another whistling rocket, another explosion. I struggled to open my mouth and yell for backup. Nothing came out. I saw a truck jolt and fly back. It was hit.

Then, like an old-fashioned television switching off, everything blinked to black. I didn't see anything anymore.

CHAPTER 1: HOMECOMING

Nikki

The thread hanging from the hem of my blouse taunted me. I licked my thumb and first finger and twisted it back inside the wrap of my top. I'd tried to have everything perfect. My hair was freshly highlighted, my nails were done, I was waxed *everywhere...* and this one little thread wanted to ruin it all.

Sitting in the terminal, I stared down the long hallway he'd walk up after getting off the plane. I remembered a time when you could wait for friends and loved ones right at the gate, and to be honest, I was a little glad those days were over. I'd need a moment to catch my breath when I saw him again.

Derek and Patrick had both moved to Wilmington a year ago, and the Princeton office of Alexander-Knight, LLC, was set to close. Until now. After six years of steady employment, I was sending out resumes when Stuart asked if he still had a place here. I got the email from Derek to prep his old office right after I got the message asking if I'd be willing to stay on as Stuart's secretary. I couldn't say yes fast enough.

Meeting him at the airport was my idea.

Again my eyes strained down the long hallway leading to the concourse. It was eleven o'clock, and I was one of a small handful of people waiting in the lobby. A woman and a little boy appeared, walking toward me. The boy excitedly skipped and ran ahead. The tired woman tried to keep up with him. Behind them a businessman held a phone and texted as he walked. A break between them, and... No one.

My mind drifted to the last time I'd seen Stuart, three years ago, the night he'd left to go back to Saudi. We'd gone out for a farewell dinner. Derek as usual called it an early night, but the two of us stayed a little later.

Stuart was eager to leave, and it made him uncharacteristically open and chatty. We laughed and shared a few drinks. I could tell he felt good by the way his hazel eyes sparkled. I was in heaven. Three years of working in the same office, dressing up every day, and he'd never shown me this much attention. It washed over me like warm water.

I'd done my best not to look like I was slugging my drink before I asked if he might drive me home. My excuse was I'd drunk too much, and I didn't like cabs. I never dreamed it would work.

That memory made my eyes slide closed as I sat alone on the bench. Stuart was amazing in bed, and his body was unbelievable, lean and lined. Strong—he carried me through the door all the way to the bedroom! His shirt was off in one swipe, and a little squeak escaped my throat at the sight of his lined torso. I couldn't get my dress off fast enough. I sat on the bed in front of him in my underwear, trailing my fingers down the ridges of his stomach.

My bra was off with a flick, and large hands cupped my breasts. He tweaked my nipples into hard little pebbles, rolling them between his fingers... *Oh, god!* I'd quickly lowered his zipper and slid his jeans down.

Heat flared between my thighs when I thought of the lump straining inside his boxer briefs. Delicately, I'd traced the outline of it before lowering the fabric and taking the large, mushroom head into my mouth. He only let me taste him a moment before lifting me and sinking deep inside.

He fucked me hard, and I guess I always suspected Stuart would be rough. It matched his controlled persona. He didn't take shit, and he expected his orders to be followed. I'd walked around feeling it for two days. It was the best fuck of my life.

Mr. Alexander, of course, had no idea I'd slept with Mr. Knight his last night in Jersey. If he had, I was pretty sure I'd have gotten my marching orders the next day. Derek didn't tolerate in-office romances. Patrick, who took his older brother's place at the private investigative firm nearly pushed him to his limit.

A little smile curled my lips. I loved having the younger Mr. Knight in the office. Patrick was flirty and fun, and he changed the mood of everything. When he said he was moving to Wilmington to be with his fiancée Elaine, I nearly cried. Derek was such a slave driver. Six months later, Derek was gone, too. He wanted to be with Melissa. *Why those ladies couldn't move to Princeton…*

Then I saw him.

My stomach flew to my throat at the image striding in my direction. He still had that confidence, shoulders back, perfect posture. A pack was on his back, and he carried a faded brown-leather jacket across his arm. His jeans were loose on his slim hips, but the olive-drab tee he wore stretched tight over his broad shoulders. I could see the cut of his muscles through the fabric, and sheer lust pooled low in my pelvis. I wasn't sure I could stand.

He was almost in front of me, close enough that I could make out the hazel of his eyes, when I pushed to my feet and cleared my throat. "Need a lift, soldier?"

I'd been scolded for calling them that when I'd first started working in the office. At first I was confused. Derek and Stuart called each other "soldier" all the time, but I later found out it was an inside joke. You *never* called a Marine "soldier."

Tonight it made my new boss stop in his tracks. He saw me and at first he seemed confused. I guess he was surprised to see me, although I couldn't tell if he was glad.

"Nikki?" His deep voice hit me like an avalanche. "Derek didn't say you'd be here."

"I figured you could use a friendly face after that long flight." I caught him in a brief hug that filled the air around me with the scent of soap and cedar. Stuart's scent. "I brought the keys and everything you need to get into the office and Derek's old place. Let's get your bags."

"Thanks." A brief smile appeared and disappeared from his face, but it was enough for that damn sexy dimple to pierce his cheek. "I wish I'd known. It's late."

"I don't mind." My voice was soft, and I couldn't bring myself to say I'd help him get readjusted in *every* way if he wanted. I had to let him call the shots. It was how he liked it.

We waited in silence as the baggage claim cycled, as one after another rectangular black pilot-case slowly passed us. I knew we were looking for his standard-issue roll. He always used it.

"So how have you been?" he finally asked.

The jacket was still slung over his arm, the backpack still in place on his shoulder. One hand was in his pocket. He could've been a fucking model, he was so perfect.

Managing a little smile, I nodded. "Good. You?"

He shrugged. "Same."

I tried to think of something more to say. When he left, he'd said he couldn't take sitting in an office all the time. He was born for combat. He missed the desert.

"I was surprised when Derek said you were coming back. How long do you think you'll stay?"

"Haven't decided."

Silence again.

It was always this way with Stuart, thousands of words left unsaid. His pack rolled around, and he lifted it in one easy sweep off the conveyer. My lip caught in my teeth as his biceps flexed, stretching his shirtsleeves. What I wouldn't give to see that body naked again.

"Ready?" I managed to ask.

"Lead the way."

I'd dressed for just such an order. The jeans I wore hugged my ass tight, and my top ended just high enough to give him a good view. A pair of stack heels did the rest of the work for me. *Eat your heart out, Mister Knight.*

No comment.

We got to my car, and he walked around to the back to toss his stuff in the trunk. I waited inside until he joined me. Before we backed out, I handed him an envelope containing a set of keys, a door card, and the passcode for the building.

He only glanced inside. "Is Derek's place still the penthouse he had back in the day?"

"One and the same, and he rented you a Lexus until you've had a chance to buy or lease something. It's parked in his space in the garage."

Stuart exhaled a laugh. "I never could tell if he was showing off with all that shit or if he was really that soft."

"You could afford the same or more if you wanted."

Family money combined with his years of active duty, being single, and what he made in private security had left Stuart with quite the net worth. In the millions the last time I'd snooped, which was three years ago.

"I don't give a shit about glamour."

His lips pressed into a frown, and I let it go. It wasn't much of a conversation anyway. I tried to catch as many red lights as possible on my way into the downtown area, but at this time of night, most of the signals were blinking yellow. We reached our destination far too soon.

"Let me out at the front." He leaned forward to retrieve his jacket, and my brow fell.

"Wouldn't you like me to walk you up? Give you the tour?"

I slowed to a stop at the entrance to the luxury apartment building. A doorman waited inside the glass entrance.

"I'm pretty sure I remember my way around the place."

I couldn't think of a thing to make him invite me inside, but my expression must have told him how I felt. He paused before getting out and leaned toward me.

"Thanks again, Nik. I'll see you tomorrow." A pat on my shoulder, and he was gone, headed to the back of the car to retrieve his bags before disappearing through the glass entrance.

A long exhale escaped my lips, and I started to cry.

* * *

Stuart

Derek's condo was as plush as I recalled. Stainless steel everything in the kitchen, and the living room was decked out with black leather sectionals and a massive flat-screen television. Both bedrooms were identical with king-sized beds, crisp white linens, and similar dark-wood furnishings as in the living room. It was all very masculine and spare, not a single rough-edge in sight.

He was a stand-up guy giving me his old place, but I couldn't stay here. This wasn't my style. Hell, I wasn't even sure I was making the right call coming to Princeton. Nikki meeting me at the airport almost killed the deal.

She was as beautiful as ever, and I knew she'd wanted me to invite her up here tonight. My last night out, I was flying high, and I'd pretty much fucked her senseless. She was a great lay, but it was a huge mistake, especially in view of my current situation. Clearly Derek never found out. *Shit.* He'd be pissed, and he'd be completely justified.

I should've asked if she was still in the office, but it hadn't occurred to me. Not that I was a self-centered prick, I was just preoccupied. It would be hard enough to keep my shit a secret without the complications of a woman sniffing around, and I needed privacy.

My hands started to shake as I stood looking out the wall of windows. Fisting them against the withdrawals, I ordered my mind to *Fight. Fight, dammit!* I was stronger than this. Nothing controlled me. I called the shots.

But I also knew the drill.

Shaking was the tickling whisper of what was to come. The easy greeting before the gut-twisting pain showed up to kick my ass and bring me to my knees. After that came the hot flashes, followed by more blinding cold shakes.

Insomnia... I hadn't slept in days. If I could just get one night's sleep, maybe it would bolster my strength to fight.

Crossing the room, I dug in my backpack for the bottle. Turning it toward the light, I remembered what I'd read. Tapering off was the least painful way to beat this addiction, but every time I opened that bottle, I took more.

Jaw clenched, I told my mind *No*. I came back to grab the reins, to get away from the easy prescriptions and the rationalizations. I was at a turning point, and if I couldn't do it here, I only had one place left to go.

The bottle shook in my hand just before the first cramp twisted my stomach.

"*Fuck*!" I shouted, as my body bent in half. I staggered to the sofa before pushing off and heading to the bathroom.

Cold sweat coated my forehead. In seconds, it would all come out again, but before it did, I twisted off the white cap and dumped the entire contents into the toilet. No going back.

Sitting there, I braced against the pain, every muscle in my body straining so hard, I saw veins. *God dammit. Hold on. I could do this.* It hurt so bad, a hoarse groan scraped through my throat, past my resistance.

Getting up, I went into the kitchen and slammed cabinet doors open. Nikki had stocked the place, but I wasn't after food. Shoving aside boxes of rice, pasta, crackers, another searing pain cut through my stomach, and a loaf of bread hit the floor. I gripped the oven door handle so hard, I thought it would break before I was able to straighten up again.

With a shaking hand, I opened the last cabinet and found the liquor supply. White, brown, golden. She'd bought a little of everything, no doubt expecting to share it with me.

I pulled out a fifth of Crown and threw the purple bag aside before I twisted off the top. I didn't even wince as the whiskey burned through my chest. One big gulp after another, I slid down to the dark hardwoods. I'd sit here and finish it. Then I'd go to the next bottle until I passed out. I didn't have a choice tonight.

* * *

My eyes burned fire as they peeled open and scanned the floor where I lay. I never left the kitchen of my partner's immaculately clean condo last night. It had only taken a fifth of Crown. Easy night. Now my tongue was stuck to the roof of my mouth, and my stomach was more torn up than before.

Shit. I'd never make it to the office this way, but I had to try.

Easing myself up, I held onto the sink before reaching into the cabinet for a glass. The water was so cold and good, I drank two before staggering into the living room, where a phone waited on an end table.

"Walter here!" The aged voice on the line was ready to serve. Clearly, he'd been informed I was moving into Derek's old place.

I'd met him before, of course, and I couldn't count the number of times my partner had mentioned how great he was. Better than a butler, connections in the service industry all over town, I vaguely recalled Walter could get a reservation at any restaurant with any amount of notice.

Food was not on my agenda this morning. "Walter, any chance there's a drugstore in the building?" I sounded like shit.

"Sorry, Mister Knight, but I can send out for something. What do you need?"

Clearing my throat, I looked out at the sun cutting through the long, grey clouds. "I need Imodium."

"I'll have it in less than five. Hang in there, sir."

"And Walter?"

"Yes, sir?"

Squeezing my eyes together, I tried to remember what I'd read. "If they have any of those pain relievers with sleep aid? I've been having trouble sleeping."

"I'll see what I can find."

Dropping the plastic phone on its base, I rubbed my eyes. Spoiled or not, Derek had brains holding onto this place—especially being single. That errand alone made Walter a true asset. I'd shower and put in an appearance at our old firm. It was the least I could do. It was why I'd come back.

* * *

Nikki was at her desk when I pushed through the glass doors. The Imodium had helped my stomach, and I'd taken four of the Advil PMs Walt had included in the discreet brown paper bag. They should hold off the symptoms for a few hours at least.

Blue eyes lit when they met mine, and my hand went straight into my coat pocket to clutch the narrow bottle of painkillers.

"You made it!" She smiled as she rounded the desk, giving me the full view of her body tightly wrapped in a green dress. I remembered why I'd slept with her—I also remembered being sure I'd never come back.

She blinked up at me. "Were you able to sleep last night?"

Was she checking up on me? "I did all right."

My tone was irritated, and her nose wrinkled. "It always takes me a night to adjust to a new place."

Right. *Stop being fucking paranoid, Stuart.* Following her into Derek's old office, I remembered the cabinets full of food. "Hey, thanks for stocking the kitchen."

"I figured you'd be hungry." She touched my arm and leaned forward so that looking down, I had the full view of the dark line between her breasts.

The memory of those in my hands caused a twinge below my belt. Whether I acted on it or not, it was a good sign. The fucking drugs hadn't taken everything.

"I've already set up your computer and the card with how to change your password is on your desk. Let me know if you need a refresher on the phone system."

Clearing my throat, I looked away from her body. "I won't stay in long today. Fucking jet lag."

"Okay!" She gave my arm a squeeze and went to the door. "Come over to my place tonight. A home-cooked meal at dinnertime will help."

Jaw clenched, I tried to think of a reason to say no. I needed to say no. So many reasons to say no filtered through my mind, but I couldn't find an appropriate one to say out loud.

"I'll expect you at six o'clock sharp, Mister Knight." She gave me a wink and twirled out the door.

Yeah, this wasn't going to work.

* * *

Fire blazed in my legs. The pain was so intense, I yelled as hard as I could against it. It didn't matter. Nobody heard me. Explosions blasted all around us, and I couldn't force my body to respond. We were so close, and we weren't going to make it. Our last fucking day, and we were both going to die.

Fuck that. I was born to die for my country, but Derek wasn't. He had Allison and plans for a family. He'd told me about his dreams, and I'd silently vowed to get him out alive no matter what happened. He deserved that.

Strong hands grasped both my arms, roughly pulling me up and dragging me toward the trucks. Looking back, I saw him lying unconscious, unprotected on the desert sand where I'd fallen.

"Put me down!" I yelled, struggling against their grip. "Get him first!"

The loud SLAM! of shrapnel hitting the ground threw us all a foot in the air and jerked me awake.

I sat straight up in the bed shaking in the twilight and gasping for breath. My body was drenched in sweat.

Dropping my head into my hands, pain radiated from my lower back down through my legs. Even sleeping on one of those expensive number mattresses didn't stop the pain of that old injury. Only one thing was strong enough for that...

No.

The clock said five-thirty. Nikki expected me at six. I considered being a dick and pulling a no-show, but that was a coward's way. Staggering across the hall into the bathroom, the shakes were back. *God dammit*, I was a wreck.

In my coat, I found the Advil PM Walter had brought me and took four more along with another Imodium. Seven to ten days is how long they said before the drugs were out of my system. Then I'd be through the worst.

Two weeks.

Until then, I had to fight.

* * *

Nikki's hair was messy and swept over one shoulder, and her green wrap dress was loose on her body, unlike earlier in the day. She'd kicked off her heels, and the whole disheveled thing actually did it for me. An image flickered across my mind of grasping her face and kissing her roughly, tasting those pink lips, but I brushed it aside.

"Come in! I've got chicken and sausage gumbo in the slow cooker. Doesn't it smell amazing?"

A small laugh followed her as she led me into her apartment, where the rich aroma of meat hit me right in the face. A responsive growl from my stomach—another good sign. Appetite gone, I'd been forcing myself to eat for weeks.

"It does smell good."

She walked into the kitchen and took the lid off a pot to give the contents a poke. "I got the recipe online. The aroma's right, but it's supposed to be thicker... I think I made more of a soup." She laughed again. "Gumbo's like soup, isn't it?"

"Sure."

Her mood was so happy, it itched the agitation under my skin. Advil helped with my cramps, but I could tell the shakes were only a half-hour away at most.

The pain radiating from my pelvis down my legs was impervious to everything. My spinal column had been damaged in the blast. It healed, but when the residual pain was at its worst, I couldn't run. It was why I'd been forced to retire.

I'd tried massage therapy, then a chiropractor, but those treatments didn't last. I needed the pain to stop for good so I could return to active duty. Narcotic-based pain relief was the only thing that worked, and I'd had an easy time finding willing doctors to give me scripts, over and over for as long as I wanted.

The pain disappeared, and even the freaking nightmares stopped. For the first time in a long time, I felt peace, like my old self again. It was a miracle drug.

Until it became a nightmare.

She handed me a tumbler of amber liquid. "They were out of Johnnie Walker. I hope Dewar's is okay?"

I nodded and took a sip of the scotch. "You have a good memory."

She held a glass of red wine, and slanted her blue eyes at me. "I remember a lot of things."

I watched her a moment, but I didn't take the bait. "Yeah?"

Her face fell just a click, but she exhaled and took a sip. "Like I remember you hate being cooped up in an office. What brought you back this time?"

The truth? I had to beat this addiction before it killed me... I'd keep that to myself.

"I founded Alexander-Knight with Derek. I should at least try to hold up my end of the agreement." It was a good-sounding lie.

"Patrick's doing a great job holding up the Knight end of the agreement. Have you talked to him?"

"I don't talk to Patrick." The mention of my little brother stirred my agitation even more. "We have nothing in common."

"That's not true. You're both handsome devils." She winked and headed back to the kitchen. "And you should see your little nephew Lane. He's following right in your lady-killing footsteps."

"Right." I took another sip of scotch. "Patrick got some girl pregnant."

"Kenny." She put her wine down and pulled a loaf of French bread from a long paper bag. I watched as she sliced it into thick pieces. "She's just over in Bayville. Maybe you could catch a ride with her next time she goes to Wilmington for a visit."

I had no intention of doing that. "He didn't marry her."

"I think it was the right call." She was now spooning chicken, sausage, and rice into bowls. "They're very different people, and he had already moved on when she told him she was pregnant. You'll really like Elaine."

All this talk about Patrick made my stomach churn. My little brother had always been a fuck-up, and clearly he hadn't matured out of it. I lifted my tumbler and caught the tremor in my wrist. *Fuck.*

"Mind if I use your restroom?" I needed to pop a few more Advil and take a few deep breaths.

"Remember where it is?" She smiled and pointed. "Right down the hall to your right."

Walking quickly down the dark passage, I stepped into the narrow bathroom and locked the door. Flipping the light switch, a loud vent whirred overhead. I took the top off the pain reliever, and *Dammit!* Only one left.

My lips tensed, and I opened the medicine cabinet. Nikki had to have something in here. Shoving aside contact lens solution, mouthwash, deodorant, eye cream, I found a brown bottle with a white top. Some old prescription, I guessed. I turned the small container to read the label, and everything went very quiet. *Percocet.*

Standing in that bathroom, I stared at what I held in my hand several long minutes.

Another turning point.

Another fork in the road.

At that moment, a cramp stabbed my stomach so hard, I barely got the toilet lid up in time to lose all the Scotch I'd just drunk. Nothing else was left. I pushed the lever to flush then turned back to the sink and rinsed my mouth.

Without a thought, I opened that bottle and popped two of the pills. Fuck it. Then I shoved the rest in my pocket and walked out. I didn't even pause as I went through the kitchen.

"I've got to go." It was a shitty thing to do, and I was doing it.

"Wait!" Nikki was understandably shocked. "Stuart— you haven't eaten!"

"My stomach's messed up." I shoved my arm into my overcoat, then the next. "I'm sorry. Thanks for the effort."

I was out the door, headed back to Derek's condo without a backwards glance.

CHAPTER 2: LEAVING

Nikki

The office clock ticked from ten fifty-nine to eleven, and he still wasn't in.

No call, no email, nothing. I'd say it wasn't like him, but since he'd returned, I didn't know what to think. Everything about his behavior was strange, from our meeting in the airport to his abrupt departure before dinner with no explanation, to this.

The airport thing I chalked up to my surprise appearance. I should've known that was a bad idea. Stuart never liked surprises — but I didn't regret it. The memory of him walking toward me in that airport... He was still so sexy.

I thought of his hands, long and elegant as he held the tumbler. It was all I could do not to make a sound as his lips parted to reveal straight, white teeth. He was a shade darker than Patrick, but they both had those hazel eyes. Stuart's always burned with his drive, his focus, but I caught a peek of something else in them last night. Something haunted.

Standing, I paced around my desk into Derek's old office, where he should be. If he was suffering, I wanted to help him. I wanted to nurse him back to health. I'd hoped last night...

Exhaling a sigh, I thought about how different I'd hoped our dinner date would go. I'd hoped it would end with me blissfully entwined with his muscular body. Maybe it wouldn't have been as wildly passionate as our first time, but I'd take whatever version of Stuart he'd give me.

Fifteen more minutes. Maybe I should go to the condo and check on him. He'd been so serious about rejoining the firm. What had he said? He wanted to hold up his end of the agreement with Derek? It didn't make sense for him not to show up or call... or email.

If it were Patrick playing hooky, I wouldn't give it a second thought. He'd most likely waltz in the next day with one of his cases closed, but Stuart was different. He didn't go missing without a word.

Chewing my lip, I wished one of the guys was still here to check on him. As it was, my dropping by would be a bridge too far. I'd already gone after him twice. Still, he'd said his stomach was bothering him. He could have a virus, and nobody would know. He could be too weak to pick up the phone. He could dehydrate...

Another ten minutes passed, and I decided I'd try getting lunch. If he didn't come in tomorrow, and I didn't hear from him, I'd call Derek. He could casually check in without making it sound like I'd tattled.

Where are you, Mister Knight?

* * *

Stuart

The pickup rumbled down the highway in the direction of Bayville. I needed to get away, but I had one errand to do before I left. Just in case I never came back.

After I left Nikki's, I went back to Derek's place and tore through a bender. When I opened my eyes again, two days had passed. I was sitting on the bedroom floor with an empty bottle of Belvedere, an empty prescription bottle, and the few mementos from after my dad died in the line of duty. As the oldest son and the only Marine to follow in his footsteps, Mom had given them to me.

With bleary eyes, I studied his medal of honor and the assorted badges he'd earned for exemplary service, the flag he'd fought to defend, and then I looked at what I'd become. My own career cut short, I'd slowly devolved into this. A shame to his legacy, a black mark on everything he'd done. Chips cashed in, I only had one last thing to try. If that didn't work…

Kicking my ass off the floor, I pushed through the headache and the hangover to the shower. For a while I stood under the warm spray and let it bring me back to life. After that, I dried off and dressed in dark jeans and a long-sleeved, white button-down. It would do for this errand.

A quick login to the firm's server gave me the address I needed. I considered calling Nikki, but immediately dismissed that notion. She'd ask too many questions, and it'd be easier if I sent her an email. Or nothing. I hadn't decided. I didn't want people following me.

I threw all my shit into my pack and grabbed the keys to the rental. I had to return it since I was leaving the state, but I had money to buy something. It was more the delay associated with going through the process. I stopped in a used car dealership and bought a late-model, black pickup. Once I finished in Bayville, I'd drive it as far as Cleveland and fly the rest of the way to Montana.

I thought about my plans. Dad's Medal of Honor should be with someone who deserved it. Lane was a baby, but maybe one day he'd do a better job carrying on our family legacy. I'd shot that privilege straight to hell.

The Jungle Gym was nicer than I expected from the tagline "Where the wild things are." I expected it to be a bunch of MTV reality-show bad actors, since that was what this area was infamous for. Instead I found a decent-sized, respectable gym.

Someone spoke, but I didn't acknowledge them. I was checking out the establishment when I said, "I'm looking for Kendra Woods. She goes by Kenny."

"I'm Kenny." The voice came from a tiny girl behind the counter. She was dressed in black and had enormous blue eyes.

Her appearance didn't make sense, and I said what I thought. "I expected someone older."

"I'm twenty-six, and you are...?"

She was pissed, but I couldn't imagine my little brother having a baby with this person. She was not his usual leggy blonde. Nikki's comment about them being very different echoed in my mind. Still, apart from the purple hair, she was cute in a waifish sort of way. Her eyes were a definite plus.

"I'm Stuart Knight. You know my brother Patrick. May I speak to you alone? It's about my nephew."

A tremor moved through my torso, and I reached up to rub the back of my neck. I needed to relax, but my action seemed to put her on guard. Probably all of this had her on guard, which wasn't my intention.

Resistance stiffened her back. "We can talk here. Mariska's my best friend."

The person behind her stepped forward, and for a second, my control slipped. A pair of hazel eyes exactly like the sunset in the place I was headed struck me. Then her cheeks blushed a shade of pink...

"Hello," I said, watching her.

"Would you like a smoothie? I make them myself, right over there." She turned and pointed to the other end of the bar, and her chestnut hair swayed in long waves down her back. I imagined lacing my hands in those soft waves, pulling her head against my shoulder... "It'll give you some privacy while you talk."

"Thank you." I looked down to break the spell, but my eyes caught on the sway of her ass as she crossed to the other side of the space. Small and perky, I wanted to see the mark of my hands on it.

Clearing my throat, I focused on Kenny. "I didn't mean to frighten you. I have something for Lane." I took out the medal wrapped in a piece of heavy black cloth and paused as she crossed to my side of the bar. "It's my father's distinguished service award. It was given to me when he died. I need you to give it to Lane as the first grandson when he's older."

Concern flooded her blue eyes, and I could tell she was smart. That's when it all clicked. Patrick was a sucker for smart chicks.

"Are you ill?" She touched my arm carefully. "Do you want me to call Patrick?"

"No. I don't want my brother involved."

My voice was sharper than I intended, and another tremor tickled at my neck. I was losing patience. I needed to get out of here and to a drug store. I was about to pay for that fucking bender, and it was going to hurt like hell.

But Mariska was back. "On the house." She held some kind of beverage. "It's full of lavender and blueberry. It'll help you relax."

Just looking at her beautiful eyes seemed to help me relax, and her cheeks blossomed with that rosy glow. My gaze dropped to her full, pink lips, and a force inside me pulled. It didn't make sense, but I wanted to explain why I couldn't stay with her, why I couldn't take her with me.

"I have to go," is all I said.

"Where will you go?"

"My uncle has a place out west where I can breathe. It's a place where I usually find peace."

Fuck. Why did I tell her that?

"Please let me call Patrick," Kenny interrupted.

"Do *not* call my brother. I don't want to see him." My tone sent her back to afraid, but I couldn't help it. I was barely fighting off the withdrawals, and her insistence pissed me off.

I went straight to the door and was just about to push through it when Mariska ran up to stop me. She was taller than her friend, but smaller than me. Her skirt swayed around her slim hips with her movements.

"You forgot this." She touched my hand before holding out the cup.

Her skin was cool against mine, and I wanted to pull her against my chest. Memorize the feel of her body, take a deep inhale of her hair so I knew her scent. I wanted to watch her as I drove deep between her thighs, see how the light changed in those beautiful eyes. I wanted to hear the sounds she made when she came.

But it was more than sexual desire I felt. Her touch, the sound of her voice, did something to me. It filled my head with images of morning light breaking over her skin. Time passing in her arms. Her stomach round with my baby.

Jesus. It was coming off the fucking drugs is what it was. I needed to get out of here, to Uncle Bill's. If I couldn't get it together there, none of this mattered. Besides, I didn't know anything about this woman. Correction, this *girl*. Up close, I could tell she was at least ten years younger than me.

"Thanks," I said and pushed through the door.

* * *

Bill met me at the airport. I'd made it to Cleveland on Imodium and ibuprofen then I'd left the truck in the parking garage and boarded a five-hour flight to Great Falls, bolstered mainly by Benadryl and alcohol.

Bill was my dad's younger brother, and like father, like son, they'd never gotten along. Still, my uncle had always been good to his nephews. He was someone I could talk to when my old man didn't have anything to say to us. I rarely had much to say myself, but when I did, I expected someone to listen to me besides our mother.

I remembered my dad saying once Bill was an alcoholic. At the time I was too young to know what that meant, but from my father's tone of voice, it sounded on par with being a murderer.

Bill conquered those demons years ago, and after, he'd owned a home in Arizona that Patrick and I visited every summer — minus our parents — and now this horse ranch in Montana. It wasn't a functioning ranch, but he liked to keep a few horses on it. It was the only place I could remember ever feeling quiet, and Bill was the only person besides Derek who I'd ever felt like I could trust.

When I saw him at the airport, despite how tightly I was wound fighting all the symptoms with everything I had, the tension eased a bit.

"Boy, you look like shit." He caught me around the neck in a hug.

"I feel like shit," I confessed, pressed against his shoulder.

He let me go and passed a hand over his mouth under his thick, grey mustache as brown eyes evaluated me. His matching steel-grey hair was slightly long and swept away from his face, and his leathery skin was lined. Bill was as tall as me, and about as slim. I guessed we had the same build. He took what I said as seriously as I meant it.

"You've come to the right place." With a nod, he started walking and I followed. "Winter's barreling in, but the old timers say we've got a Chinook coming this year."

"Think they're right?" We went from the baggage claim out to his old blue Ford. Tossing my roll in the back, I was in the cab slamming the metal doors before I got my answer.

"They usually are."

"I only remember one since you've lived here."

"There's been a couple. Could last a day, might last longer. Either way, it'll make everything downright tolerable for a little while."

It would be an unexpected gift. We headed down the two-lane dirt road out into the middle of nowhere— exactly where I wanted to be. I wasn't planning to lean on him. I wasn't planning to ask anybody to help me out of the mess I'd made, but it was nice knowing I had someone close by who'd been there. Someone who loved me. It was the shit withdrawals making me weak, but it was how I felt.

We drove most of the way in silence, and I held on through the growing pain and nausea. I had more sleep aids and Imodium in my pack. It was going to be a helluva night, but I'd make it through this. What came after that, I hadn't decided yet.

"You can take the east wing of the house if you want." Bill said, once we were at the sprawling ranch. His expression was calm, but I knew he had a read on me. He wouldn't crowd, which I appreciated. "You know Winona. She'll be in tomorrow morning to cook. After supper, she heads back to her place in Black Eagle."

"Thanks." I nodded, not bothering to say I hadn't felt like eating in weeks. "And thanks for taking me in. I can't tell you—"

"Then don't."

We exchanged a nod, and I headed to my room, preparing to face the night.

* * *

Derek

Stuart was missing.

He'd only been back... *shit*, a week? Nikki called last night to say he'd stopped coming into the office. When she checked with Walter, he'd left the condo without a word.

He wasn't acting like himself, she said. What the hell did she know about how Stuart acted? He was my partner, and I hadn't even had a chance to talk to him. I had no idea what was going on with him, and now here I was, lying in the bed with my beautiful Melissa curled against my side not able to sleep for worrying about a man who was fucking as close to me as a brother. *Dammit, Stuart. What the hell?*

I'd been surprised when he'd wanted to come back. After his injury, he had to leave active duty, but my idea of us starting our own firm hadn't satisfied him. To his credit, he stuck it out for years, but the pace was too slow for him. He needed action—I understood that. It was who he was. So he did Middle East private security a while.

Still, even the most fulfilling work has a season, and I'd never deny his place at Alexander-Knight. Even though his little brother was far more suited for the job.

Shit, I'd have to get Patrick in on this. Those two got along like oil and water, but of the three of us, he was the best at tracking people down.

Melissa stretched and sighed in her sleep, and warmth stirred my insides. I cherished few things in life, but at the top of the list was the way she moved against me when she slept. I'd told her I wouldn't leave her again after Princeton, and now I might have to break that promise.

37

Her voice was thick when she spoke. "Are you having trouble sleeping?"

I reached down and smoothed a lock of dark brown curls away from her face. Her eyes were still closed. "Just thinking about Stuart."

She sniffed and rose up, wrapping her slim arms around my neck. "Why are you thinking about Stuart?"

Her bare breasts were against my chest, and I couldn't deny the rise that provoked. It was morning, after all, and images of last night drifted through my memory. Why she was only wearing panties. "He's apparently gone off the grid."

Sapphire eyes filled with concern, so beautiful. "Is he in trouble?"

"Don't know. I haven't talked to him." Kissing her brow, I moved my hand up her side until I could slide a thumb across her tightening nipple. I didn't want to think about Stuart right now or possibly having to leave her.

"You don't seem too worried about him."

I kissed the line of her jaw, feeling her smile. That smile was just the beginning of what I had in mind. "Worrying won't help anything. I'll take care of you and call Patrick in a little while."

My mouth moved down the length of her neck. I spun her around and pulled her back firmly against my chest. She let out a little squeal.

"Do I need to be taken care of?"

My hand continued down her stomach, lower, until I found the edge of her panties. Pushing them down and off, my fingers explored the cleft between her thighs, locating that little bud hidden in the folds. Her head dropped back, and she let out a low, *Mmm...*

"Always." My middle finger took a dip, and she made another little noise. She was already wet. "You tasted so good last night," I whispered. "Open for me."

Her thighs parted, and I slid into her from behind. God, it was the most amazing thing—hot, clenching. Her fingers rose and threaded into my hair as I kissed the side of her neck. Another little noise, a shiver. Looking down, I watched her breasts spilling over my forearm, rising with her gasps, as I held her tight against me. The sight was hypnotic.

"Your body is so beautiful." My lips were close at her ear, and I kissed her beachy-rose scented hair. "I love the way you smell." Circling harder on her clit, I hit her deeper from behind. Another noise and her insides clenched. My eyes squeezed shut. "The way your pussy holds me... You make me so hard. Just thinking about you—"

"Derek!" She squeezed my hand between her legs, where I rubbed her faster.

"Make that sound." It was a low command. She whimpered in response. "I want to remember how you feel on my dick."

"Oh, god!" She was getting close, and her ass bucked against my pelvis, pumping my shaft inside her. *Shit*, I was even closer. *Hold on...*

"Are you coming?" My voice strained. Nodding fast, her fingers curled tight, pulling my hair.

"Please don't stop..." she gasped. Her hips bucked faster and all at once she strained then broke into trembling, a little cry came from her lips, and her insides pulled me.

It was more than I could take. Changing positions, I braced her hips and rocked hard into her. I needed to go all the way, pull her closer as I came. She moaned against the mattress. It was so good.

Two more deep thrusts, and my orgasm shattered through my pelvis. I held her, my eyes closed, savoring the intensity of this moment with the woman I loved more than my soul.

A deep exhale, and I rolled us together onto our sides, wrapping both my arms around her waist and burying my face in her hair. Her hands slid down my arms until our fingers entwined, and we held each other through the whispers of afterglow.

All those nights in the desert, all those conversations. I never could get Stuart to see how great a wife, a home could be. Now he was pulling me away from mine.

I softly kissed the top of Melissa's shoulder, and she struggled to get free, so she could turn and face me. Sliding closer, she wrapped her arms around my neck, and our bodies touched everywhere, shoulders to chest to hip to knee, even our noses met—just before she kissed my lips. I pushed her onto her back and parted them, sweeping my tongue inside for a deeper kiss that earned me another little noise.

My lips moved to her cheek, and I held myself over her. "Stuart wouldn't be lost if he had this."

Reaching up, she held my face, lightly tracing her thumbs over my cheeks. "Aren't you the same age? And he's never had a serious relationship?"

My brows pulled together as I thought about it. "If so, he's never told me. I mean, he can get laid whenever he wants, but he never lets it go far. He says women are a distraction."

Blue eyes narrowed. "How many distractions did you have in the service?"

That made me laugh, and I moved to lie beside her. "None. I was with Allison, and then... I guess I shared his opinion for a while. Until you."

Those dark years after my first wife died seemed so far away now that I had Melissa and Dex. When the cancer took Allison so cruelly and so fast, I turned to stone, my heart a ball of rage and bitterness. I'd done my duty to God and country and came home planning a long life with my wife, starting a family, building a home. She was gone before we ever even had the chance.

When I met Melissa, everything changed. She was beautiful and kind and strong and so sexy. She soothed the anger in my heart. She healed me with her love, and she gave me a son. I could remember my past, of course, but it made my present so much more precious.

She rolled up beside me. "I love you."

"I love you more." I smiled, touching her cheek, and she continued.

"So what does all of this mean for us? What are you thinking?"

My eyes went back to the ceiling. "I might have to leave you for a bit if he needs help."

"Derek! He's a grown man." She fell back on the bed, arms crossed, and it was my turn to prop up beside her.

"He saved my life, Mel. If he's in trouble, I have to be there for him."

"Doesn't he have a family?"

"His dad was killed in the service. It's just his mom, Patrick, and their little sister Amy." With a big sigh, I rolled onto both elbows, onto my stomach. "Amy's a college kid, and he'd rather punch Patrick in the face than take help from him."

"Sounds like a prick."

I couldn't help laughing again. "I know you love Patrick, but I had that initial response to him myself."

"Patrick is one of the good guys. If you can't see that—"

"Settle down, I can see that. He might color outside the lines, but he manages to turn it around and come out on top. He's a good man."

That satisfied her. She smiled and relaxed her crossed

arms, I reached out and pulled her against my side. "It's more than an obligation. I want to be there for Stuart. You'd feel the same way if it was Elaine."

She couldn't argue with that, so we were quiet a moment. A tiny squeal from down the hall broke the silence, and we both grinned. I was out of the bed first, heading down the hall without bothering to grab underwear.

Of course, Mel catcalled after me. "Holy shit! Check out that rear view!"

Dammit again. Stuart had better have a good reason for pulling me away from this.

CHAPTER 3: BIG SKY COUNTRY

Patrick

Sunset in Montana is one of the greatest sights in the world. I looked out my window at the golden pinks and oranges just beginning to touch the horizon. The ground was so flat, it made the sky seem to go on forever.

"I've got to get Elaine out here," I said under my breath as Derek and I taxied into the Great Falls airport in a small, private jet. I hadn't been to Uncle Bill's place since I graduated high school, and I'd honestly forgotten how much I loved it here.

"We've got to take care of your brother first." Derek's tone was as irritated as it had been since we'd started our search.

It hadn't taken long to track down a credit card transaction in Bayville, and Kenny was quick to point us here. Or I guess her friend Mariska was. I only paused a moment to remember the girl's unexpected interest in Captain Asshat, my not-so-affectionate nickname for the guy who lived to bust my balls. Now he had us running all over the country searching for him.

"Either way, winter's way too cold for what I have in mind." It involved me, Elaine, an Indian blanket, and nothing else — except possibly a bottle of wine.

"Hopefully we can get some answers and head on back. Your uncle didn't give us much to go on."

We weren't just running after him like a couple of old ladies. Stuart wasn't returning any of our calls, emails, or texts. I was willing to bet he'd flushed his phone down the toilet, knowing his aversion to communication.

When I'd called Uncle Bill, he said he gave him a wide berth to work out his issues, but he'd gotten worried when Stuart took off for the little cabin out on the plain and hadn't come back.

"Bill's too old to be running around playing nursemaid. Stuart knows better than to do him like that."

Derek's lips tightened, and I could tell he was equally worried. "Unless he didn't have a choice."

We took our bags, thanked the small crew, and walked through the terminal to the parking lot. I knew he was concerned about my brother. I also knew his thoughts were on Melissa.

"You don't have to stay. Once we know what's happening, you can go back to Wilmington."

His eyes cut to me. "More like you can."

It was true. Captain Asshat would rather die than come across as weaker than me. "How about we just play it by ear."

Bill had left a truck for us in the PJ lot. It had enormous, ridged tires and was perma-frost ready. Winter hadn't set in yet, but I knew how bad it could get in another month. My hope was we wouldn't have to stay that long.

Many miles down a lonely road heading way out of town, and we were at the ranch. The sun was low as we stepped onto the wood porch, but I couldn't stand and admire it. Derek wanted answers, and he wanted them now.

The house was designed in a U shape, with the kitchen and living areas in the middle and two long wings. The east and west sides were identical, each with two bedrooms that shared a bath and two suite rooms.

Across the yard from the house was a large barn with ten stables and a paddock off to the side.

Bill was in the kitchen when we made our way in. He caught me in a big hug.

"You're filling out, boy!" He squeezed my shoulder. "You've got some muscle in there. Leftover from your military days?"

I laughed, thinking about all the ways I'd avoided exercise in the Guard. "Nah, this guy got me started working out."

Derek's irritation eased enough that he cracked a grin at our greeting. "Derek Alexander," he said, stepping forward to shake my uncle's hand.

"Good to meet you, Derek. Bill Knight." My uncle nodded and shook back. "Stuart mentioned you a few times. You served together in the Marines?"

"I was his commanding officer." He looked out the window at the darkening sky. "If you don't mind, I'd like to try and see him tonight."

Uncle Bill took a deep breath, which put me on alert. On the phone he'd said Stuart had taken off, but now I could see there was more to the story than he'd told us.

"I don't know if I can let you do that, son." His hands went into his pockets. "I kind of gave my word to let him have his space."

"What's going on, Bill?"

My uncle's lips puckered, but Derek broke the silence. "I appreciate we're putting you in an awkward position, but I've left my job and my family to come here. I'd like to see for myself he's at least alive."

Bill nodded. "I think you might be the only one he'll see right now."

"I'm not losing sleep over it. I'll show Derek the way and head on back here."

That struck a deal, and I led my partner out to the barn where eight horses were housed in separate stables. Bill showed us the tack room, and we went inside to grab bridles and blankets. We'd be back for saddles.

"Take Dakota and Cheyenne," he said, pointing to a pair of Saddlebreds looking curiously over their stalls. "They're the easiest to handle. How long has it been since you've ridden a horse?"

Rubbing my chin, I thought about the question. "When was the last time I was here?"

My uncle shook his head and preceded me into the small area. "Hand me that bridle, and I'll get her ready."

"I remember how to do that much." Still I stood back and let him slide the leather straps over Dakota's ears and ease the silver bit between her teeth.

"Dakota's a good mare. That Appaloosa Freckles spooks easy. Watch out for her."

Derek was already carrying a saddle from the tack room. "You almost ready?"

I grinned back. "I never took you for a cowboy."

"I've been around a few horses."

Minutes later, we walked the tall, dark-brown mares out, and I was glad I'd worn jeans. Looked like we were fast-tracking this recovery operation.

"Cabin's due west." I threw my leg over Dakota's back, and gave the reins a gentle flick. We'd be there in ten minutes at an easy gallop.

* * *

Stuart

Sitting out by the small campfire I'd built, I watched the sky gradually turn from blue to burning orange, pink and amber, stretching for miles away from me. It was beautiful, and it signaled the start of the worst. The days were hard, but the nights were unbearable.

I'd been here a week, and I couldn't tell if anything had changed. Two years of escaping the pain and the nightmares had left me with an opium addiction the size of that big sky, but this was where I'd see if I could climb out of the shit hole I'd dug. It was the only place outside the desert I loved.

The fire popped, and I stared at the orange flames licking around the edges of the wood the way the first of the night's tremors licked at the edges of my legs. They'd moved from my hands to my lower extremities, and I wanted to believe it meant they were on the way out. Next stop my feet, then gone. At the same time, I remembered reading about restless legs and withdrawals. I was most likely holding onto false hope.

I'd drunk the last of the whiskey. Tonight it would just be the campfire and me facing the monster. The stars, my horse Ranger, and getting through this night. I'd have been lying if I'd said I wasn't nervous. Darkness growing, the sound of hoof beats was not what I expected to hear.

Looking up, I saw Cheyenne and Dakota headed across the flat landscape in my direction. I couldn't make out who was riding them, but considering I was AWOL and my slip in Bayville, I was pretty sure I could guess. Damn females and their big mouths.

The horses slowed as they got closer. One dropped back, but the other kept coming. A few paces more, and I recognized Derek pulling up at the side of the cabin. He swung a leg off, dropped the reins, and walked straight to where I sat watching him. His pace was either determined or angry. Or both.

Once he'd reached the fire, he stood for a moment and simply looked at me. His brow clutched, and I could tell he was sizing up the situation, trying to decide where to begin. I didn't feel like waiting.

"You're a pretty good rider." It was a less adversarial greeting than my first choice, the obvious, *What the hell are you doing here?*

"My mom thought it was a good skill for kids to learn." He continued standing, watching me from the other side of the orange glow until finally, after a few long moments, he spoke again. "Are you sick?"

My eyes went to the fire, and I thought about his question. I was pretty sick, but not in the way he meant. "No."

The flames danced hypnotically on the wood, but instead of soothing, they were the soundtrack of my wrecked nerves—crackling and spreading fever from the middle of my back across my shoulders, down and up my injured spine. I tried rubbing my face, but it only made the pain worse. I wanted to be alone.

"You should head on back to the ranch," I said. "Cabin's only got one bed."

He didn't move. "You planning to stay out here all night?"

"I don't know." Truth was, I didn't know what to expect from this night. I'd considered taking Ranger and riding until we ran out of ground to cover, but my back wouldn't tolerate riding that long. *Dammit.*

"We'll just take it as it comes, then. Won't be the first night we've had to share close quarters."

I started to argue, but a cramp seized my insides. I tried to play it off, but it grew harder. I had to pull a knee up and brace myself until it passed. My eyes squinted shut, and I pressed my fingers against them holding on as hard as I could to avoid yelling. *Fuck*, if I was alone, I could yell as loud as I needed.

Hold on.

Five...

Four...

Three...

Two...

...

The pain didn't stop, but it backed off enough for me to breathe. I opened my eyes, and Derek was gone. *What?*

I blinked a few times wondering if I'd hallucinated the whole thing. Scanning the horizon, which was only a sliver of light now, I found him. He'd walked back to the other rider. They had a short conversation, and then whoever it was turned and headed back the direction they'd come.

Looked like my partner was staying the night.

* * *

Derek

God dammit, Stuart looked like hell. His skin was pale and his eyes had dark circles under them. He'd lost weight. If I had to guess, I'd say he hadn't slept in days. I couldn't be sure what was going on here, but I'd seen withdrawals before. It looked like my partner was coming off a long run of some powerful shit. Only I didn't know what or why.

"Head on to the house," I told Patrick, who'd followed my order to stay on his horse. He might not like his older brother, but the concern lining his face said he still loved him.

"What is it?" His voice was low.

"I'm not sure, but it looks like he's coming off something."

My younger partner's eyes moved back and forth. "Coming off something? As in related to his injury?"

"Could be. Either way, I'm staying. Head back and get the truck and bring us supplies. He needs painkillers and a bottle of whiskey. Make that two bottles. See if you can find us some food, and bring any clean clothes in his room."

Patrick nodded and turned his horse before heading back to the ranch at a gallop. The last of the horizon was disappearing fast, and a blast of what looked like a million stars scattered over our heads. This was it. Big Sky country. It was beautiful, and we were in no position to enjoy it.

Turning, I took a deep breath and headed back to the campfire. The closer I got, I saw Stuart leaning forward, face in hands. He was hurting bad, and he was proud. I'd have to work with him through this. He wasn't going to take help from anybody.

"I've got supplies coming," I said, pretending not to notice how hard his muscles were flexed. "Supper, clean clothes, pain killers. Whiskey."

He let out a grunt in response, and I figured that was all he could manage. I didn't expect an answer, but after a few moments, he took a deep breath and eased himself straight again. "Who was that with you?"

"Patrick."

His didn't speak, but I knew he was pissed. For a little bit, the only sound was the crackling of the last piece of wood on the fire. I looked around and saw a decent-sized pile of wood freshly chopped and stacked near the cabin. I went over to grab a few logs to throw on it. It was good to see he'd been exercising.

The cabin was small. I guessed it was used for a shelter when the winter came and hands needed to be out in this part of the territory. A quick glance through the window showed Stuart's things scattered around, but mostly, I noticed the overturned furniture.

I walked back and threw the wood onto the bright orange coals. "I haven't seen you since you've been back. I wondered if you changed your mind."

His hand passed over his mouth, and he nodded. "It probably wasn't the best idea to go to the office."

No more beating around the bush. "Looks like you're dealing with some serious shit here."

His arm dropped, and he made a fist before unclenching it. "That old injury was giving me problems."

A million other things would have hurt less than that. I knew he didn't mean it, but that old injury tied me directly to what was happening here. He saved my life when it happened, and the damage to his back had sent him home with a purple heart and an honorable discharge. It was the worst thing that could've ever happened to him, and guilt stung in my chest.

"This looks like more than just your back."

Quiet filled the space again. It wasn't clear if he wasn't answering my question or if he was thinking about what to say. Stuart had never been overly talkative.

We watched the fire pop until he spoke again. "Remember that time we had tower duty, and we had to stay awake all night?"

Rubbing my hand over my eyes, I thought of all the shit we'd been through the two years we'd served together. "Seems like we had more than one of those."

"You told me about being a kid and getting through the scary times with your dad." His elbow bent and he rubbed his eyes. "You said something like... you imagined the two of you doing your favorite thing together? You would think, the next time you saw him that was what you'd do?"

I'd only told two people that story. The other was home with my son. "Yeah, I remember that."

He stared at the fire again, not speaking. I wondered why he'd brought it up.

"When Patrick and I were kids, we had a pain test. It was mostly tough guy shit, the worst pain you could endure." He waited a moment, and so did I.

"The pain in my back and legs wasn't the worst pain. I could endure that. I got through it by imagining me back in the shit. Once I'd recovered, I'd go back to doing what I loved. Fighting, serving, defending—what I was born to do."

He'd never said this much to me, and I was afraid it was because he was giving up. He'd reached the end. I wouldn't let him do that. We had to find a way back from this.

He stared at the fire, never once looking up at me. He only paused a moment to take a breath. I couldn't tell if he was hurting physically, but it looked like he was straining against some level of pain. When he spoke again, his voice was rough. "You never said what to do when the thing you were hoping for was taken away."

It was a question I'd been asked before. It was almost the exact thing Melissa had said the day she'd shown up in my office after finding my email to her abusive ex-husband Sloan. It was a question I'd asked myself when Allison died. I knew the answer, but I wasn't sure he was ready to hear it yet.

He pulled a knee into his chest, and I watched helpless as he clutched against whatever force tormented him.

"Two years ago, I started the meds. Narcotics. They took away the pain... all of it. From both injuries."

"Two years is a long time."

"I can beat this." Veins showed in his arms, and his voice broke. "I hope."

His hand went over his squinted eyes, and for a moment, he only held on. I wasn't sure how much longer he could endure. *Where the fuck was Patrick?*

He took a breath, and I did as well. I was fucking holding my breath. *Shit.* I hadn't done that since Melissa had given birth to Dex. She'd insisted on no drugs, and I'd nearly lost it watching her suffer through labor.

My back was turned, and the pain must've passed because he spoke in a haggard voice. "I'm proud I was able to save your life. You were a life worth saving, and I did what I was born to do—serve, protect. *God dammit!*" He clutched again, and I pushed against my legs, pacing in front of the fire and straining my eyes into the dark night.

Far away, I saw two points of light, and it was like the fucking cavalry. "Hang on," I said. "Relief is coming."

The points grew larger until the noise of the truck drowned out the quiet. I hustled over to the cabin. Patrick parked on the opposite side, and I went around to help him unload.

"How's he doing?" Patrick's brow lined as he helped me carry in food, clothes, and the other supplies I'd requested.

"Not good." Inside, I picked up the table and set it on its feet. Next I straightened the chairs.

Patrick put a cardboard box on the counter. "Sorry it took a while. Bill's a recovering alcoholic, so he didn't have whiskey in the house." He handed me a brown bag. "I had to drive into town to get it, but I figured you needed it the most."

I nodded and took it from him. "You made the right call."

"Any idea what's behind all this?"

I thought about how much I should tell him. Stuart's pride wouldn't want Patrick knowing everything, at the same time, Patrick had a right to some version of the truth. "He took being discharged harder than I knew."

"No shit, he'd been preparing for that gig his whole life."

I paused a moment. Patrick was smarter than either of us gave him credit for being, but I was catching up. "So you knew it was a pretty significant blow?"

"Look, Stuart's a dick, but I grew up with that asshat. He lost his identity when they put him to pasture."

"Your brother was a great Marine." I put the dinner plates they'd prepared for us in the refrigerator and grabbed two cups out of the cupboard to go with the liquor. "He saved my fucking life."

"Hey, man, I get it. You two have that bond of brotherhood. Forged under extreme pressure." Patrick leaned against the counter, crossing his muscled arms over his chest. He was the image of Stuart the last time I'd seen him — bright, thoughtful, strong. I had to help him get back to that.

"He seemed to like working in private security."

"Are you kidding me?" Our younger partner laughed. "It's nowhere near the adrenaline rush of being on all the time. Stuart lived for that shit."

I nodded. "It's true."

The weight of what was happening here warred inside me, pushing against my commitments at home. Stuart was dealing with withdrawals, but more than that, he was facing demons that would go on after he'd beaten the physical pain. I couldn't stay with him that long, but I wouldn't leave him to suffer alone.

"Thanksgiving is in another week. I'll talk to Mel and stay here until then, but I need to be with her and Dex for the holiday."

Patrick nodded. "I can stay. Elaine is out of school, and I'm sure she wouldn't mind coming out here for the break."

"What about Lane?"

"Kenny takes him to Bayville for Thanksgiving. They do a family reunion-type thing."

Nodding, I looked back toward the fire. "You don't mind hanging around here?"

"Look, Stuart's my brother. If he's in trouble, I'm staying."

"Sounds like a plan."

CHAPTER 4: WHERE THE WIND BLOWS

Mariska

Pain. Burning. Explosions. All around me is confusion and yelling. The bright beige of the desert contrasts sharply against the dark green and brown of the armored vehicles, and figures in white robes and sand-colored fatigues rush by without stopping.

I can't control what's happening, but I've got to complete this mission. I've got to get him to safety. Someone grabs my arms and drags me roughly away. A whistle grows louder from above, then BOOM!

We're all lifted a foot off the ground then slammed back again...

Gasping, I sat straight up in the bed and stared into the darkness of my bedroom. *What the hell was that?*

I'd had vivid dreams since I was a little girl. My Yaya said it was because I was more sensitive than others, and she liked to note that I dreamed in color. Very unusual.

Still, all my dreams were about me—a solution to a problem or a premonition of something coming. Nothing in my life was like the images I'd just seen. My body shook, and my heart beat too fast. I was afraid. My dreams also never scared me. I could control them because they were mine.

Only... this dream wasn't mine.

My grandmother taught me to keep a dream journal. She said it would help me understand when the events came to pass. I just had to write them down and wait.

She'd taught me to read coffee grounds in the old Turkish style and to detect auras. She would smile and say everything was connected. If I paid attention, I'd see how. Thinking of her calmed my frayed nerves. I missed her so much.

Reaching for the notepad I kept on my bedside table, I quickly jotted down everything I could remember from the brief nightmare. By the time I'd finished recording as many details as I could, my eyes had grown heavy again.

Curling onto my side, I looked up at the window over my bed. From this angle, I could see the night sky. It was clear, and a million stars blanketed it. Since she'd passed, stars always made me think of Yaya. They were mystical and magical. They held secrets, and if you could read them, they gave answers. They granted wishes…

Tonight, however, was different. Tonight, I thought of him. He'd said he was going west, somewhere to find peace. A streak of white, and a star shot past. I closed my eyes and made a quiet wish. Then I imagined him under a sky filled with stars just like the one outside my window.

* * *

Stuart

Derek sat with me through that long first night. He kept the fire going, and he kept the pain relievers and whiskey coming.

"Was your uncle always a rancher?" He asked after our third round of Jameson.

"No," I said, taking another sip. We were having too much, but it dulled the pain significantly. "He was a fucking hippie. My dad hated him."

"What the fuck is up with the brothers in your family?"

I laughed with him. The fact that I could do that right now told me I was one sip away from being shit-faced. "Too many strong personalities. Too little patience."

"No shit." Derek took another sip before lowering the glass beside him.

I'd set up a few logs around the fire, and it looked like we'd spend the night out here sitting in front of it drinking. It was cold as Valley Forge, but we were both wearing Carhartt jackets and the fire burned hot. Derek kept it stoked, so I didn't have to move if I didn't want to.

"When Patrick took your place, I thought I might have to kick his ass." My partner laughed. "I couldn't understand why you'd sent him to work with me."

Grunting, I thought about Derek in those days. Allison had died, and he'd turned into a bigger, darker version of me when it came to women. He was angry, and he was mean. It wasn't who he was.

"I was a bad influence on you." I finished my glass before reaching for the near-empty bottle.

"You didn't have anything to do with how I was back then." He went quiet a moment. "Melissa is the skeleton key to that mystery."

"Melissa's your fiancée?" He'd only mentioned her a few times, but from the way his voice changed, she had to be pretty special. I knew how he'd felt about Allison.

"She's fucking adopted your little brother." He rubbed his face. "He took care of her at a time when I couldn't."

My lips tightened against another cramp twisting my midsection. "You owe him one," I managed to grunt out.

His eyes cut to me then. "Need another ibuprofen?"

I held out my hand in an attempt to say no. He didn't press it. Another thirty seconds, another minute, the pain finally eased. We were back to quiet. I thought he'd fallen asleep when he spoke again.

"You can't fight for your country now. I get it." He rubbed his forehead, probably trying to think against all the alcohol we'd consumed. "There has to be something you can fight for, though. Fuck, Stuart. Find something."

Staring at the fire, I thought about it. He was working hard. He was doing what I'd do in his place if the tables were turned. He wouldn't let me give up, and I appreciated the effort, even if I knew it was futile.

"Yeah," I said, wanting to let him off the hook. "I'm going to work on that."

My eyes rose to the stars spread over us. Nothing interested me as much as being in the service. Nothing fulfilled me the way working hard, being on a team, defending millions of Americans who never even knew my name did.

Derek's breathing grew steady, and I knew he was asleep. I pushed myself through the pain and staggered back to the cabin. We both needed heavy blankets to get through this night.

A streak of white passed overhead, and I thought about shooting stars. They were pretty common out here, but some people had never seen them. Some people made wishes when they did. As I watched it fade, my mind drifted to a pair of sunset eyes I'd only seen once.

* * *

Mariska

Kenny had come so far since Slayde left. She wasn't crying anymore. She ran all the time. I was ready to suggest she sign up for a marathon, wait for summer and become a triathlete, go for broke and do an Ironman.

What I couldn't do was burden her with my problems.

Last night I'd woken up screaming. *Screaming!* My whole body was on fire, and the noise and explosions had my heart beating out of my chest.

The man with the dark hair was in a limp pile on the sand. I couldn't tell if he was dead, and I couldn't make my body move to get to him. Then those hands returned, dragging me away. The overwhelming stress of needing to get back, of him being out of reach, the anger at being dragged away... *I was supposed to die, not him!*

Oh god, it was too much. I couldn't take another night of this, but I didn't know what to do.

Flipping to the back of the notebook where I kept my smoothie recipes for the Jungle Gym, I sketched the outline of a face I'd only seen once. He was beautiful. Sexy, powerful, determined, and so wounded. I spent a lot of time on his eyes. They were more green than brown. I only shaded them lightly.

The more I drew, the more his soul emerged on the page looking back at me. My eyes burned and my heart ached for him. *Why was I having his dreams?* I was convinced the only way to make them stop was to go to him.

I needed to talk to Kenny. We'd been best friends since we met in art class at college, and we'd always told each other everything—from Yaya's passing to Lane's birth and her fears that Elaine hated her to our plans for the future...

No. I couldn't burden her with my suffering right now. She needed a break. Still, I didn't know what else to do. Yaya said sometimes you had to follow your heart, even if it seemed to be leading you in an unexpected direction. Was it possible she'd tell me to follow this strange path and see where it led me?

Closing my eyes, I filled out the vacation slip for a week off of work. I wouldn't think about it. I wouldn't back down. This could either be the best decision or the biggest mistake I'd ever made.

Maybe I should talk to Kenny.

* * *

Stuart

We made it to the end of the week. Our second whiskey delivery was almost gone, and we'd talked about everything that had happened over the past two years. He'd told me about Melissa and having his son. I'd told him about private service and why it wasn't the same as active duty.

We talked about the flashbacks. He didn't have them as much as I did. Actually, he didn't have them at all owing to the fact he'd been knocked unconscious by the grenade blast.

"They don't upset me," I said, watching the wind outside the cabin push the brown grasses flat as it crossed the open space. Ranger and Dakota were in a pop-up shelter my little brother had included in the supplies he'd brought. "I expected to have them. Honestly, I figured I'd have *more* before my career ended."

Derek tilted the heavy glass back and forth, watching the amber liquid move side to side. "You're the only person I've ever heard say something so bat-shit crazy."

He wasn't drinking as much as he had the first night. I was still fighting the pain, but whether it was the presence of a familiar friend or simply the passing of time, something had shifted. I was stronger. I was coming out of it.

"It goes with the territory." I pushed out of my chair and made myself a small glass of water. I'd been popping a vitamin complex since I'd arrived at the ranch. Uncle Bill had suggested it based on his own private battles. "With the stress we were under, and what we faced every day…"

Derek watched me take the pill. "I guess there's some logic there."

Our conversations were like tower duty all over again, and again we'd come out on the other side.

When he spoke this time, he sounded almost guilty. "I'm headed back tomorrow. Melissa wants me home with her and Dex for the holiday."

Nodding I put the glass in the sink. "It's a family time."

"We've only been out here a week, but you look better."

"Two weeks is how long they said for the physical symptoms to subside." Staring out the dark square window over the sink, I thought about the other side of the coin. "They suggest self-help or meditation for the mental shit."

Derek studied his palm. "It's not a bad idea."

I almost laughed, but I didn't. "I've never been much for meditating."

He nodded. "We can talk about it when I'm back." Walking over to the small sofa, he glanced around the room. "You planning to sleep tonight?"

"Maybe."

"If you change your mind, let me know so I can have the bed."

"Take it now." He was as tall as me and twice my size in straight muscle. "I sleep sitting up these days."

He laughed and grabbed a pillow off the sofa. "Wake me if you need anything."

We turned out the lamp and sat in the quiet for a while until I knew he was asleep. Sleep had eluded me so long, I couldn't remember what it felt like to lie down and drift to that other place. In the darkness I thought about our conversation from the first night. Something to fight for, some reason to stay.

My partner would leave, my little brother would stay, and my future sister in law would arrive. The coming week was definitely shaping into a mental challenge, but I didn't see a way around it.

* * *

Elaine

Thanksgiving break was here, and I was going to be with my man. I couldn't throw my shit in my suitcase fast enough. Sweet baby Lane was with his family in Bayville, and as much as I loved that little boy to pieces, I was more than ready to have some alone-time with his daddy. I'd be on a plane headed west in less than two hours to spend my first holiday with the Knight men. I was practically skipping with excitement.

Stuart was a mystery to me. Patrick didn't like him, and call me biased, but for Patrick not to like someone, he had to be a royal jerk. I mean, he would be my family soon, so I had to be nice. Still, I wasn't letting him get me down. We'd deal with that situation, and in the meantime, I'd be with my guy.

I was almost ready to go when my phone sang out the special tone I'd reserved for Kenny. My stomach clenched, and I dropped everything, digging in my bag as fast as I could to find it.

"Is Lane okay?" My words flew out in a rush.

"Oh my god!" Kenny spoke so fast, I could almost see her clutching the sides of her hair. "Lainey, I'm sorry! He's fine! I didn't mean to scare you."

"No, no! It's me," I laughed, grabbing the reins. *Take a breath, dial it back.* "I didn't expect you to call. What's up?"

"Well…" she hesitated, and I was completely confused. If this wasn't about Lane, I couldn't imagine. "Just say it, goose. It can't be that bad."

She laughed in my ear, a soft little noise. "It's silly is all. I have this friend. My best friend, actually. Mariska." She hesitated again.

"Okay?"

"She wants to go with you to Montana."

My brow lined. *Kenny's best friend wanted to go with me to Montana?* "Okay. You know we're friends now, right? So I'm just going to say it: What the hell?"

"I know!" she laughed. "But you don't know her. I mean, you'll like her a lot, but she's like… well, she's kind of umm… I don't know the right word." Her voice dropped, and I could tell this next bit embarrassed her. "She needs to go with you."

"Oh!" I, by contrast, brightened at that. "Does she know Stuart?"

"Sort of."

"Well, that's good. He needs all the friends he can get from the way it sounds." I especially liked the idea of having another person to take the focus off Patrick and me.

Kenny's voice was skeptical. "Have you ever met Stuart?"

Stuffing the last of my things into my suitcase, I grunted as I dragged it off the bed. "Nope. This is going to be my first encounter with Captain Asshat."

Peals of laughter met my ear. "Oh. My god. What did you just call him?"

"That's what Patrick calls him."

"Have I told you I love your fiancé?" She was still laughing, but I squinted one eye.

"Now I'm completely suspicious."

She caught her breath and suppressed another laugh. "Just hold that thought until we talk again. In the meantime, would you be okay if Mare tags along?"

"Actually, I'll kind of like it." Making my way quickly through my condo, I stopped outside the door. "I didn't want to be the only female at our first meeting, and if she's friends with Stuart, me and Patrick can have more alone-time."

"Of course!" Kenny laughed. "Always the most important thing."

"*Always.* Can she meet me at the airport?"

She hesitated a moment. "I think she's going to meet you in Great Falls. When are you getting in?"

Hitting speaker, I lowered my phone and scrolled through my flight details. "Eight-fifteen."

"I'll let her know." I could tell she was making notes. "And seriously. I can't wait to hear what you think after you've met him."

My curiosity was at an all-time high.

* * *

Getting off the plane in Great Falls, I realized I'd forgotten to ask Kenny anything about her friends' appearance. I had no idea what I was looking for. Just then my phone dinged with a text.

Thought you might need this. Kenny had texted a picture of the two of them to my phone while I was in flight.

Mariska was actually really pretty. She had long, light-brown hair and a slightly olive complexion. In the photo Kenny had sent, the two of them were hugged cheek to cheek. As usual, Kenny's crystal blue eyes stood out against her fair skin and dark hair. Mariska was more sultry—hazel eyes that hinted at all sorts of layers of mischief against a caramel background. She looked fun, and I liked her right away.

"Elaine?" Looking up from my phone, I spotted the girl in question headed towards me. Her voice was slightly higher than I'd expected, and she wore black leggings and a black bodysuit with a sheer floral tunic on top and black booties. A long, sparkling-green scarf was around her neck, and her light-brown hair hung in loose waves down her back. "Kenny's shown me pictures of you with Lane! It's so great to meet you!"

She stepped right into a hug, and I didn't resist. I hugged her back. "Of course! So you're here for Stuart?"

Her expression wavered, and her lip caught in her teeth. "Umm... Yes?"

"Perfect. I'm here for Patrick, so we can all go our separate ways when we get there. Meet up at dinner." I elbowed her as my bag appeared at the top of the carousel. Turning away quickly, I thought I caught a worried glint in her eye. When I looked back it was gone.

It didn't matter because just then I spotted Patrick walking through baggage claim, looking for us. He was dressed in jeans and a tan, canvass jacket, and he actually had on cowboy boots. I squealed and took off towards him, leaving everything at Mariska's feet.

He'd spotted me just before I jumped into his arms, and I caught the spark in his eyes as our mouths crashed together. Lips parted, tongues entwined, his arms were strong around my waist, and I didn't give a shit who was watching.

Lowering me to my feet, he smoothed both hands on my cheeks. "I am so damn happy to see your face."

I laughed and kissed him again. "You are so damn fine in cowboy boots, Mister Knight. You have to wear those all the time. Nothing else."

He grinned and that sexy dimple pierced his cheek. "I'm ready for you to be wearing nothing else. Let's get back to the house."

"What's taking so long!" Our hands entwined, and I pulled him in the direction I'd come. "I already got the bags, and do you know Mariska?"

She was hanging back, smiling shyly as we approached. Patrick's sunny voice greeted her first.

"Oh, yeah—Kenny's friend?" He stepped forward and gave her a hug. "You were at the gym... and you made that really good stuffed cabbage."

"Right!" she nodded, a smile replacing her worried expression.

I shook my head. This man never met a woman who didn't love him, and he never forgot a good meal.

"Cool earrings." He pointed to the little skulls she wore in her ears. "You were right about Stuart being here. Thanks for the tip. Did he ask you to come?"

"Oh, well—"

"Let's chat on the road!" I interrupted, scooping Mariska's arm into mine. "I need to freshen up. Maybe take a shower?"

Patrick's eyes twinkled at me, and I couldn't stop a grin. This week was going to kick ass.

* * *

Mariska

Reality slammed into me like a thousand-pound medicine ball. *What the hell was I doing here?* It was like I'd had some moment of pure, one-hundred percent, temporary insanity! I'd cashed in all my frequent flyer miles, traveled halfway across the country... to do what?

Stand around and lie to everybody, apparently.

My hands were clammy and I could barely breathe. I was going to see him again in less than an hour. If Elaine hadn't been gripping my arm as we strode out to Patrick's pick-up, I would have turned and run all the way back to the ticket counter and taken the first flight home.

She was so pretty in faded blue jeans and a grey cowl-neck sweater. Her long blonde hair was over one shoulder, and of course, she had on cowboy boots. Patrick was handsome as always, and the only saving grace was they were too busy touching each other and swapping innuendo to notice how badly I was freaking out. They put me in the tiny backseat of the extended cab, and we headed out on some lonely road into what looked like the middle of nowhere.

Great. This was just great. With each passing mile, I was getting further and further from any way out of the mess I'd created. I was rapidly moving toward complete and total humiliation. My stomach was so tight, it was very possible I'd throw up before the night ended.

Elaine took a break from touching her fiancé to turn and smile at me. "Do you like horses, Mariska?"

"Sure." My voice cracked, and I looked down at my trembling hands clutched in my lap. "I-I hope you don't mind me tagging along for the holiday."

"No way! Friends are always welcome." Patrick was so easygoing, I completely understood why he drove Kenny crazy—and why she called him her big brother. "The house is huge, and my uncle is going to love you."

Blinking up at him, my brow lined. "Why do you say that?"

"He's an old hippie himself."

"Patrick!" Elaine slapped him on the arm. "Mariska's Boho Goth. Pay attention."

Her humor only escalated the panic I was feeling. I

kind of already liked Elaine. I wondered how angry she'd be when I told her I'd lied about knowing Stuart. Would she yell at me? Would she think I was a complete whack-job?

"I'll show you attention." He grabbed her face and kissed her quick before putting his hand back on the wheel.

I looked into the darkness outside my window. "We're really far from town." My stomach was sick at the prospect of the awkward drive back to the airport. Maybe I could call a cab?

"Wait until you see it on horseback," Patrick answered. "If the Chinook comes down, we'll ride out to the lake. It's beautiful... well, it's beautiful everywhere."

"I can't wait to see it with you." Elaine's nose crinkled, and she slid her hand behind his neck. I watched her fingers thread into his hair before glancing out the window again.

It was too cold to hitch a ride back to town. Temperatures were already dipping into the teens, and snow wouldn't be far away. Coming here like this was the craziest thing I'd ever done in my entire life, and now I'd have to face the consequences.

At the same time, maybe it was the right thing? Oh, god, I shivered, I couldn't even hope for that much. All I knew was I couldn't have that dream again.

CHAPTER 5: NEW BEST FRIEND

Mariska

The windows of the sprawling ranch house were lit by lamps, and a strand of twinkle lights twined around a large side porch. In the starry evening, it was a beautiful place, and my stomach was so tight, my head hurt.

"Here we are!" Patrick hopped out of the truck and left his door open for me while he pulled our suitcases out of the back.

"It's gorgeous!" Elaine skipped out of her side and slammed the door. "Which room is ours?"

"Hold your horses." Patrick laughed as he stopped at the cab where I sat frozen in the back. "You need a hand?"

His question forced me to move. I shook my head and carefully eased myself out of the large truck. Elaine had already dashed up the porch and rung the doorbell. As the heavy wooden door started to open, I felt my head getting light.

"Elaine!" A deep male voice I didn't recognize spoke. "I'd know you anywhere."

"I take it you're Bill!" I watched her embrace what could only be Patrick's uncle, and then it was my turn. Kind brown eyes assessed me. I slowed my pace, but Patrick bumped me with the suitcase.

"This is Mariska," he said. "She flew in with Elaine."

His uncle's thick grey brows rose. "Pleasure to meet you, Mariska."

I was literally going to die. All these nice, attractive people were going to think I was a psychopath when they found out why I was here. If they could figure out why I was here—I wasn't sure myself.

"Thank you." I managed to answer.

"Come on in. We were just sitting down to supper." Bill led the way, and I followed behind Elaine, dread twisting my insides with every step.

The short hallway ended at a large, open kitchen with a dining area on the side. A massive wooden table with long bench seats filled the opposite end, and a short, stocky woman with graying black hair moved around, stirring pots and taking down plates. The whole room smelled delicious from whatever she was cooking.

"Winona, we've got one more for supper," Bill said. "Mariska came out with Elaine."

Patrick walked over and put the suitcases by a hallway I assumed led to where we'd sleep. I frantically scanned the room for any sign of his brother. He wasn't here. *Would he even join us for dinner? Was he staying somewhere else?*

"Stuart's putting Ranger in the barn." It was like Bill read my mind. "He'll be in shortly."

"Is he…" Patrick didn't finish the sentence, but his uncle nodded.

"He's doing real good. Your coming here was the right thing, I think."

His uncle was still talking when a tall figure walked through a doorway I hadn't even noticed off the side of the kitchen. Stuart stepped into the light, and my heart jumped to my throat. He wore a brown shirt and jeans, cowboy boots and the same type of canvass overcoat as his brother. I could barely breathe as he slipped it off his broad shoulders. Then he took off his cap and raked his fingers through his dark hair. He looked even better than I remembered.

"Ranger's brushed down and in his stall." His deep voice sent a tingle across my stomach, and when he looked up, our eyes met.

It was just like that day at the gym. Quiet filled the space around us, and the world seemed to disappear. Deep satisfaction warmed my chest. His face was the only thing I wanted to see.

At the same time, I was here without an invitation. When we met, he was there to see Kenny where she and I happened to work together. He hadn't asked me to come here. I shouldn't even know how to find him. Would my appearance change his feelings? What was I talking about? He'd never expressed feelings to me!

Panic snaked up my insides like a vine. Somebody spoke, but I couldn't hear them. Heat burned in my cheeks, and when his brow lined, I spun on my heel.

"Excuse me." I took off down the hall where Patrick had left our suitcases.

Door after door passed. I ran on tip-toe, hoping not to make a sound. I had no idea which door to choose, so finally, I just picked one. Pushing inside, I closed it, turned the lock, and collapsed. My body was shaking so hard. I tried to calm my breathing as I scanned the room for signs of occupancy. A queen bed was in one corner, but otherwise the space was bare. It seemed I'd picked an unclaimed one.

Pushing off the door, I rubbed my clenched stomach. All I could see were those gorgeous hazel eyes under a brow lined in confusion. *Oh, god!* I couldn't imagine what they were saying. Stuart and I were not friends. If I were lucky Patrick would laugh it off. Uncle Bill was a mystery, and Elaine...

A soft tap on the door made me squeal. I waited, holding my hand over my mouth. It tapped again.

"Mariska?" Elaine called from the other side.

Slowly, I went over and opened it. She stood blinking at me, her green eyes a mixture of curiosity and mischief.

"What's going on?" She spoke softly as she walked into the room. "Why did you run out like that?"

Pushing the door closed again, I put my forehead against it. This was going to be so bad.

"Are you okay?" she repeated.

Taking a deep breath, I turned around and faced her. Being honest seemed like the best course of action at this point. "I lied."

Her face lined, but she still was almost smiling. "About... what?"

"I don't know Stuart. I'm not his friend." I started pacing, wringing my hands.

"Wait... what? But you said... I don't understand. Why?"

"This is going to sound crazy. This actually *is* crazy. Oh my god, I'm going to be sick."

Elaine caught my hands and stopped me. "Calm down and just tell me."

I turned and sat on the bed. "I only met him that one time at the gym. He came in to see Kenny, and we only talked for like a minute. Maybe less. He probably doesn't even remember it."

Her eyes sparkled. "And you came all the way to Montana? Are you stalking him?"

"No!" I nearly shouted. "I mean... No."

She started to laugh. "Liar! You're totally stalking him!"

"Oh my god!" I pulled my knees up to my chest. "It's not like that... I can't believe I came here. I don't do things like this!"

"Come on." She sat beside me on the bed and threw an arm over my shoulder. "Tell me what happened."

I hesitated to say it out loud. It really did sound nuts. "I had this dream."

For a moment, the only sound was the bedside clock ticking.

"And?"

"That's it."

She leaned back and gave me a look. "What was the dream about?"

I knew she was going to say that. "It doesn't make any sense." In my mind, I replayed the dream I kept having. "It's all fire and explosions and pain. It doesn't match anything that's happened in my life, but..." *Oh, god, this was the crazy part.* I couldn't say it.

"But...?" Elaine leaned forward.

"I think it has something to do with him." Her nose wrinkled, but I charged on. "Because it started after I met him, and every time I wake up after having one, he's the first thing I think about."

"He's definitely something to think about." She shook her head and stood, pacing to the other side of the room. "Not that I expected anything less of Patrick's brother."

I chewed my lip watching her as quiet again filled the room—all except for the ticking of that damn clock. If this were my bedroom, that thing would have to go.

Finally she spoke. "What did you think was going happen when you came here?"

"I don't know." I stood and started pacing, too. "Now he's going to run as far and as fast away from me as possible. He's going to think I'm a total head case, which clearly I am—"

She shook her head. "None of that's going to happen. You're my new best friend. We met through Kenny, and I didn't want you to be alone at Thanksgiving... so I brought you with me."

"What?!" My eyes were instantly hot. "You'd say that for me? Why?"

"Because I love that you're a crazy romantic!" She hopped over and caught my hands. "What if you're right, and you are dreaming about him?"

"I can't even look at him. I feel like a total fool."

"Stuart's just come off a really tough time. Patrick said he can't go back overseas, which is a huge deal for him... Maybe you're onto something coming here." She pulled me toward the door, but when she got there she turned back and squared her shoulders, looking me right in the eye. "Before we go one step further, you have to answer two questions."

I nodded. "Okay..."

"Are you going to be fun?"

"I-I'll try."

She pressed her lips together and nodded. "Good enough. Are you going to turn into a psycho?"

That made me snort-laugh. "Despite all appearances up to now? I never have before."

"Then as long as I get to spend most of my time having sex with Patrick, we're going to get along great." She threw her arm around my neck. We were the same height. "How old are you, Mariska?"

It was an odd question, but I answered it. "Twenty-six."

"Sounds to me like the perfect time to do something completely impulsive and utterly romantic." She kissed the side of my head. "Kenny said you're her best friend, and she's usually right about people."

I remembered how much my friend had worried about Elaine hating her. "She wasn't sure what to think about you..."

Elaine threw an arm out. "See what I mean?" I liked her even more.

"If we're besties, you'd better call me Lainey."

"And you'd better call me Mare."

"On a horse ranch?!"

I shrugged. "That's what Kenny calls me."

Her arm tightened around my shoulders. "Come on then, Mare. Let's be reckless and have some fun!"

* * *

Dinner was awful.

No, that's wrong. Winona prepared an amazing dinner for us. It started with French onion soup that was incredible, followed by juicy beef tenderloin with mashed potatoes and a rich, dark gravy. It all smelled divine, and I couldn't eat a bite.

Bill sat at the head of the table with Patrick on his right and Stuart on his left. Naturally, Elaine was beside Patrick, and I tried to be very small on the other side of her.

Uncle Bill put his elbows on the table and clasped his hands just before we all picked up our forks. "We thank thee for this bounty." Four additional heads ducked. My eyes sneaked to Stuart's, which were open but looking in his lap. "We thank thee for time with family and friends. We thank thee for the strength you give us in times of need..."

Movement to my left caught my attention, and I glanced just in time to see Elaine's hand cross Patrick's thigh and take a fast turn into his crotch. He jumped back with a loud cough just as his uncle said "Amen."

Elaine ducked as a blast of air exploded from her lips. I snorted myself. I had a feeling being Elaine Merritt's bestie was going to be fun.

Bill cleared his throat as he glanced toward his younger nephew.

"Good prayer." Patrick said clearing his throat.

Stuart was not smiling. The air between him and his brother was tense, and he only gave Patrick an annoyed glance. His reaction puzzled me. I thought of his sharp response to Kenny wanting to call Patrick for help when he stopped in at the gym. It appeared they didn't get along.

Stuart turned to Bill. "I'm sorry I wasn't more help last week."

His voice smoothed through my insides like hot chocolate. So good.

Bill gave his arm a squeeze. "Don't even think about it. I'm glad you're back with us now."

"What can I do? I'd like to help out somehow."

"I understand that." His uncle nodded, and Patrick jumped in.

"The girls want to ride. I can take them on some trails and show them around the place."

Stuart turned his attention to his plate and didn't answer. I tried not to die inside. He didn't want us here.

"If that Chinook comes down like they're saying it will, I'm putting you all to work," Bill laughed.

"Okay, what's a Chinook?" Elaine was quick to join the discussion.

"Weather phenomenon," Patrick answered her. "I've only experienced one since Bill's lived here, but it can raise temps from negative four to sixty-eight in a day. The word actually means 'snow eater.'"

Elaine's mouth dropped open. "That's unbelievable."

"Yep," Bill added. "They can hang around for a day, sometimes longer. I'll put together a list in the morning, and we can figure out what everyone wants to do."

The rest of the meal, Patrick and his uncle tossed around old memories of the brothers visiting him in Arizona and later here. Elaine interjected funny quips throughout, but Stuart ate in silence. Occasionally he'd nod if his uncle addressed him. His behavior didn't seem to bother any of them, but it was killing me.

When he finished, he rose and patted his uncle on the shoulder before putting his place setting at the sink and going into the living room to stand by the fire. My eyes followed him the entire way. He stopped and rested his arm on the mantle. His back was turned, and my eyes drifted lower to his butt, narrow and firm in dark jeans.

"You're blushing," Elaine whispered, elbowing me in the ribs.

"Shut up!" I whispered back.

"Here's something," Patrick announced, sliding his plate forward on the table. "Name the one book you absolutely cannot live without."

"Hmm..." Uncle Bill's voice was slow and deep like he was considering every word before he said it—even if it was a joke. "It can't be one book, because everyone would say The Bible." He paused and glanced at each of us. "Right?"

Nobody spoke, and Elaine snorted a laugh.

"That's true," Patrick said. "We should name two."

"What if one of us is Buddhist?" Elaine jumped in.

Bill's eyes caught her teasing tone. "Are any of us Buddhist?"

"I don't think so, but I actually had a student who was Buddhist once."

"In Wilmington, North Carolina?" It was clear he was already in love with his future niece.

"I know!" Elaine cried. "I was trying to make some point about religion, and she just blasted it all to hell."

"I'm not even going to ask what point you were making." Patrick's eyes shone in the lamplight.

It was all so warm and lovely, and my gaze kept drifting to the fireplace where Stuart stood. Naturally, that time, he was looking right at me when I peeked. Our eyes clashed, and my stomach clenched. I quickly blinked to my lap again.

Ultimately the "one book" game was abandoned and Patrick, Elaine, and Bill all rose to join Stuart in the living room. I hung back, wishing there was some way I could escape to my room without seeming rude.

"So you're friends with Stuart?" Patrick said as I lingered by the table. Stuart's eyes again cut to mine, and my stomach dropped.

"No!" Elaine jumped in. "That was my mistake. Mariska said they'd met once, and I misunderstood. But we can all get to know each other this week, right?"

Stuart didn't speak, and I couldn't breathe. I reached for my second glass of wine and took a quick gulp. Their uncle was a recovering alcoholic, but he didn't mind if we had wine with dinner.

I watched as the three more animated members of the group took seats near the fire. Stuart said something I couldn't hear, and they nodded. His uncle held out his hand, and he clasped it before turning and taking that fine ass down the opposite hall of where the three of us were staying. I felt the light slowly fading from the room when he stopped and turned back. He was headed toward the kitchen, toward where I stood by the table.

My heart jumped, and I reached for the other plates to stack on top of mine, hoping he didn't see my hands trembling. He didn't speak as he went to the cabinet and took down a glass then stepped to the sink to fill it with water.

I was just about to take my stack to the sink when I felt a gentle touch at my elbow. Looking up, I almost dropped everything when I met his gorgeous eyes.

"Uhh... Hi," I stammered.

"You dropped your scarf." He was so close, and I could see my chest rising and falling with my rapid breaths.

The sparkling length of green silk I'd looped around my neck this morning was in his hands. Apparently it had come loose during dinner.

I set the plates down. "Thanks."

His hands were beautiful. Long fingers, elegant, but not pampered. He was clearly strong. In a flash, I pictured them on my body, and my cheeks flamed red.

"You're friends with Elaine?" His voice was a low vibration straight to my core. He waited in front of me, and I knew I had to look up.

Blinking several times, I met his intense gaze again. "We met through Kenny." At least that much was true.

He nodded. "Hope you like it here."

With a small, breathtaking smile, he turned and walked away. I couldn't decide if I'd melt into a puddle or burst into flames as I watched him disappear down the hall.

* * *

Stuart

She was as beautiful as I remembered with those long, brown waves and sunset hazel eyes. When she moved, I thought of nights wrapped in an Indian blanket by the fire, holding her on my lap, claiming her lips, every part of her…

Derek's challenge had been on my mind since he'd issued it, and I'd decided once I cleared the last hurdle in my recovery, I'd go back to the desert. I'd return to the job I was meant to do. I'd prove I still had honor, and I could rise to the challenge.

Then she appeared.

Why had Elaine brought her here? She presented an entirely new obstacle for me to overcome. Or maybe it was the weakness talking, the mental side of my recovery. She was a girl, after all. I'd had plenty of girls, and they never lasted. I didn't let them last.

Women only got in the way of what I wanted, or they became a liability down the road. I didn't need that, and there was no reason why this particular female should stick in my mind the way she did.

When I got back from the cabin, Bill put me in the east wing with him. Patrick, Elaine, and... she... were all on the west side. I liked this arrangement. I'd go to my room, shower, and go to bed.

"Good to have you back in the house." Bill met me in the hall on his way to bed.

"Thanks," I said with a nod. "I'm glad to be back."

"Listen to me." He caught my shoulder and gave it a squeeze. "You're stronger for what you've been through. Don't let anyone tell you it makes you weak. Weaker men would ignore a problem like that, and eventually it would destroy their lives. Possibly even kill them. You faced that demon, and you beat it. You're still a hero."

Words failed me, and I could only nod in response. He was being way more generous than I deserved, but this man had always been more of a father to me than my own.

"Now," he continued, "Get some rest. You're welcome to stay here as long as you need. I'm glad for the company."

Rubbing my chin, I glanced up. "I was serious about helping out." I hadn't planned to stay indefinitely, but while I was here, I'd carry my own weight.

He just laughed. "Don't worry. It's a horse ranch. You come here to experience the lifestyle, not to have a holiday."

"Sounds great." I patted his arm, and he continued on to his bedroom.

That was it: hard work, recovery, back to the desert. I could resist the pull of temptation. I'd already left one casualty behind. I wasn't leaving another.

CHAPTER 6: CHINOOK

Mariska

That clock was wrapped in a thick blanket and hidden in the bottom of the trunk at the foot of the queen-sized bed where I slept. I was curled up in a warm ball beneath the covers when my new bestie jumped in beside me.

"It happened!" Excitement bubbled in Elaine's voice. "The Chinook blew in last night. It's like heaven outside!"

I squinted out of my burrow at her. When Patrick explained it last night, I didn't say I'd heard of such a thing. "What's the temperature?"

"A nice sixty-eight and breezy. Total shorts weather."

"Except we're going to ride horses, right?" I sat up slowly, rubbing my eyes and pushing a lock of brown hair behind my shoulder.

"Hmm…" Elaine looked around the room. "You're right. We'll have to figure that one out. Nothing sexy about chafed thighs."

She hopped off the bed and went to my closet and pulled out a cream, crocheted shrug that hung to my knees. "This is so cute. You have to wear it." She tossed it on the bed before going to my drawers. "And these! You were really thinking ahead." A beige crop-top and high-waisted denim shorts joined my long sweater on the bed.

"Now for the shoes." She dragged out a pair of tan-leather, open-toed platforms.

"Lainey." I cocked my head to the side. "What about the trail ride?"

"You know what they say," she winked. "Save a horse, ride a cowboy."

"Oh my god!" I fell back laughing. "You did not just say that!"

"Here's your hat." She tossed a royal blue Stetson at me. "Hurry up, now! The guys are already in the barn. Meet you in the kitchen."

"What time is it?" I tossed the quilts back and jumped out of bed.

"Time to get your man!"

She was out the door and shouting down the hall. *Shit!* I cringed, hoping the whole house hadn't heard her. Picking up the pieces of the outfit she'd chosen, I figured what the hell. It was why I was here, wasn't it?

* * *

Elaine wore a short black top, denim cutoffs and Miranda Lambert boots. Her Stetson was brown, and she let it hang on her back while her long, blonde hair was in a messy braid tossed over one shoulder. Patrick took one look at us and pushed his straw cowboy hat up.

"You can't ride in that." The dimple in his cheek was visible from the front porch. "We'd better figure out something else to do."

Elaine hopped down the steps and into his arms. "I've got a few ideas."

The air outside was noticeably warmer, and I hung back to scan the yard as they walked over to the truck. The wind pushed through in hard gusts, and nobody else was around.

"Hey, Mare?" Patrick called, and I wrinkled my nose at him using my nickname. "Bill has something for you to do in the barn, I think."

"Okay—thanks!" It was nice that he wanted me to help with the chores. Made me feel less like a party crasher.

When I entered, I was confused. The barn seemed empty, other than five stalls with horses peeking over the doors. Two were dark brown with black manes, one was brown and white, and another was a Palomino. At the far end was a gray mare with white spots. I decided she was my favorite and headed in her direction.

"Careful around Freckles." The familiar voice stopped me in my tracks. I spun around to see Stuart coming out of the brown and white horse's stall. "She spooks easily."

"Thanks for the warning." I tried to keep my voice calm as I waited for him to close the door. He held an oval-shaped brush and a comb, and he seemed to be keeping his eyes on those items and not me. "Were you grooming your horse?"

"Just checking him out." He continued past me into what I assumed was the tack room. I followed. He nodded in my direction. "That's some hat."

"Elaine loaned it to me." Inside I was flying, and I was far less freaked out than I'd been last night. At least now I was welcome, and I wasn't lying to everybody.

He put the brush and comb on a shelf and turned back to the door. Looking up, he seemed surprised I was behind him. *Was it possible I threw him off balance, too?* Doubtful, but it was encouraging to imagine.

"Patrick said your uncle had something for me to do in the barn?"

Stuart's did a fast, tingling sweep of my body, and got caught momentarily around my legs. Now those smoky hazel eyes held mine, flooding heat to my lower half.

"Bill went into town."

"Oh. I must've misunderstood him." *Or not.*

I had a pretty good idea what my new bestie and her fiancé were up to sending me in here. "Do you need help?"

Stuart cleared his throat and straightened, rubbing his palm across his toned midsection. The grey tee he wore stretched across his broad shoulders, and his faded jeans hung sexy around his waist. The same tan cowboy boots were on his feet as from last night, and I wished he had a hat to complete the outfit. He looked so good, my mouth watered.

"I was just brushing down the horses, checking their coats for any lumps or swelling."

I picked up an oval brush the size of my hand. "Which ones are left?"

"I'm finished." He looked at me only briefly before averting his gaze to the wall and taking a turquoise halter off a peg. "Ranger was the last one."

Looking over my shoulder, I noticed three additional horses for a total of eight. "What time did you get out here?"

He stepped out of the small room, and I caught the scent of soap and cedar in his wake. It was a warm, masculine scent I immediately loved.

"I wake up early, so I came out and got started."

He was headed to the Appaloosa's stall, and I noticed the slightest hitch in his gait. Frowning, I hurried to catch up with him.

"Did you hurt yourself?"

My question seemed to irritate him. "No."

"Sorry. I just... you're limping."

He stopped and leaned against the stall, looking down on me. His expression seemed angry, and a mixture of fear and excitement tickled in my stomach. "I'm not limping," he growled.

My mouth dropped open. *Why was he lying to me?* I studied his back as he entered Freckles's stall and slipped the halter over her head. His muscular lines appeared and disappeared through the thin fabric of his shirt as he moved around the horse. Chewing my lip, I stepped back as he led her out and toward the tack room where we'd just been.

"Come here, and I'll show you how to scrape the hooves."

I followed him to where he left the horse standing while he retrieved a metal hook from inside the small room. Then he stood beside the large animal and patted the front of her shin. Her leg bent in response, and he caught her foot in his hand. My lip caught in my teeth at the deep line in his triceps.

"Get closer and look at this."

Stepping closer to him, I could feel the heat of his body against my torso. Shimmers of electricity seemed to pass between us as I tried to concentrate on what he was saying.

"This triangle here is the frog." He pointed with one long finger that I could only imagine touching me in very naughty ways. I suppressed a sigh. "If you hit that, it'll hurt her and she'll kick you."

I straightened beside him, and he glanced up at me with a look that melted my insides. "I don't want to get kicked," I said softly.

He scraped the hook down the horse's hoof along the sides toward the rounded front then he stood in front of me again. His back was to the horse, and we were so close our breathing seemed in sync.

"Never mind, I'll take care of this." He spoke low, and longing moved through me. I wanted to step forward into his arms.

The green in his eyes shone against the light tan of his skin. Straight, white teeth peeked behind his full lips, and a light shadow was on his cheeks. My fingers curled wanting to slide over that scratchy face, jaw to chin. I'd follow it with my tongue.

"Isn't there anything I can do for you?" I asked.

He studied me a moment longer, and I almost believed he pictured the same thing as me — our bodies entwined together. But he pulled away, going around to the other side of the horse. My breath slowly returned along with severe frustration.

"You could bring me something to eat. I didn't have breakfast."

"Okay!" I stepped around the horse's head. "Any special requests?"

"Whatever Winona made is fine."

I did a little wave, intending to say I'd bring him anything when my sweater flared out in the breeze and the horse made a whinny sound. Her head flew back and shook side to side as she pawed the ground.

"Oh!" I cried, throwing up my hands, which seemed to startle her more.

She did a little jump, and Stuart was quickly in front of me, pulling my body close against his back.

"Ho, girl." His voice soothed, and he held a hand out, palm down toward her. "Easy now."

I clutched his sides, burying my face in his soap and cedar back as the horse pawed the ground a few more times. His arm rose with each movement, and he continued speaking in that dulcet tone until Freckles was at a tentative calm.

I trembled all over when he turned. His arms were still around my waist, and I was acutely aware of his palm against the skin of my back. It did not help me catch my breath.

"You okay?" He searched my eyes, speaking in the same tone he'd used with the startled horse.

"I think so." I blinked up. "I'm so sorry. I didn't mean to scare her."

He glanced briefly at my mouth. One dip, and our lips would touch. He stepped away.

"It's okay. I'm glad you weren't hurt." His voice didn't change, but his mouth was now sadly too far from mine. My hands were on his forearms, and I wanted to hold onto him. I never wanted him to let me go.

"Did something happen to make her act that way?"

Our eyes mixed and mingled as I watched him think about what I'd asked. Maybe he was thinking about himself?

"I don't know." One hand went into his pocket, and the other only held my elbow. Stupid distance. "You can take a break if you need to."

Moving my arm so our hands met, I shook my head. "No, way — I owe you breakfast."

"Are you sure?" Concern filled his eyes, and I was certain I'd never seen anything sexier in my life than this man right now protecting me.

"I'll be back in a few minutes."

He gave me a little smile, and I headed toward the barn entrance. His continued talking to the horse, and I glanced again to see him moving towards Freckles, a definite limp in his step. A new idea drifted through my mind, a way in.

* * *

Stuart sat on a bench against the back wall of the barn to eat his breakfast of scrambled eggs and ground sausage wrapped in a tortilla, while I stood nearby sipping coffee. I watched him make short work of his meal.

"Winona was more than happy to make you two of those."

He'd just taken a big bite, so he nodded. The muscle in his jaw moved as he finished before speaking. *Swoon.*

"She's been stuffing us since we were kids." He winked and finished the last bite, quickly wiping his mouth with the napkin. I seriously was ready to kiss that mouth, but I had to play it cool.

"You must've loved being able to come here growing up. It's like your own personal summer camp."

"Bill's always been good to Patrick and me." He cleared his throat and stood, tossing his trash in a nearby can.

Just then Elaine popped in. "Hey, Mare, Patrick said he's got a surprise for us. But you've got to change into jeans, okay?"

I tried to think of any reason to say no. Coming up with nothing, I shrugged. "Okay. Give me a second."

She turned and disappeared the way she came, and Stuart was already heading out to the paddock where a young colt waited.

I followed him a few steps. "I hope you don't feel like I'm ditching you."

He only waved. "No way. You're just here for the week. Have some fun."

Something about the way he said it, so dismissive, made me want to cry, which was stupid. "See you later," I said.

He nodded and went out the door. I exhaled, feeling my shoulders drop and started for the house.

* * *

We paused in running our horses to look across the prairie. It stretched on for miles with the mountains rising misty in the distance. Over it all, the clouds formed a strange-looking orange arch that made me feel uneasy.

"Are you sure it's safe to be riding in this?" I shouted. My horse didn't seem to want to stand still. "The wind's so strong."

"It never stops blowing out here, even when there's no Chinook," Patrick called back. "It's like—have you ever been to west Texas or Oklahoma?" I shook my head. "On these flat open plains like this, nothing breaks it."

"Still…" I couldn't explain how I was antsy, while at the same time it was so warm and lovely.

"It's like nothing I've ever experienced." Elaine's eyes sparkled.

"Don't worry. We'll be fine," Patrick said, turning the Palomino he rode. "Let's head down to the lake. I've been wanting to show it to you."

The last bit was said to Elaine, but I didn't mind. We gave the dark-brown mares a flick, and set off after him at a fast gallop. Occasionally the wind would blow so hard, it felt like I might fly out of my saddle, but I laughed it off. Patrick had grown up coming here, and he loved Elaine. He wouldn't put us in danger.

Over a small rise and down into a little valley was a dark pool with a few trees sprinkled along the banks. The lake was beautiful—a big black splotch in the middle of a sea of beige. We rode up and slid out of our saddles. I was actually a little sore from gripping the sides with my thighs. Patrick collected the reins and tied them loosely over a tree limb.

"Race you in!" He shouted, tossing his hat aside and whipping off his shirt to reveal a lined torso.

Elaine was right. The Knight brothers had a lot in common physically. His jeans were down in a flash, and I only caught a quick glimpse of black boxer-briefs before he did a cannonball off the pier. Elaine laughed, and without hesitation, she tossed her brown Stetson on Patrick's pile of clothing.

"I love this guy," she said, pulling off her shirt, so she was only in her black bra. Jeans off, I stood watching with my mouth open. "Don't be a goose," she said. "It's more material than the bikini I wear."

"I think I'll keep my shirt on." Shrugging out of my boots and jeans, I was glad I'd opted for a tunic top and ditched the thong in favor of boyshorts.

We ran along the wooden pier, our feet making staccato thumping noises. Patrick grinned at us from where he waited in the pool. A brief flight through the air, and then complete and total shock as we burst through the water.

I came up screaming. "It's freezing!"

Elaine shrieked as well when her head broke through the lake. "Patrick! It's like ice in here."

She quickly swam to him and wrapped her body around his. I was shit out of luck.

"What did you expect?" He laughed, giving her a squeeze. "It's late fall in Montana!"

"You almost gave me a heart attack!"

That made me laugh, even though I was shaking too. I swam around, pumping my arms to build up heat, but it wasn't working. "I wish I'd brought a blanket."

"It's a relief after that dry wind, don't you think?" Patrick's arms were around Lainey, and she was practically fused to his body.

Nodding, I kicked and dove under, letting the frigid wetness soothe my parched skin. When I resurfaced, they were kissing. I turned my back and took a small mouthful of the water. It was icy and tasted like a penny. I spit it out and went under again, kicking to the other side. This time, when I reappeared, Elaine was behind Patrick, holding onto his neck.

"Go under and listen," he said. "It sounds like roaring."

I tread water slowly toward them. "Okay." Dunking my head I held my breath and listened. The noise was like a fire burning or a microphone hum. Popping back up, I nodded fast as I pushed my hair out of my face. "It does!"

Elaine bounced on his back. "Did you ever do that game where you yell a word underwater and the other person tries to guess what it is?"

"When I was like nine," Patrick said.

She pushed his shoulder. "Do it!"

"See what I have to put up with?" But his hazel eyes sparkled. They both went under for a few seconds, and I heard the muffled echo of a shout.

"Bubblegum!" Patrick said, when they came up blowing air and splashing.

"No!" She splashed him.

He splashed back. Then she splashed me. "Hey!"

I shot a stream of water right at her face, and for the next several minutes we engaged in a vigorous battle that sent water flying everywhere and almost ended in me drowning laughing.

The wind howled, and I couldn't help looking up again at the arc of yellow clouds over the horizon. I wasn't sure how long we'd been out here, but I sort of wanted to head back.

* * *

Stuart

Patrick and the girls rode out like they'd just robbed a train and the sheriff was on their tails. My lips tightened as I watched the horses run. Had he even checked if they were experienced riders? Did they know how to stop without falling off? How to handle a sudden break? Cheyenne didn't act like herself when the weather changed, and he'd put Mariska on her. Tightness spread across my chest with anger close behind. I should have gone with them.

Mariska had followed me around the barn this morning like some kind of cute little kid eager to learn. Only she wasn't a kid. She was a gorgeous, sexy young woman, and it had taken all my strength not to pull her to me and kiss the shit out of her beautiful mouth in the tack room. Her eyes danced, and everything about her was light and happy, talking to me about the horses, asking about Bill, bringing me breakfast. When Freckles reared back at her, my stomach flew to my fucking throat. I tried to cover, but I was as startled as she was. Then I was confused.

My need to protect her was overwhelming. I'd never felt anything like it. She was sunshine and warmth and fire under my skin. Leaning against the rails of the paddock, I tried to figure out what the fuck was happening to me.

Long nights spent talking to Derek pressed on my mind. He'd told me about Allison and how any time she took a road-trip, he was plagued with images of how she might be killed on the highway. I was fucking turning into that guy.

My little brother's careless attitude had me ready to punch him in the face, and I'd done a damn good job keeping my cool with him at the house. No confrontations, moving past our differences, and now he was fucking with Mariska's safety. It was possible I might have to kick his ass after all.

What. The. Fuck?! I had to grab the reins on this shit. I was acting like a fucking husband. The images I'd had in Bayville of holding her, waking up with her in my bed, watching her body change as she carried my babies floated around the periphery of my mind. In Bayville I'd been sick with withdrawals. Now I was well, my appetite was back, and I was hungry. My desire for her was forceful and demanding. It was different than I'd ever felt for a woman.

The colt made a little bray and trotted around his small yard. He was Cheyenne's foal, and apparently he'd inherited her dislike of strange weather. Bill asked me to help break him. I needed to focus on that job and tone down the irrational lust. I was just entering when the sound of hoof beats echoed in the barn. Turning to check it out, my stomach revolted when I saw Cheyenne standing at her stall, stamping her hooves and wanting to be let in. The whites of her eyes shone as she lolled her head around. *Where was Mariska?*

I was in the tack room in under a second. Bridle over my shoulder, I snatched a blanket and saddle off the rack and headed to Ranger's stall. Before I left, I opened Cheyenne's door and let her in then my horse and I were out the barn faster than the beating wind.

My stomach hurt, and my vision tunneled. I couldn't seem to steady my breathing. All I could picture was her thrown, hurt, she could have a broken bone. If she fell wrong... She could have a broken neck. *Fuck! God dammit, Patrick!* Fighting back the red in my eyes and the panic in my brain, I tried to remember what my brother had said. They were headed to the lake. I gave Ranger a nudge, and he ran faster. I had to get to her. She had to be all right.

* * *

Our splashing had quieted down, Elaine drifted back to hanging on Patrick's shoulder. I trailed a reed along the dark surface, watching the tension break and swirl when Patrick grinned. "Well, look who's here."

Spinning around, I quickly spotted Stuart riding up fast on Ranger. My stomach jumped, and I swam away from them, toward the pier. I held a post and watched as the elder Knight dismounted, his muscles flexed and for a moment, he stood, beside the saddle.

He seemed to be waiting for something, or maybe he was trying to calm down? He was breathing as hard as his poor horse. Finally, he wrapped the reins over a limb and started in our direction. I couldn't help noticing his slight wince as he walked.

"Hey, bro, coming in for a swim?" Patrick called out.

"What the fuck, Patrick?" Stuart shouted. His eyes were furious, his lips tight. He looked at us, and I noticed his fists clench. "It's dangerous to race in this wind. Someone could get hurt."

The younger Knight pushed himself up onto the pier, water droplets tracing down the lines on his back and arms. Standing together, I couldn't help notice their similarities — and differences. They were both slim with drool-worthy bodies. Stuart was a bit taller, a shade darker, and a lot less playful. In fact, I was a little scared he might hit his brother. Why was he so angry?

Elaine swam up next to me, her growing annoyance clear. I felt guilty, like we'd been busted playing hooky from school, which was silly. We were supposed to be having fun... Right?

"Where is Mariska's horse?"

Stuart's voice was barely controlled. His brother's by contrast was still playful, as if the older Knight's agitation was an everyday occurrence.

"Well, what the hell." Patrick rubbed his chin. "That little sneak. But you know Cheyenne. She always gets jumpy in a Chinook."

"How were you planning to get back?"

"The girls can share a horse. Or better still..." He glanced at us in the water and winked. "Elaine could ride on my lap."

"My favorite!" She called from where we were attempting to pull ourselves out of the lake.

Stuart turned to me, and heat replaced the cold I'd been feeling. He reached down, and I didn't have time to think. I took his hand, and in one quick sweep, I was up on the pier. The ease with which he lifted me was impressive, but now I stood in front of him, my wet tunic dripping.

"She could've run into a fence and been killed. As usual, you're not thinking, putting the women in danger..."

Patrick reached down to pull Elaine up. The nonstop wind had already started to dry my hair and my shirt, but it was still relatively see-through, and even the beige bra I wore had turned almost clear. Stuart's eyes drifted to my breasts and bare legs, and I wasn't shivering anymore — at least not from cold.

"You're riding back with me." It wasn't a request, but I didn't mind. The way he looked at me had heat sizzling between my thighs.

Elaine, however, marched up to him and shoved his arm. "Hey, Captain Asshat!" Patrick reached for her, but she jerked away. "I guess you equate women with little children?"

"Easy, bossypants," Patrick laughed as he caught her around the waist.

Stuart's jaw tightened. "I expect my brother to use his brains."

She poked his chest with her finger. "If Patrick used his brains, he wouldn't have come all the way out here to check on a jerk who isn't even grateful."

"That's enough, now." Patrick ducked and swept Elaine over his shoulder. She squealed, but he kept walking toward the horses. "Did you insult me just then?"

"You'd better cut the shit, or I'll kick your ass myself!" She shouted, pointing to us as Patrick carried her away.

Stuart glared in their direction, but as soon as they were gone his expression dissolved into a smile. "Looks like my little brother made a good decision for once."

I didn't want to be jealous of my new bestie, but his obvious approval irritated me just a bit. All that disappeared when his hazel eyes met mine. They were hot and interested, and they made me tingly and light.

"Are you cold?" He asked, leading us back to the horse. "That lake is like ice."

"I'm okay," I managed to breathe.

He scooped up my jeans and hat while I held my boots. "I have a blanket you can sit on so you don't have to get your jeans wet."

He spread an Indian-print blanket over the front of his saddle. I stepped into my boots, and he helped me up. The wool scratched my thighs, but I didn't have time to complain. He grasped the reins in front of me and the saddle behind. His eyes raked over my thigh, and all at once, his firm chest was pressed behind me in the seat. Absolutely nothing was wrong at that point. One hand moved to my stomach, and butterflies surged through the arches of my feet. I had to work hard not to make a sound.

The reins were in his other hand, and he turned us back in the direction of the ranch.

Starting out, the nonstop bounce of the trot and my lack of access to the stirrups made me feel like I was falling, but soon we eased into a loping gallop.

"We'll take it slower." His voice was beside my ear, and the horse moved in smooth ripples. "If you're uncomfortable, let me know."

"This is perfect."

Patrick and Elaine had already taken off at full speed toward the house. Patrick's cowboy hat was on, and Elaine's blonde hair flew behind her. They were both shouting and having fun, but I was focused on the hard body at my back and the firm grip he had on my midsection.

All my anxiety was gone, replaced with pure bliss. Nothing could be wrong with Stuart's arms around me, holding me close and safe against his body. From the front of the saddle, I had a panoramic view of the mountains surrounding us, the vast sweep of prairie grasses, and gradually coming into view, the sprawling ranch house. The wind continued to blow warm, and above us, the arch of yellow clouds was gradually turning deeper orange with the sunset.

We didn't speak—mostly because it was difficult between the wind and the speed of the horse, but I'd already perceived this man favored quiet over the noise of voices. When I was comfortable with Ranger's movement, I carefully lifted one of my hands from the saddle horn to cover his on my stomach. Threading our fingers, his muscles tensed at my back, but he didn't pull away. He accepted my hand, and warmth flooded my chest. We rode through the colors of the sky, the roar of the wind, and the heat of our bodies pressed together with our fingers entwined.

We held each other all the way until we pulled up at the barn and Ranger slowed to a trot, breaking our moment, sending me scrambling for anything to grasp. Still, a small bridge had been built. A tiny step forward.

He pulled Ranger to a stop and quickly swung his leg off from behind me. From the ground, he held up a hand to help me down before I could catch my breath.

Dropping in front of him, I looked up, expecting things to be different, some kind of change, but his expression was back to closed, distant.

"I didn't brush down Cheyenne when she got back." He turned his back on me and went to the small closet, leaving me bewildered where I stood. "You can take care of her."

With an exasperated breath, I stomped into the tack room, past him, and snatched up an oval brush and a comb. Perhaps I was being ridiculous, but so was he. How could he act like nothing just happened between us?

"I'll get her saddle for you," he said, but I didn't stop.

I almost told him I didn't care. He could do whatever the hell he wanted, but that would've been a lie. No matter what was going on right now, I still cared very much what he did.

Cheyenne was in her stall fully tacked. I took a deep breath before opening her door, not wanting to agitate her with my frustrated mood.

"Hey, girl," I said in a quiet voice, running my hand down her velvet nose. She made a low grunting sound.

"The warm wind feels nice, but it bothers some of the animals." Stuart stepped past me into the pen and loosened the strap that ran around her belly.

In a matter of minutes he lifted the blanket and saddle easily. I stayed at her nose holding her bridle, not wanting to care how his muscles looked when they flexed or how sexy his profile was with that straight nose and slightly full lips.

"I'll be back for her bridle," he said as he passed. "You can start brushing her down."

He was gone, and I released the breath I didn't even realize I was holding. Going to Cheyenne's side, I pulled the brush across her back in long, firm strokes. I traced it over and over, down to her rump, across her belly then I pulled out the comb. With a few quick pulls, I brushed her mane, and keeping to the side of her rear, I quickly combed her tail. I was just finishing when Stuart returned for the bridle.

"Dinner's ready, but you probably want to shower." He reached up and casually lifted the bridle off her ears and slid it down her face. She released the bit at once.

"I don't care. I can eat like this." I pushed past him in a pout, but he caught my upper arm and pulled me back, nearly lifting me off my feet.

He was too close, his grip on my arm too firm, and with his lowered brow, the clenched jaw—it was overwhelming. "Don't set your sites on me, Mariska." His voice was tight. "When the time comes, I will leave."

My voice, by contrast, was surprisingly calm considering my skittering insides. "What makes you think I'm interested in you?"

A light sparked in his eyes, and before I could think, his mouth was on mine. Bodies crashed together, a small noise escaped my throat and was lost in him. I dropped the brush—it hit the ground with a clatter as I pushed my fingers into his soft, thick hair.

He was forceful and strong and delicious. His tongue found mine in a sweep, and I made another little noise as his hands moved to my waist, lifting me against the post of the stall door. Soap, cedar, the pungent smell of the barn filled my senses. My arms tightened around his neck as my mouth chased his. I wanted more, I wanted all of him. He caught one of my lips between his teeth, giving it a pull before releasing me with an exhaled groan.

We stood there, foreheads touching, arms entwined, both breathing hard. My lips throbbed, and my legs trembled. His brow clutched again, and he looked almost angry. Without a word, he went straight to the tack room, bridle in hand.

My body was throbbing, and I could only hold the stall door, trying to calm myself. How could he walk away so calmly?

I could see I had a fight on my hands. Deep in my heart, I knew he belonged to me, but that wounded warrior wasn't letting anyone in. He had his plans, and for whatever reason, they didn't allow room for love.

Stuart Knight had locked his heart up tight, but I was determined to break in and steal it. He might be strong, but that kiss told me what I needed to know. He wanted me.

CHAPTER 7: MASSAGE THERAPY

Stuart

My safe place was ruined. First, Patrick showed up, killing any hopes I had of finding calm — at least he was occupied with Elaine and out of my way, and we'd figured out how to coexist without actually hurting each other through the years.

I had no strategy for Mariska.

She intoxicated me like nothing I'd ever experienced. No drug compared to her, and then I went and kissed her. *Jesus*! I don't know what the hell made me do that. I fucking had to leave now.

Thinking back, I remembered my visceral reaction when her horse ran into the barn without her. Adrenaline surged in my veins, and my vision clouded. Ignoring the pain in my back and legs, I'd saddled up Ranger and taken off after her.

God, she was beautiful standing on that pier. The shirt she wore was transparent wet, and her dark nipples hinted through the fabric making my mouth water. Her chestnut hair hung in gentle waves over her shoulders, and her hazel eyes glowed like the sun behind the clouds.

Which was exactly the problem. I was no fucking poet. Now I had all these bullshit lines flooding my brain over a girl who looked half my age.

All I could think about were her soft lips, the feel of her in my arms. Riding back, I'd had to fight not to respond physically to her body moving with mine in the saddle. She held my hand, and the pull between us...

I was like a fucking teenager.

Worst of all, I kissed her. She tasted like cool liquid and she smelled... like heaven. Shit, if she didn't make the most amazing noises. I picked her up, and she was so light in my arms. I wanted to carry her up to the loft, take her, claim her, make her mine, cover every inch of her skin with my mouth. Visions of her riding my lap tormented me. I was healthy, I was over the meds, and I wanted her.

Growling, I rubbed my forehead hard, trying to scrub these thoughts and images away. I'd beaten one drug. I could do it again.

* * *

The kitchen was dark when I finally took the chance to enter. I waited until everyone had eaten, visited and gone to their rooms in the hopes of avoiding her. It was beneath me to act this way—hiding from a woman. The problem was I was still getting my strength back.

When I entered the dim room and saw I was alone, disappointment tightened my stomach. *Ridiculous.* I'd talk to Bill about taking a few days at the cabin. I was close to being one hundred percent, but I needed a little more time.

Winona left a plate of fried chicken, a baked potato, and rolls in the microwave for me, and I poured a glass of wine to go with it. The fire burned low, and I walked over to sit on the hearth and have my dinner as the orange flames caressed the black coals.

It reminded me of nights under the stars. Healthy nights when I'd camped alone and enjoyed the solitude and majesty of the open plain. It was the remedy that would get me back to whole. Then I'd return to the desert.

A soft creak on the floor made me glance up, and I hated the anticipation burning in my chest. I hated the disappointment when I saw it was only my uncle.

"Sorry to disturb your quiet," he said, giving me a kind smile. "I'd wanted to talk to you about this at dinner."

"I didn't feel like company." I took a bite of roll, and the two of us watched the flames a moment.

Finally, he cleared his throat and propped a boot on the hearth. "Well, I won't take all your time. Evan Robertson rode over while you were away this afternoon. A few of his cattle got loose, and he's worried about them getting lost, electrocuted. Asked if we could help track them down and round them up tomorrow."

"Think it's wise to wait?" Metal fences often became electrified during a Chinook, and unsuspecting livestock died as a result.

"Not my call to make." Bill straightened and walked over to the hall leading to our rooms. "He asked if we could join them at sunup. I thought you might like to ride along."

Today's unplanned trip across the plain had irritated my back, but I wasn't about to stick around another day with temptation so close at hand.

"I'll be ready when you are."

* * *

Evan Robertson owned a cattle ranch several miles west of us, toward Vaughn. In addition to cows, he was one of several ranchers who'd added bison to his herd, and those animals, it seemed, led yesterday's escape.

Dressed in jeans and a brown leather jacket and chaps, Evan hopped up on a flatbed trailer before shouting over the wind to the group of about twelve men on horseback, who'd come to help.

"Got about ten of the big ones running ahead of the wind," he said. "If we split, half going north, the other half east toward Benton Lake, we should spot them and circle them back around to the pen. I picked two leaders, we each have a flare gun to shoot when they're spotted."

Conway Hendricks, who was from a spread near Benton, held up one of the large-barreled flare guns. His thick, grey beard was unmistakable, and he had two guys, one wiry and one stocky, with him. In addition to cowboy hats, they had bandannas tied around their mouths and noses. It seemed like overkill to me. A few other guys had joined us. From the looks of them, they had ridden up from the Air Force base, probably looking for some adventure.

Bill and I stayed with Evan's group. We wore jeans and canvass jackets. Even at dawn, with the sun just cutting across the mountains, the warm winds made jackets unnecessary. They were good protection, though, against flying debris or electrified objects.

I turned Ranger's head to follow my uncle, who was on Scout, the Palomino Patrick rode yesterday. He along with my paint Ranger were the best herding horses on the ranch. A sharp whistle rang out, and two groups of six took off at a gallop in opposite directions across the tan grasses.

For miles, all we could see was nonstop brown dotted by the occasional green or blackish scrub. Evan was in the lead with my uncle not far behind. I'd dropped back to keep my eyes open in the direction from which we'd come, making sure we didn't miss anything. It was a tough day of riding hard and squinting harder, doing our best to distinguish brush from bison.

After a while, it became monotonous, and I struggled to keep my thoughts from drifting to memories of soft lips and sunset eyes. I tried to focus on my recovery and my plan. I was getting better. The physical symptoms had receded, and truth be told, the mental side wasn't as hard for me. I hadn't taken the drugs to escape or to find some mental respite. That was a bonus. I'd only sought relief from the pain.

The wind blew, the clouds arched, and my mind said *Mariska*. Her name lingered and turned over in my thoughts. Why was she here? Elaine said she didn't want her to be alone at Thanksgiving. Why would she be alone?

It didn't matter. My goals were established—I'd get well, give myself time to be firmly back on my feet, and I was gone. Still, this person stood there in my way, silhouetted against the burning fire of the sun, taunting me with her presence.

I didn't want her.

I wanted her.

I needed to stay away from her.

I needed to be with her.

Dammit.

By afternoon we'd combed miles of open land between Sun Prairie and Benton Lake without seeing a single rogue beast. Evan was determined and wanted to keep riding, but Bill convinced him the horses needed a break. We stopped at a pond near one of the rocky outcroppings off Bootlegger Trail to breathe and eat.

I led Ranger over to a spot by the water, and shocks of pain radiated through the backs of my legs. *Shit*, I'd overdone it between yesterday's hard ride and now this. Holding the side of my horse's saddle while he drank, I closed my eyes against the blazing ache, remembering what had driven me to start the drugs in the first place. Nothing eased this.

Here was where the mind battles began, the bargaining and rationalizing. If I got another script, I'd be smarter this time. I wouldn't think I was stronger than the docs did. I'd only use them on the worst days. If I was ever going to get back to the desert, be as strong as I used to be, I had to have something to help me with this wound.

I hadn't even noticed Bill at my shoulder until he spoke. "You doing all right, partner?"

Pushing away from my horse, I stepped back, but a muscle spasm caused me to wince. "Just taking a breather."

His brow tightened. "This is a fool's errand if you ask me. I want you to head on back to the house."

"I came to help. I can do this."

Bill's hand closed over my arm like a vice. "Listen to me, son. Conway's all the way down to Black Eagle, and he hasn't seen a thing. Those bison could be as far as Conrad with the head start they got. Maybe farther."

I knew he was right, and even my pride wasn't strong enough to override the misery radiating through my pelvis. Ranger was watered, I'd had a few bites of the cold chicken Winona had packed us.

"Anything you need tending to when I get back?" I could do that much at least.

"Nah. With all the work you did yesterday, we're pretty set for a few days. Take a break." Confusion lined my face, but he only laughed. "You forget when you and Patrick are gone, it's just me and Ron doing chores. You two've gotten us more than caught up."

My expression relaxed, but at the same time, I didn't want to sit around the ranch house with the internal battle I was waging. "Would you mind if I spent some time at the cabin?"

"Wouldn't you rather spend some time with our guests?" He glanced at me, and a hint of mischief was in his eyes. "Some of them are right easy on the eyes."

Exactly. "I'd do better with some quiet time."

He sniffed and his eyebrows twitched. "Suit yourself."

* * *

I'd taken my time riding back to the house. We weren't as far out as I'd thought, but Ranger was thankful for a restful lope after two days of tearing across the prairie. None of our house guests were apparent when I made it to the barn, and I hoped to get in the stall, brush Ranger down, pack quickly, and head out again.

Considering my plan, I decided to take Freckles with me back to the cabin. Patrick wouldn't use his fucking brain to keep Mariska off her, and the least I cold do was protect her against a flighty horse. The idea that I wouldn't be here to protect her from anything else gnawed at the back of my mind, but she was a grown woman, even if she was young. I had to give her credit for being able to keep out of trouble.

Ranger in his stall, I removed his saddle and blanket and was just making my way toward the tack room when she ran through the doorway off the side paddock. She was laughing, and her hair blew around her face in silky ribbons. My chest tightened, but I kept my pace steady, determined.

"Oh!" The soft note in her voice hit me right in the stomach. "I didn't hear you get back."

I didn't plan to answer her, but when I turned to go back for the bridle, she was standing in the doorway blocking me. Today she wore an Indian-print poncho and what looked like nothing else except cowboy boots. She was delicious with that long hair wrapping over her shoulder. *Stirring below my belt. Fighting that.*

"Patrick said you'd be gone all day." Her light brows clutched over those eyes. "Did something happen? Where's your uncle?"

Clearing my throat, I tried to find balance in the midst of the internal storm she provoked. "He asked me to head back. Check on the place."

Scooping up a brush, I started for the door, but she didn't miss a thing.

"It's your injury." I kept moving, and she was right behind me. "You never gave me a chance to tell you. I know massage therapy. If it's muscular or nerve damage, I could probably help you."

Massage therapy had been one of the most effective treatments before I'd gone on the meds. Still, I couldn't think of anything more dangerous than her small hands touching my bare skin, relieving my pain.

"That's okay. I'll manage." Pulling the stall door open, I moved Ranger to the side of his pen so I could quickly pull the brush over his coat.

When she spoke again, her voice was soothing, sexy. "Don't be that way." I kept my eyes on the brown and white horse in front of me, but I could hear her smile. "You're clearly in pain. Won't you let me help you?"

The way her voice rolled across my ears, low and sultry, tightened the muscles low in my stomach. Yesterday's kiss blazed in my mind, but I fought it back with anger.

"I'm taking a few days' rest." My voice was sharp, but it was for the best. "I'll be fine."

"Are you afraid?" Flashing a glare at her, I had to look twice. My anger hadn't stopped her. She actually reached for my arm.

Everything froze when she touched me. This small, beautiful creature inserted herself between me and my horse, holding my arm and my gaze. She wasn't going to run, and she wasn't letting me go.

"What do you want, Mariska?" The muscle in my jaw tightened. I was too tired for fighting.

Another hand on my other arm, she held me against her body and whispered. "I want you, silly."

I moved my arms away and grasped her by the shoulders. She blinked as I shook her once. "I already told you. I'm leaving."

"Take me with you." Her hazel eyes burned into mine. *Was she casting a spell on me? Take her with me? God dammit!*

Loosening my grip on her, I stepped back, and a flare of pain shot through my hip. "Fuck!" I hissed, and she was right with me.

"Come on." Her voice was patient yet insistent.

Lacing her fingers in mine, she pulled me toward the door. She took the brush from my hand and set it on top of the stall. Once we were out, she locked the pen. Our eyes didn't meet as she caught my hand again, pulling me in the direction of the house. I didn't fight her. Ron walked across the yard, but he didn't acknowledge us. Patrick and Elaine were nowhere to be seen.

The sway of her poncho across her ass revealed she was wearing short denim cutoffs underneath. Her legs were smooth, and I followed the movement of her hair up the length of her back. I couldn't tell if the poncho was a shirt or if there was more to her outfit.

She didn't stop once we were in the house. She kept walking, leading me to the hall where Bill's and my bedrooms were located.

"Which is your room?" she asked.

I wasn't getting out of this easily. I wasn't sure I wanted to. Taking the lead, I walked us to the third door on the right. It was a spacious bedroom with a bathroom attached. A small desk was just inside, and a recliner sat near a wall across from a medium-sized, flatscreen above a large dresser. Mariska was only interested in the king-sized bed in the far corner.

She turned to me and pulled my shirt out of my jeans. "You don't have to take off everything. Just strip down to your boxers."

Her hands fascinated me as she unbuttoned my shirt. They were slim but strong, and several needs I'd put on hold for a long time sprung to attention.

"I need a shower." My voice was thick.

Sunset eyes flickered up to mine, and I wanted to kiss her again. "You can shower when I'm done. Or you can sleep and shower tonight."

"I don't sleep during the day."

"When I'm finished, you'll want to rest."

One of my eyebrows arched, and I couldn't stop a grin. "That sounds highly unlikely."

"This is therapy, Mister Knight." Her eyes slanted, but I caught the gleam there. "I'm a professional."

"Are you licensed?"

Her lips pinched in the most adorable way. "A minor technicality."

If I weren't so curious about what was coming, I would've ended this doctor-patient game she was playing and crushed her against my chest in that moment. But I *was* curious.

"Now," she said, once my shirt was off. Her eyes didn't leave my chest, and I saw her breathing change. It was the fucking sexiest thing she'd done yet. "Sit down, so I can take off your boots."

For a moment, I stood in front of the girl in the Indian poncho, denim cutoffs, and possibly nothing else, contemplating all the things I wanted to do to her. After another beat, another damn sexy blink, I sat on the bed.

She started to breathe, and a grin curled the side of my lips. Her eyes moved from my mouth to my chest, and I noticed her slim hands tremble as she caught the heel of my boot.

"I have a boot jack over by the door," I said.

"I'll use it for mine."

Stepping in front of me, she caught my heel in her palm and pulled. A sharp tug, and the boot slid off my foot. While she carried it to the door, I reached down and pulled off the other one. A small frown creased her eyes when she walked back to take it from me. She carried the second boot to the door, and I quickly slid my jeans down and off.

This time when she turned back around, her pink mouth dropped open. She closed it fast, but I almost laughed as she visibly fought for control. She hadn't touched me yet, and my muscles were already relaxing.

"Okay, then." Her voice wavered just a bit. Lifting an arm, she pointed to the mattress. "Lie on your stomach."

"I thought massage therapists used special tables." It was a stall. I wasn't quite finished watching her squirm.

"We're having to make do. Now lie down."

No one told me what to do. It was that simple. But her standing here in front of my bed, tentatively giving me orders, was a definite turn-on. I followed her cute demands and whipped the covers back before sliding across the cool mattress.

Relaxation settled over my shoulders. I heard her use the bootjack to slide her first boot off. A thump and a shush later, I knew she'd removed the second. She didn't come to me right away, though. Soft noises, the sound of heavy cloth hitting the floor preceded the indentation of the mattress, the movement of her climbing up the bed beside me.

My eyes were closed when she touched me the first time. Warm hands slid back and forth across my lower back. It felt so good.

"I'm going to do deep-tissue massage, but I need you to tell me the extent of your pain. Is it from an old injury?" Her touches turned deeper, kneading as she spoke. It was painful, but I could feel the ache releasing. "I'm assuming since you can ride, it's not delicate."

"Nothing on me is delicate." My voice was muffled from lying on the mattress.

"Do you mind if I remove your boxers?"

Yes. I minded very much. I wasn't sure I'd have the strength to stop myself if things went further. "No," was what came out of my mouth.

With careful movements, she slipped off the bed, taking the boxer briefs I wore with her.

* * *

Mariska

If you asked where this sudden surge of bravery came from, I'd have to be honest. I had no fucking idea. Stuart rode into the barn looking like sex on two legs... very tired sex on two legs, but sex on two legs all the same, and I made up my mind. After the way he kissed me yesterday, I didn't care what type of bullshit line he tried to spin, Stuart Knight was in the same space as me. He was fighting hard, but he wanted this.

Now I was in his bedroom ordering him around, and he was actually allowing it. Humoring me, more like it. Not for one minute was I suffering from the delusion that this man took orders from anyone. Still, for whatever reason, exhaustion or simple curiosity, he let me take the lead.

Once his shirt was off, I couldn't hide the hitch in my breath at the site of his lined torso. Ridges crossed his abdomen, lines stretched across his broad shoulders and down his arms. He lay on his stomach across the mattress, and it was all I could do not to run my tongue over every inch of his beautiful body. Instead, I quickly took off my boots, and for increased mobility (yes, that was my excuse), I removed my denim shorts.

Lightly I smoothed my palm across his lower back, trying to remember the touches I'd learned in the few massage therapy classes I'd taken. *Why hadn't I taken more?* Kneading a little harder, I knew I had to get lower, down into the pelvic area to give him relief.

"Do you mind if I remove your boxers?" My voice was breathless and trembling. Those snug, dark briefs didn't hide much, but I knew once I saw that ass, I'd be a goner.

"No."

One word. He'd sounded almost as cautious as me when he said it. Closing my eyes, I shook myself. Now was the time. This was my man. If I was going to make it happen, if I was going to make any of this make sense, from the day I left Bayville to this moment, I had to go for it. Fate had dropped this opportunity straight in my lap.

Inhaling a quiet breath, I gently pulled the waistband out and lowered it down his legs. I knew what was on the other side, pressed between his pelvis and the mattress, and I didn't want to hurt him. Miraculously, I got his underwear off, and

Oh.

My.

God.

Square and tight, with palm-sized indentations on each side... For a moment, I could only stare at his backside. Perfect and golden as the rest of him.

Climbing back onto my knees, I took the quietest deep breath in the history of recorded time. It trembled going in, and my hand trembled reaching out. I touched him. He seemed to breathe at that exact moment as well — almost as if he'd been holding his breath, too.

Pressing with my palms and circling with my thumbs, I kneaded the tightness out of his left side. Moving down that perfect curve of muscle, I went to his hamstring and repeated the process moving back up. Thumbs circling, palms pressing, more circling, more kneading, and I moved to the other leg to repeat the process, down then slowly working my way back up to that perfect ass.

He let out a few quiet groans throughout, and after ten minutes that felt like a mixture of ten seconds and ten hours, I'd done all I could do. I was finished.

Sitting back on the bed, I looked at the sculpted physique lying before me.

"You should take an ibuprofen to head off any pain tonight. Massage releases lactic acid, and you might actually feel worse at first. It'll be a lot better in the morning."

His head turned, and smoky hazel eyes blinked under thick lashes. He was tired, but he was still so handsome. "That felt really good." Husky voice. The man was pure sex. "Thanks."

Dropping my chin, I looked at my hands. "Glad to help."

Neither of us spoke. He didn't move. My work was done, and it was time for me to go. I had to go.

My insides twisted, and my stomach cramped at the thought of walking away from him, at the prospect that he might not follow. Still, I knew Stuart Knight, and I couldn't be easy. He had to decide what he wanted. He had to come after me.

Clearing my throat, I turned and slid off the bed, scooping my shorts from the floor. "I hope you feel better," I said before heading to the door where my boots lay next to the jack.

He didn't speak, and from what I could tell, he hadn't moved. He was letting me go. Heat blurred my vision, my stomach ached, and I started moving faster. I would *not* cry—at least not here. I'd run all the way to the other side of the house, to my room, before I lost it.

Reaching for the door, I'd just turned the knob and started to pull when it flew from my fingertips and slammed shut. The noise made me jump, and a boot dropped from my arms, hitting the floor with a loud *thump*. Stuart's arm was over my head. He'd pushed the door closed, and my bottom lip sucked between my teeth when his hand slid slowly down to turn the lock.

Lined stomach, broad chest, strong arms, he was naked before me. I wanted to look lower, but instead I cautiously blinked up to his eyes. They were hot and angry and desperate and hungry, and my heart ricocheted all around inside my chest. He was losing the fight this time.

"Stay." His voice rumbled low, and my arms went slack.

I dropped my other boot, my shorts, and stood in front of him waiting, ready for whatever was coming.

Chapter 8: The Cabin

Mariska

Time seemed to stand still for several moments as Stuart fought an internal battle I could see in his eyes. He told me to stay, but he was still fighting. Like a deer in headlights, I couldn't move.

"Take off your top." He gave the low order, and I obeyed it. My top was off in an instant, and I stood before him in only my bra and panties.

"Braid your hair."

Blinking, I wasn't sure where this was going, but I pulled the length over my shoulder and without breaking our intense eye contact, I started weaving my wavy locks into a thick rope over my shoulder.

"Bra." I reached around and unfastened it. The straps tickled my hypersensitive skin as they fell down my arms. The entire garment fluttered to the floor, and his eyes broke from mine to study my body. I couldn't breathe.

Reaching out, he cupped the bottom of my breast and slid his thumb across a tightening nipple. The rough touch of his palm against my delicate skin, the circling of his thumb around my straining buds. Hungry eyes darkened as he watched my body respond to him. Heat pulsed deep between my thighs. My breath hitched then became shallow and fast. I had no idea what he'd do next. I didn't expect him to turn and go to the bed.

He climbed onto it and leaned against the headboard, eyes fixed on mine. I wanted to look down, to gaze at all of him, but I couldn't.

"Remove your panties." His voice had changed, but it still commanded. I only hesitated a moment before catching the thin sides around my thumbs and pushing them down. Standing before him completely nude, I couldn't stop a shiver. My arms crossed over my stomach, and I tried to cover myself.

"Stop." He spoke sharply. "Don't cover yourself." His eyes raked over me in a look so predatory I felt it on my skin.

I looked at him as well. His powerful, lined body was tense, ready, and his erection rose up his belly. Thick and long, I shivered at the size of it. Nothing like that had ever been inside me, still I ached for it.

"Come to me." It was a lusty whisper speaking words I'd longed to hear since before I'd flown across the country. I crawled up the bed, but just as I reached his waist, he stopped me. "Do you want this?"

"Yes." My voice was only a little shaky.

"I want be inside you, but first I want to be in your mouth."

Moisture pooled between my thighs. I'd never been with a man who made demands, who told me exactly what he wanted and expected me to deliver, but it only intensified my feelings for him.

I leaned down to follow instructions, but he stopped me. "I want to taste you as well. I want to hear you come before I sink between your thighs."

My brow must have lined because the slightest grin softened his stern face. He pulled me against his chest, and warm breath drifted across my cheek as he spoke to me.

"Beautiful Mariska." Hands in my hair, he consumed my mouth.

A moan ached from my chest and was lost in him. Strong fingers tightened against my skull, holding me forcefully, taking no prisoners. I moaned again as he pulled my lip between his teeth before pillaging my mouth once more. I held his wrists, my head light.

In that moment, he pushed me back against the bed. Stunned, my eyes blinked open, and I tried to get my bearings. It was all happening so fast. He sat back on his heels and gripped my thighs, pulling my hips to his mouth. He gave me one slow, lingering look before licking his tongue from the top of my clit all the way down to my opening, wet and throbbing.

"Oh, god! Stuart!" I cried, flexing my ass in his hands. I was so close, I would come for him fast.

He didn't stop, tracing his tongue back again and slowly circling that small, powerful bud. I whimpered as he repeated the figure eight pattern, circling and sucking until I saw stars. My thighs began to quiver, and he lowered me, shifting his body around so his hips were positioned near my head.

"Suck," he breathed against my thigh.

His enormous cock was just at my mouth, a clear drop at the tip. Pushing against the mattress, I rose above him, lifting the heavy muscle to my lips before tracing my tongue around the tip, down the side and back up.

He rolled to his back, holding my ass so my knees were on each side of his head. A low groan vibrated against my clit, and my entire pelvis jerked. My head dropped against his thigh. I was right there, quivering on that sparkling edge. I managed to take him into my mouth, giving him a firm squeeze. At the same time, his stomach muscles flexed, and he gave me another hard suck, sinking a thick finger deep inside me.

I arched, moaning against him, lightly touching his tip with my teeth.

"*Shit,*" He groaned against my clit, and the muscles low in my pelvis tightened harder. One more pass, and my orgasm would shatter through me. Heat flooded the lower half of my body, and a delicious ache raged in my core.

Moving my head up and down, I gripped his base, pumping him, drawing him out as I whined and moaned from the delicious pleasure his skilled tongue was teasing from me. He didn't stop, and I tried not to stop, but my body shook as I came on his mouth.

Lowering my head, I sighed his name as pleasure snaked up my thighs, curled through my belly, and exploded from my chest.

Before I knew what was happening, he rolled me onto my back. The orgasm still shimmered under my skin as he leaned toward the nightstand to retrieve a condom. No hesitation, I watched as he tore it open with his teeth.

I remembered a line from some class I took in college: Condom on a banana. *Big banana.* The thought made me giggle, and he leaned forward, catching my cheeks and pulling my mouth hard against his. I wrapped my arms around his neck. This time, I kissed him back with equal force, pulling his luscious mouth between my lips and teeth. He lifted me by the waist, and I was on his lap, holding him, tasting him.

In my dreams it had been this way with him, blazing, familiar, orgasmic… I wanted to push him back against the headboard and spend the next several minutes exploring his mouth, but large hands held me back.

Commanding eyes fixed on mine as he reclined against the headboard. "Fuck me."

My body was still buzzing with our kiss, my orgasm, but I hesitated. It was only for a moment, but he didn't miss it.

"What's wrong?" Again, those lines across his stomach deepened as he sat up, pulling me closer. I tried to look away, but he caught my chin. I knew he wouldn't ask me again. Still, he let me lean forward and press my face against his neck as I said it.

"It's my first time."

Everything stilled. Silence echoed under my fingertips. Fear stronger than my first-time jitters twisted in my stomach that he might push me away, that my revelation might change how he felt about me.

Without a word, I fumbled my hand to his straining cock. His desire was strong as ever, and as I circled my fingers around him, he lifted my head from his shoulder. Tilting it back, he looked straight into my eyes. "You're a virgin?"

"Technically."

It was so hard to explain. I knew I was ready. I knew I wanted this. I knew the wetness from the incredible orgasm he'd provoked would smooth his entry. I knew all of these things, but I was scared. He was so strong and demanding and so... big.

Before I could say anything, he moved me onto my back. Propping his head on one hand, he looked down at me. I couldn't decide if he was exasperated or if he was amazed.

"But just a moment ago..." His brow creased, and he shook his head slightly. "You give a hell of a blow job for a virgin."

Tucking my face against his chest, I exhaled a little laugh. "I didn't say I was a nun." My voice was low, and he made me look at him again.

"What are you telling me right now? Do you want to stop?"

"No." Lifting my hand to his neck, I slowly threaded my fingers into the side of his hair. "Just this one time... be gentle?"

"Mariska." He exhaled my name, leaning into me.

I shivered in his arms as his mouth traced my jawline, nibbling, biting. "My Mariska."

At those words, joy radiated in my chest. He seemed to want this even more. His arms were all around me, his mouth covering my skin. His sparse chest hair teased my nipples as he moved, and his delicious scent clouded my mind. He was so strong and so forceful, yet in this moment, he softened.

His hand traced down my side, lightly following my curves, shaping around the base of my ass. With a knee, he spread mine apart then he propped himself on his forearms. Desire smoldered in his eyes, and I could feel his erection on my belly. Still, he was holding back, touching me with care. The idea that I could give commands as well as take them drifted across my dazzled brain.

"You could be on top... If that helps?" The slightest strain was in his voice, and I knew he'd gone as long as he could.

"I trust you."

Holding my thighs open, he lightly touched the sensitive skin at my entrance. His fingers tested my wetness, stretched gently, and I tensed, holding his shoulders.

"I don't want to hurt you."

Placing my hands against his chest, I looked into his eyes. "Why did you have me braid my hair?"

Heat flared in his gaze, and I knew I had asked the right question. "This changes everything."

"Does it?"

Leaning down, he claimed my lips again, and with one strong thrust, he pushed inside me, tearing through my virginity. Our mouths broke apart, and we both cried out in response.

Mine was a cry of pain, a gasp of shock at the intense sensation of fullness, and a sudden need to move around, to figure out how to accommodate him.

His was the guttural response to claiming new territory. "Jesus, god, Mariska. You're so tight."

With every shift of my hips, he groaned, until at last he gasped, "I need to move."

Nodding, I tried not to whimper as his hips moved against mine slowly, allowing me to adjust to the incredible sensation of him inside me. Mentally, I'd prepared for the pain. I'd even done a little research on how to minimize discomfort, but nothing could get me ready for the actual sensation of him being there, inside me, stretching the limits of what I'd ever felt.

As if unable to hold back, he moved faster, going deeper. The discomfort gradually dulled, transforming into the heat of our bodies working together. Slowly, the pain receded, and my senses focused on our bodies united. It was amazing. I didn't want him to stop.

The sounds of his climb were dizzying. Noises, groans, a bead of sweat rolled down his cheek. I leaned up and licked the salty drop. How many times had I wanted to run my tongue along that scratchy jawline? He was delicious.

"Mariska..." His voice ragged, his lips caught mine. Mouths sealed together, his tongue left no part of mine unclaimed.

His thrusting became more forceful. My hips arched involuntarily, and his skin massaged the top of the cleft between my thighs. With a jolt of pleasure, I saw how well our bodies fit together. Arching my hips again, I scrubbed that part of me against him until the friction, the incredible fullness of him inside me, the shuddering groans of his building orgasm, tightened the muscles in my core. Large hands gripped my ass, and with three more violent thrusts, I dropped my head back and cried out his name.

His head fell against my collarbone, and he held still inside me, pulsing. My thighs quivered as I felt him jerking, coming. We held each other, both breathing fast. His lips touched my skin before he reached between us and held the condom as he came out, sliding it off and disposing of it quickly.

He was back with me, and I curled into his chest. Strong arms circled me, and we held each other, buzzing in the afterglow as our breathing gradually returned to normal.

* * *

Stuart

She fit perfectly in my arms. Holding her this way, after making her body mine, I began to understand why Derek couldn't talk about anything but Allison all that time we were in the desert.

I'd been with other women. I'd been with a lot of other women in a myriad of ways, but nothing was like this—and not just because she was a virgin. *How was it different? Why?* Answers to these questions escaped me, but I knew, holding her in my arms, I was seriously screwed.

Her head moved, and she leaned back to meet my eyes. The moment sunset hazel hit me, all my future plans disappeared. I didn't care about being screwed. I only wanted more of her.

She started to giggle, and my arms tightened around her slim body. I felt the smile curling my lips. I was actually smiling. I was fucking happy. *When was the last time I'd felt this way? Shit, for that matter, had I ever felt this way?*

"Why are you laughing?" My voice was a low rumble against her skin as I kissed a trail behind her ear.

She squealed and pulled up her shoulder. I mentally noted that spot for future reference. "We probably undid all the massage therapy I just gave you."

My lips sealed against the skin at her temple. They trailed over her brow before I leaned up to meet her eyes. "I have to confess... I couldn't care less."

Eyes twinkling, she smiled bigger, and I was pretty confident nothing could be more beautiful.

"I care," she said, reaching up to trace a finger over my brow. "I don't want you to be in pain."

"I can assure you, baby, I'm feeling no pain."

She laughed again, and I ducked down to nibble the skin along the base of her jaw.

"You never told me why I had to braid my hair."

She communicated so much with her eyes. Excitement, curiosity, knowledge. For example, in this moment I could see she knew exactly why her hair was braided. Testing that theory, I put it out there.

"So it's easier for me to pull your head back when I fuck you from behind."

I had to work to hold my expression neutral. I waited for her to cower or draw back, but instead, her eyes sparkled. Cautious excitement. Heat tightened low in my groin.

"You like it rough... But just now you were gentle as a lamb."

"I'm no lamb, angel. I want you to enjoy this as much as I do."

Her lips pressed together as she considered my words. I took the opportunity to slide a hand up to her breast, to roll a nipple between my fingers and watch it tighten. Her body arched to mine, and her bottom lip caught in her teeth.

"You are so beautiful… so responsive."

A shaky breath passed through her throat, and she didn't answer.

I knew exactly what I wanted to happen next.

* * *

Mariska

Stuart held me against his chest, and I was so afraid, I could hardly breathe. His embrace was like iron. He smelled like heaven. He was the most amazing lover, and I was falling so fast. It was dangerous and frightening, and nothing could keep me away from him. I suspected it when I stepped foot on the plane in Bayville, but now it was concrete in my mind. I'd do anything for him.

"I want you to go with me to the cabin." He'd kissed every inch of my skin, leaving a trail of sparkling shivers in his wake, noting every way my body responded to him. Now he threw out this challenge, and of course I'd say yes.

"What will we do there?" Impressive how I managed to sound aloof as his thoughtful gaze traveled over my body. After his braid revelation, I couldn't even imagine what he might say in response.

"It's pretty remote. One room, no television or phone." His head propped on his hand as he thought about the answer. "In the past, I'd go by myself to get away, think, find peace."

It was his place—the one he'd told me about at the gym! Still, I acted coy. "So you're saying it'll be me and you and nothing else?"

Again a small smile. Again, I melted. "Is that something that would interest you?"

I traced my finger down his shadowed cheek, not squealing the *Yes!* echoing in my brain. "Some men go hunting to get away from it all."

"Not much to hunt around here." He turned and caught my finger between his lips, giving it a quick suck before releasing it. "I'd rather hunt you."

Oh, god. Shivering, I let my eyes slide closed. "What should I tell Elaine? I can't disappear without a word."

He loosened his hold on me and sat up. My eyes traveled down his lined back now turned to me then lower to that perfect ass when he stood into his jeans and pulled them over his hips. "Tell her you're going with me to the cabin."

Tee scooped off the floor, it was over his head and down, leaving his hair in the sexiest bedhead. Mine still hung in the thick fuck-me braid he'd asked me to weave.

"I suppose she'll know what that means." Sliding to the edge of the bed, I reached down for my poncho, but he caught my shoulders before I made it.

"Hey." Our eyes met, and his were a disconcerting mixture of authority and wariness. "I want to know you better. That's all."

The little tag at the end pricked the balloon expanding in my chest. *That's all?* We'd get to know each other better, but don't expect more? Was it possible for me to do such a thing?

Another little smile, and I knew it didn't matter.

* * *

Lane's voice was the first to greet my ear when Kenny answered. "Mommy paint." Kenny was right behind him. "Hello?" She said over the chatter of her son. "Mariska? Are you okay? I didn't expect to hear from you!"

I'd left Stuart to pack his bags and ran over to my side

131

of the house to collect whatever I could think of to bring. Something about the way he'd set up this trip told me I wouldn't need much in the way of clothing.

"I'm fine!" I quickly eased my friend's concern. I needed to hear her voice. I needed that reinforcement. "What's happening back home? Has anyone complained about my lack of smoothie artistry?"

"Pete misses the cinnamon bun protein shake you invented for him." I heard her transfer the phone to her other ear and the baby to her other hip. "That's not really a thing, is it?"

Ugh! Pete. For a whole year he'd tried to take things further with us, and I'd turned him down. I couldn't help a little twinge of guilt over how hurt he'd be if he knew what I just did… And how much I looked forward to doing it again. And again.

"It's a real thing. Check my recipe notes… I think it's in the middle."

"God, you spoil that guy," she sighed. "No wonder he can't move on."

I stood in front of my closet chewing on my lip, trying to decide what I should pack for a three-day sex-weekend. "He asked for it specifically. It was more of a dare."

"Hmm…" Her voice was skeptical. "I found it!"

Nodding, I pulled out a strapless dress that had an asymmetrical hemline. "Now you can be his forever crush."

She snorted in my ear. "I'm not ready for anyone new." Lane said something, and I heard sounds of her putting him down. "By the way, this is a really hot sketch of you know who—"

"Oh, Kenny! That's why I called you." Spinning away from the closet, I collapsed across my bed, pulling my knees to my chest. Deep between my thighs, I still throbbed from where he'd been, set up residence, and made it impossible for me to forget him. "So much has happened, and not enough!"

My friend sighed in my ear. "You are so freaking dramatic. What the hell is that supposed to mean?"

Squeezing my eyes shut, I told her. "We just did it."

"Shut the fu — front door!" Her hand muffled over the phone. "Lane's holding my leg, but eff! Eff! EFF!!! Tell me all about it!"

Rolling onto my stomach, I pressed my forehead into my arm. "It was amazing. I came like five times." She made a little squeal as I continued. "Okay, I exaggerated a little. But he wants me to go away with him — "

"No! I don't care if he's Patrick's brother, you are not leaving the country with him!"

"I don't think we've made it that far." Propping my head on my hand. "He wants me to go to this little cabin with him for a few days. He said we'll get to know each other. That's all."

Kenny was quiet. I'd attempted to infuse the last bit with all the weight I'd felt when he said it.

"That's not very encouraging." And *that* was why we were so close. "Can it be that way for you? I mean, I feel like it can't or you wouldn't be there to begin with."

Rubbing my closed eyes with my fingers, I thought about everything. "Of course it can't, but I knew this, Ken. When I came here, I knew what he was like. We both saw him that day in the gym."

"Stuart Knight is no one to fu — front with." Lane's little voice said something, and she covered the phone to answer him.

"Oh, god!" I dropped my head against my hand again. "Why the hell am I here?"

Kenny was back. "I'm still not really sure, but you *are* there. You're going to go with him. What can I do?"

Comfort warmed my chest at her words. "I'm going to have to be strong with him." She made a noise of agreement. "I have to hold my own if I ever expect to be a part of his life. He won't respect anything less."

"I can see that."

Pausing a moment, I thought about what that meant. Then with a little laugh, I touched the corners of my hot eyes. "Help me pick up the pieces when he breaks my heart."

"I bet Pete would be more than happy to help you." The tease in her voice gave me the tiniest nanoparticle of relief. "And who knows? You've been right before. Maybe 'That's all' is the cry of the defeated."

"Ha. In my dreams."

* * *

Stuart

It took less than an hour to pack clothes, food, drinks... pretty much everything we'd need for a three-day stay at the cabin. I hadn't given myself time to question it. No time to second-guess what I was doing or back away. I wanted to spend the next three days exploring every inch of her beautiful body, unraveling the layers of her mind. Finding the answer to why she captivated me so thoroughly.

She didn't question or protest. She seemed to understand I needed to be away from the house, the people there, everything. I needed to understand why she was different. It was potentially setting us both up for a world of hurt, but I couldn't let that stand in the way.

I'd stripped the bed and deposited the sheets in the machine while I waited for her to shower and change. She'd emerged from her end of the house wearing a leather-fringed jacket over a thigh-high, mint-blue dress. I wanted to pull her to me and slide my hands up that skirt, but not yet. Winona was in the kitchen observing for one thing.

Irritation built as she lingered to text Elaine. Not hearing back immediately, she decided to leave a note, which prompted a search for paper and a pen.

"Just so she won't worry." The sound of her voice, her fluid movements, made me impatient to be gone.

"Winona can take care of it."

"I'll only be a second."

Leaning against the doorframe, I watched, arms crossed as she fussed with paper, finding a pen. A few times she glanced in my direction, and her cheeks flushed. For some reason, it did something to me. Made it even harder not to catch her around the waist and thread my fingers in her hair.

Once she was satisfied no one would worry or come looking, I put her in the pickup Bill loaned me and told her to follow as I rode Freckles the short distance across the prairie. I'd wanted her in the saddle with me, secure against my chest the way I'd held her on our ride back from the lake, but her body was tender from this afternoon. I didn't want to prolong that state of affairs, so she kept a comfortable distance following as we chased the sunset west.

Now we were back together again. It didn't take long to unload our bags from the truck and assemble the portable shelter for Freckles. We were outside again near where the campfire would be built.

"What's this place for?" Mariska watched as I stacked wood. I had something special in mind for tonight.

"It came with the ranch." Stepping back, I surveyed the small house lonely against the vast horizon. "We think it was an outpost when they used to raise cattle here. I'm the only one who ever uses it now."

Her eyes followed mine before returning to my face. Taking in the wind pushing the soft waves away from her cheeks, I pulled her to me.

"Give me a few minutes to get the fire going."

She blinked up. "Winona sent dinner for tonight. Want me to make our plates?"

"Are you hungry?"

With a shrug, she looked at her hands trapped against my chest. "Not particularly."

"Good." I leaned forward and kissed the corner of her mouth before releasing her.

The fire was blazing a short time later, and I took her hand, leading her back toward the cabin. She followed without question. Everything she did was somehow perfect, from the way her body felt in my arms to the way she could alternate between resistance and surrender.

Inside, I pulled a large Indian blanket from a trunk at the foot of the bed. The cabin was only three hundred square feet. One room with a kitchen, living area containing a couch and fireplace, and a double bed in the corner. A small bathroom was down the hall. It had been too small when Derek had stayed to help me. Now it was almost too big. I wanted her close to me at all times.

"It's really only designed for one person." She started to push past me, but I caught her cheeks and lifted her face.

Her eyes traveled around mine briefly before I kissed her. A small groan came from her throat, and like before in the bed, she held my neck and kissed me back. I caught her under the ass and lifted her, and her arms moved around my neck, her mouth chasing mine with a desperate hunger.

Damn, I loved the force of that kiss. It showed how strong she was, and it made it even sexier when she gave in to me. I hated weak women, but nothing about Mariska was weak.

Lowering her, I scooped up the blanket and caught her hand. "Let's sit by the fire."

My back was against one of the big logs, and she sat in front of me, leaning against my chest. The blanket was around both of us.

"The stars here always blow me away." My mouth was at her ear, and again she shivered when I touched that little spot. The semi I'd been sporting all afternoon was getting harder.

"They're beautiful." Her head dropped back against my shoulder, and I took a deep inhale of her scent. Some kind of flower. "I don't know if I've ever seen so many stars in my life."

"You smell good." I caught the skin of her neck between my lips and gave it a tiny bite. She winced away with a laugh.

"It's jasmine." Reaching for my hand, she threaded our fingers around her waist. "Tell me about you. What made you want to be a soldier?"

Exhaling a laugh, I pressed my lips against her ear. "A Marine."

"Is that different?" A frown was in her voice.

"Very."

She sighed. "I never had any friends in the military. It wasn't something we did."

"What did you do?"

"Art. Music…"

"Massage therapy?"

Her grip on my hand tightened. "That came later."

"Why would you have been alone at Thanksgiving?" Elaine's comment had troubled me since she'd made it.

She paused a moment, and when she answered, her voice was quiet. "I wouldn't have been completely alone. I could go to Kenny's if I wanted."

"Where's your family?"

A little sigh, I felt the tension in her body. "My dad was never in the picture. My mom died when I was a baby. I grew up with my grandmother. My Yaya."

"Where is she?"

Again quiet. Then longing, sadness, the little crack in her voice tugged at my chest. "She died a few years ago."

Hugging her tighter, I buried my nose in her hair. "I'm sorry," I whispered before kissing her head.

She took a shaky breath. "She taught me everything. She listened to all my dreams and gave such good advice. She was so wise."

I thought of how Bill had always been there for Patrick and me, and I thought of losing him. I hated her feeling pain like that; I never wanted her to be alone. "She sounds amazing."

"I feel close to her when I look at the stars." We were quiet several minutes, listening to the fire then she squeezed my hand. "You never told me why you wanted to be a Marine."

I got this question a lot, but my answer never satisfied me. Maybe I was still looking for the answer. "My dad was a Marine." The words came out automatically, but as I said them, I knew they weren't right.

"Like father, like son?"

"No." Thinking about the man who had never been a part of my life, I shook my head. "I never wanted to be like my father."

She was quiet a moment. We were both quiet, and the only sound was the crackle of the fire. In the distance, I saw a streak of white light.

Clearly, Mariska saw it, too. "Make a wish," she whispered.

"Make it for me."

Turning to the side, she leaned her head against my cheek and traced a slim finger down my jaw. Her expression was so thoughtful, I had to ask.

"Did you?"

A pretty smile crossed her lips. "I did." She was quiet a moment longer, and I wanted to know what it was. I didn't get the chance. "So if you didn't want to be a Marine like your dad, what kind of Marine did you want to be?"

It was such a strange way to ask the question. I liked it better. It helped me get closer to the answer. "The best kind. The kind that is always faithful. The kind that stays to the end."

"Have you reached the end?"

I couldn't answer that. I believed I still had years of service left ahead of me, but the Corps had told me to retire. I was injured. They didn't know how strong I was. I'd spent these last three years working to get back, to show them how much fight I still had in me.

Another light touch on my jawline. "You're angry," she said quietly.

Glancing down, I caught the light of a million stars in her eyes. She was so beautiful.

"What do you want?" Her voice was soft, sexy.

"To die for my country."

"Why?"

Pressing my lips together, I thought about my answer. "Honor? Courage? It's what my dad did."

"I thought you weren't like your dad."

"I'm not." With a deep exhale, I confessed. "He was better than me. I ended up broken." As much as I wanted to distinguish myself from him, I couldn't get away from the truth. "Still, it's who I am. It's all I ever wanted. Now I have to redeem myself. Redeem his honor."

She placed her palm flat against my face stroking her thumb lightly across my lips. "Sometimes it takes more courage to give up one dream for a new one."

A new dream. Derek's challenge drifted across my mind. "How old are you?"

"Twenty six."

Leaning my head back, I thought about that. *Ten years.*

"Is that a problem, soldier?"

Her sassy tone made me smile. I answered both her questions. "No. And I'm not angry."

I captured her lips again. They were open and giving. Sweeping my tongue inside, I found hers. Tonight she tasted faintly of mint. Disentangling our fingers, I ran my hand up her thigh and under that short skirt. She let out a little moan, and that was enough. She was all I wanted to think about, her soft body warm in my arms, secure against my chest.

"Stuart..." Her voice was thick as I touched her under her panties.

A question burned in the back of my mind. It was too much with the way she moved, the way she looked. This girl was too sexy to have waited so long. "How were you a virgin?"

Her breath hissed through her lips as I massaged her clit. "It wasn't really a conscious decision." Her forehead pressed against my shoulder. "I had plenty of boyfriends..."

The thought of another man touching her angered me more than I expected. I leaned forward to take her lips again, needing to possess them. A moan scraped from her throat, and her thighs tightened around my hand. She was moving with me. I'd be inside her soon.

Still I wanted answers. "So why not?"

Her hand fumbled to cover mine between her legs. "It never felt right. I wanted it to be... Mmm..." She was wet, and I slipped a finger inside. A little gasp. "Magical."

Her voice changed, and I rotated her on my lap, shifting so I could move my jeans down my hips. I jerked her panties aside and lowered her down my shaft. *Fuck. Me.* "You feel amazing."

Inside, all around me, her muscles flexed. I caught her neck and moved her mouth down to mine. Another consuming kiss. I rocked my hips up, and she broke away with a gasp. Now she was moving faster, riding me. It was scorching hot, and I was close. Everything was falling away except her luscious body riding my dick.

"Are you on the pill?" She nodded fast, and relief moved through me. I wouldn't stop this for the world.

I gripped her ass and her knees ground into my hips as she struggled for traction. She was getting off as good as I was.

"Stuart! Oh, god!" Her mouth was right at my ear as she fell apart, gasping and moaning. Her insides pulsed around me, milking and lengthening my orgasm.

With a low groan, I came hard. My hips flexed, jammed into her, filling her. Being against her skin was the most acute pleasure. Damn, she felt like heaven. I never had sex without a condom. I wasn't sure what the hell possessed me this time.

Holding her close, I breathed through the warmth of afterglow. The scent of jasmine was all around us combined with the scent of sweat and sex. It was incredible. Through the haze I was struck by what I'd just done. I trusted her. *Why?*

"I'm sorry," I said, clearing my throat. She lay against me, arms limp around my neck.

I could feel her expression change with my apology. "Why?"

"I'm clean. I should have told you before."

She pulled away, and pink flooded her cheeks. God, she was beautiful. "It didn't even occur to me. I guess I trust you."

"I would never put you in danger."

She blinked a few times before allowing a small smile. "But you like to be rough."

A flicker below my waist, inside her. I was sure she felt it, too. "Yes." My tone was serious as I caught that beautiful chin and lifted it. "So will you."

* * *

Mariska

I couldn't deny a sizzling thrill at Stuart's words. I'd never liked anything rough, but the tone of his voice, the promise in his eyes, made me believe whatever he did would be amazing. Holding him, feeling him inside me was more than enough, but there was so much more to this man.

Lifting me, he carried me back to the cabin. The warm blanket he deposited on the bed, and he didn't stop until we were in the small bathroom.

One swipe and my dress was over my head and out the door. I laughed and reached inside the small shower stall to turn on the hot water. Noises behind me, and he discarded jeans, boxer briefs, the shirt he was wearing. I felt him unhook my bra moments before rough hands reached around to cover my breasts, rolling my taut nipples between his fingers. My panties were stretched and drenched from our activities by the fire, and he slid them down next, kissing my ass along the way.

That made me laugh. "Do you want to shower or not?"

He rose in front of me, tall and smiling. Hazel eyes burned with desire. I traced my fingertips down the lines of his chest to the ridges of his stomach. He was slim, but it only made his muscles more pronounced.

"We'll see what happens." His voice was that deep vibration I felt through my core as he carefully helped me into the closet-sized stall.

My back was against his chest as the water rained down on both of us. Taking a bar of white soap off the ledge, I rolled it in my hands making a lather before I turned and rubbed them all over his body. Closing my eyes, I let a groan of satisfaction escape my lips as I followed the broad outline of his shoulders down his arms to his hands waiting to clasp mine. He pushed my back against the wall and kissed me deeply. Mouths open, the fresh taste of water touched my tongue with his.

Curling his fingers in my hair, he pulled my head back, kissing my chin. "You make this shower sexy."

Blinking through the haze, I reached over my head as his soapy hands moved down my sides. Large thumbs circled my beaded nipples before diving lower, down my stomach to my thighs. He reached under the water, giving his fingers a rinse before threading them in the folds between my legs.

"Don't want to miss a spot."

I exhaled a shaky laugh as he grinned down before kissing my nose, my mouth. "I don't think it matters. You're only making me dirty again."

"Getting dirty while getting clean. I like that."

In a flash, I was up against the wall. His legs bent as he lowered me onto his straining cock. *So big.* "Oh, god!" I gasped as he stretched and filled me, rocking into me hard.

He was thrusting fast, not waiting for me to come. It didn't matter. The way his shaft rubbed my clit, I was coming anyway. We'd been here, doing this only minutes ago, but we were insatiable. Neither of us could get enough. Strong fingers bit into the sides of my ass as he came with a loud groan. The pain of his grip mixed with the pleasure of the orgasm rocketing through my legs was the most intense feeling. I tightened over his thighs, trying to push myself higher on him.

His mouth made its way behind my ear, sending a charge straight to my core. "Oh, god!" I shrieked, gripping his broad shoulders as I finished, throbbing around him inside me.

The water continued to run over us. I held him against my chest for a moment, feeling the movement of his lips as he kissed me. After several more breaths, I felt myself drifting back to this planet.

"Bonus," I panted, and his mouth curved against my skin.

He lowered me, melting me again with that sexy smile. "You can't expect to be naked, wet, and touching me like that and nothing happen."

That made me giggle, and I snatched up the washcloth to quickly clean up once more and step out. He followed suit, wrapping a towel around his waist and heading for the small dresser near the bed.

I used a fluffy white towel to scrub the damp from my hair, and I scooped up his discarded flannel shirt to wear. It smelled just like him, and I wanted to bury my nose in it. I'd tossed a pair of long, grey thermal leggings in my suitcase, so I pulled them on along with thick, wool socks.

It wasn't as cold as it might be for a November evening, but it was still chilly. By the time I joined him in the living room, Stuart had dressed in a dark grey Henley and jeans, and had a fire going in the small fireplace. Two plates were on the coffee table holding the food Winona had sent.

Sitting cross-legged on a cushion, I took the small container of dressing and shook it over the salad on my plate. We also had pork and sweet potatoes. "Winona is such a great cook," I said, stabbing a forkful of dark greens. "Has she always worked for your uncle?"

Glancing up, I noticed he was smiling as he watched me from the couch. Feeling the heat in my cheeks, I placed my fork on the napkin beside my plate.

"Don't stop." Stuart's voice was warm.

"You have to eat dinner, too."

He nodded and picked up his knife to slice a bite of pork. "I went for a long time without much of an appetite. I'm still getting used to its return."

"Why?"

His brow lined as he chewed, and I watched as he decided how to answer me. "Bad choices."

Thinking about the day he appeared at the gym, I couldn't help wondering. "Is that why you stopped in at the gym that day?"

Another slice of meat. "Partly."

Picking up my fork, I stirred the sweet potatoes on my plate. "I would love to have someone cook like this for me."

That broke his frown. "Don't you cook?"

"Yes, but it's not my favorite thing."

"What's your favorite thing?" His fork was down, and he leaned back with a tumbler of whiskey.

"Kenny and I met at art school. I'm more of a painter, I guess."

Interest lit his eyes, and they moved to my hands. "I'd like to see one of your pieces."

"Maybe I'll show you one."

We were quiet again, and the fire hissed and popped behind me. I cut a sweet potato slice in half and popped it in my mouth. Stuart leaned forward again and did the same.

"So you didn't tell me about Winona."

Clearing his throat, he nodded. "She came with the ranch. Just like this cabin."

"Do you always spend Thanksgiving here?"

He sliced more pork and took a bite before answering. "No, we usually spend it in Chicago with my mother."

"What's your mother doing this year?" I had finished my serving, and now my knee was bent, my elbow propped on it. I tried to imagine what their mother might look like. Clearly, she had to be beautiful.

My question seemed to change Stuart's mood. His expression darkened. "I don't know what she's doing. I wasn't in a position to work out the details with her. I left it to Patrick."

"Is that bad?"

"It might've been a mistake."

He put the fork down, and picked up his place setting. Pausing, he picked up mine as well and carried it to the small sink. I watched for a moment before hopping up and following him.

"Don't wash." Reaching out, I covered his hands, but he was looking out the small window over the sink. "Stuart?"

When he turned back to me, his expression was still clouded. I didn't understand.

"I'm sure she's fine," I said quietly. "Patrick's actually very responsible."

Taking his hand away, he made a little noise before going back to the couch.

"Did something happen to make you not so close?"

His foot was propped on the table, and I studied his profile as he watched the fire. "He's just a lot younger than me."

"So am I, but we do all right."

He didn't answer, and another glance back, I wasn't even sure he'd heard me. Leaving the dishes in the sink, I went to sit beside him, facing him with my elbow bent under my cheek. "Hey," I said softly. "Where did you go?"

Eyebrows pulled, he cleared his throat, glancing at me. "I'll have to check in with her when we get back. We haven't talked in a while, and I'm sure she's worried."

"The hazards of not having a phone in the cabin?"

"I could use the mobile, but I'd rather wait."

"I can go outside if you'd like. Or you could sit in the truck?"

He traced the back of his finger down my cheek. "It can wait."

Reaching up, I took his hand in mine and laced our fingers. My heart was growing, making a place for him that he kept saying he would leave, but I didn't care. "How's the back?"

"Good." He nodded, standing. "Only a slight twinge when I move too fast."

"That's not good!" I hopped up and pushed him toward the bed. "Time for another session. Take off your clothes."

He laughed and turned to face me, pulling me close against his chest. "You know what happened the last time we did this."

Staring at his mouth, I touched my bottom lip with my tongue. "I went from being a virgin to being officially yours."

A little groan, and he pulled me up to his mouth. Strong lips sealed over mine, moving them apart. Our tongues met and curled together, but I couldn't hold him. He had my arms pinned against his chest in his firm embrace.

One more pull on my lips, a little nibble, and he turned. "You might set me back a week in my recovery."

"I will not!" Pretending to be offended, I struggled out of his embrace. "This time it's just therapy then mandatory rest."

"You know that's only going to make me want you more."

"We'll see."

CHAPTER 9: LAYERS DEEP

Stuart

All the things I decided, my plans, what was coming... all of it went out the window with Mariska. I didn't know what I wanted. It was all fucked up and wrong, but I'd brought her to this place. My place.

I'd done my best not to think about her, to forget the feel of her lips against mine, the taste of cool water on her tongue. I'd gone back to Bill's with one goal in mind — I'd gather my things and stay at the cabin until they were gone. I'd be safe here.

Then she appeared. She touched me, and what did I do? I deflowered her, brought her here, and proceeded to fuck her four more times. *Shit!* Now she lay beside me asleep, looking like some gorgeous promise of a different future, new plans.

No. I shook my head and slipped from the bed, away from her. This was part of the process. My will was still in recovery. It wasn't her fault. It wasn't anyone's fault, but if I let it go further, it would all be on me.

Walking to the coffee pot, I pulled it out and started the process. Water in the carafe, grounds in the strainer. My back didn't hurt. Putting the machine back together and hitting the On button, I leaned to the side. No pain. Leaning to the other side yielded the same result. I felt strong.

Glancing at the bed again, I thought of last night. She'd spent more time working on my back than she had the first time — most likely because we were pretty well satisfied sexually. When she finished, I actually did fall asleep. I awoke later in the night in the darkness to find her curled next to me. In the past, I didn't spend the night with the women I slept with. As a result, I never knew how immensely satisfying it could be to wake with a hard on and pull her to me. Arms around her waist, I couldn't tell if she was completely awake, but she didn't resist. My hands went under her shirt to cup her breasts. My face was in her jasmine hair, and I kissed that sensitive spot behind her ear. A little moan, and I slipped between her thighs from behind. She was slippery and wet. Bracing her against me, I moved hard and fast. Her back arched as I drove deeper, and it didn't take long before we finished. Another moan, a sated kiss, and we were asleep again. God, it was fantastic. *What the hell was I doing?*

I heard her sigh, and she stretched an arm over her head. The coffee finished dripping, and I turned away from the hypnotic sight of her, trying to think this through. I brought her here so we could get to know each other better. That's all. Sure. What the hell kind of lies was I telling myself these days?

"How long have you been up?" Her voice was high and thick with sleep. I reached for mugs and poured two cups of coffee.

"Long enough to make this." I carried them to the table. "Cream and sugar?"

"Just cream." She pushed the pillows up against the headboard as she watched me. She pulled my flannel shirt over her naked torso, and I averted my eyes, pouring cream into hers, nothing in mine.

Stepping over to the bed, I handed her the mug then sat on the sofa. "Sleep well?"

The fire had gone out, but it was still warm inside, the result of it not getting very cold out.

"Yes." She spoke around a sip of coffee. Then a sly tone filled her voice. "It seems I remember another little bonus around midnight."

"I'm detecting a pattern."

"I wasn't wet or naked!" Her voice was still teasing.

"You did touch me, however."

At that she started to laugh. I couldn't help a smile curling my lips. *Dammit.*

"So what are we doing today?" She took another sip. "Besides more of the same, of course."

"Glad you're finally onboard with the program." Another giggle from the bed. "Actually, there's a lake close by. I'm pretty sure no one goes there but me."

She was quiet, sipping. My eyes moved from the dying embers to her. She only watched me over the rim of her mug.

"I'd be very interested to know what you're thinking right now, Miss...." I thought about it. "I don't know your last name."

"Heron." Her reply was quiet. "I don't know your middle name, Mister Knight."

"William."

"Same as your uncle?"

"It's a family name."

She took another sip, and I watched her thinking. "What's your middle name?"

"Renee."

"Mariska Renee Heron." It rolled off my tongue like music.

"Stuart William Knight."

Quiet again filled the cabin. Serious quiet. The exchanging of names. I ended that moment. "Do you feel like swimming?"

"Yes." She sat up and placed her mug on the side table. Scooting to the edge of the bed, I caught the twinkle in her eye. "That should cover wet, and I'm sure at some point I'll touch you."

Damn if that didn't provoke a rise in my jeans. "Is it still a bonus if it happens repeatedly?"

"Don't be such a stickler for the rules, Stuart William." She skipped across the room to where I sat, lightly kissing my lips. Things only became tighter across my fly.

"It's who I am, Miss Heron."

"Maybe some things can change, Mister Knight."

* * *

Before we left for the lake, I checked in on Freckles. She'd stayed quiet in the shelter, and she wasn't in danger of getting too cold. Horses in this part of the country developed longer coats that made them look almost plush. She nickered and pushed at me as I filled her food bag.

"Hey, girl." I scratched behind her ear while she ate. "This is all your fault, you know?"

No response. She chewed as I remembered the day she reared on Mariska. I remembered the flash of adrenaline in my veins at the thought of that beautiful girl being hurt. It was only slightly less than my panic when Cheyenne returned riderless. The fucking protective instinct was only growing stronger the more time I spent around her.

Rebellious anger twisted in my gut as my mind insisted what had to be done. A knot ached in the front of my throat. This battle was different from coming off the drugs. Drugs sucker-punched me when I was down, hitting me with pain and nausea I couldn't fight. What I was dealing with now was completely different, and I was stone-cold sober.

The swish of feet moving through the grass followed closely by the scent of ham and cheese broke through my angry thoughts.

"Hungry?" Mariska held out a small parcel wrapped in a paper napkin. Taking it from her, I recognized eggs mixed with a slice of the pork from dinner last night and cheese.

Taking it, I gave her a little nod of thanks. "I thought you didn't like to cook."

"Just because I don't like to doesn't mean I can't." She stood back and crossed her arms watching me.

Giving her a reluctant smile, ignoring the battle waging in my chest, I took a bite. *Shit* it was fucking delicious. "Mmm..." I couldn't help a groan. Months of eating poorly were catching up with me.

She laughed and shook her head before going back to the house. "I'll put on my swimsuit."

Standing beside Freckles, I finished breakfast in three bites.

* * *

Mariska

The smaller lake was secluded and gorgeous. I wasn't sure how much longer we had of this Chinook, but every day felt like borrowed time. Sort of like every day I spent with Stuart. The fight was back in his eyes, and I knew we had gotten too close this morning. Or perhaps it was last night when he pulled me to him in the darkness.

Either way, as he alternated between playful and hostile, I knew his resistance was raging back. As for me, I'd brought a leopard-print bikini, because... well, why the hell not? All my cards were in. I had nothing to lose now, and I planned to fight dirty.

Discarding the bandeau top, I pulled on a loose-weave beige cover-up. The knit was essentially a series of open circles that created an even sexier effect than topless. My breasts played peek-a-boo at every turn. Just for fun, I braided my hair in a thick rope over my shoulder.

Stuart took one look at me and cleared his throat, facing the water. "I'm pretty sure this is a mineral spring."

"Do they have those in Montana?"

"A few resorts south of here, near Elkhorn and Helena, are famous for them."

Stepping into the pool, I was intrigued. "You know, hot springs are known for healing properties?"

He stepped forward as well. "FDR bought one to cure his polio."

The water was warm and lovely. I took off my top and pushed gently through the waves. "It feels amazing. Like a spa."

Stuart seemed to forget his internal battle. He slipped off his shorts and continued into the spring completely naked. My whole body sizzled at the sight of him submerging in the pool. I wanted to wrap around that again.

"Now I feel overdressed." I pulled off my leopard-print bottoms and held them over my head, giving them a little spin. "Skinny dipping for the win!"

He cracked the tiniest smile. "I'm thinking about what you said."

Dog paddling toward him, I tossed my bottoms onto the bank. "You don't need a mineral spring. What you have with will heal on its own with regular therapy and time."

His brow lined. "I don't have time."

Stuart William Knight... I couldn't help a tiny growl moving through my brain. As much fun as I loved to have, I managed to fall for this gorgeous, strong, sexy, absolutely impossible man.

"What's the rush?" I pushed my arms, moving back out toward the middle of the lake.

He glanced up at me. "You wouldn't understand."

A new response. "Try me."

His brow lowered. Damn his angry, determined look that made my insides go all gooey. I matched it with my own, and he turned his back, giving me the full view of those broad shoulders, the nice *V* at his waist, and of course, that perfect ass. I loved running my hands all over him during "therapy."

Since he wouldn't answer, I decided on distraction maneuvers. "Do you think I might be getting a tan?" Inspecting my arm, it seemed a shade darker, and I was sure I saw more caramel in my brown hair.

"It's possible." His back was still turned, and I admired the golden glow covering his skin.

"I've always tanned easily, ever since I was young."

He stretched his arms out and did a long push across the small pond. "I feel good," he said quietly.

"You look good," I said equally quietly. Then a little louder, "What did you want to be before you wanted to be a Marine?"

Looking up, he seemed to think. "Cowboy."

That made me laugh. "I can believe it." He drifted closer to me, his lips just at the surface.

"What about you?"

"I played My Little Pony." He rose a bit in the water so I could see his lip curl. I laughed again. "You disapprove?"

"I don't know. What is it?"

"Rainbows and the magic of friendship." A laugh pushed through his lips and splashed the water. I swam to him. This man had fucked me five ways from Sunday. I'd be damned if I allowed any distance between us now. Going straight into his arms, I wrapped mine around his neck. "What was your favorite cartoon?"

"Shazam."

Now my lip curled. "What's *that*?"

"Captain Marvel." His hands lightly traced their way around my waist, and I shivered. His voice was more relaxed. "What was your favorite band?"

"Oh, no," I shook my head. "You'll only make fun of me."

"Let me guess. Backstreet Boys."

My laughter danced across the water, and he turned me so my back was against his chest. I leaned my head on his shoulder. "Mmm... I love your skin against mine."

Lips touched my neck before he spoke again. "First sexy movie?"

"*Henry and June.*"

"Artistic sexy." Lips touched higher, behind my ear. "I should've guessed."

"How about you?" I turned in the water so we faced each other again, nose to nose, lips a breath apart.

"I think it was... *Nine and a Half Weeks*?"

"You like playing with your food." He smiled, and I leaned forward to kiss him lightly on the mouth.

"I like playing with you."

A thrill surged straight to my core. "Do you bring many women here, Mister Knight?"

I was teasing, but his expression changed. "I've never brought anyone here."

"Why not?"

His shoulders lifted me with his shrug. "It's always been my place."

Under the warm, mineral spring, my nipples lightly grazed his chest. Whatever it was doing for him, it was sending all kinds of sensations through me.

"Now it's ours?"

That brought him up short. "No."

He took my arms from around his neck, but when he turned, I felt something hard and stiff brush against my hip. His erection made me giggle.

"I felt that."

He didn't respond. He was back to being broody and distant, and it was pissing me off. "What's the matter with you?" I pushed against him, and he flashed.

"Dammit, Mariska." We were both angry now, our voices raised, but I wasn't afraid anymore. I knew he wanted me.

"Do you remember that day in the barn?" he said. "After we rode back from the lake?"

"The day you kissed me?"

He was undeterred. "I told you I would leave. It hasn't changed. I'm going to leave."

Nodding, I traced my finger through the water. "It seems I remember suggesting you take me with you."

"When I go, I go alone."

Blinking up at him, I tried to understand this. Here we were, granted it was only Day 2 of our getaway. Still, we had this connection. We talked about everything. We could barely keep our hands off each other. It was hypnotic and passionate, and it had all the makings of something real and lasting... And this is what he did.

"What's so great about being alone?"

His eyes narrowed, but he took the question as seriously as I put it. "No one gets hurt except me. I have no weaknesses."

"You're thinking like a soldier."

"A Marine."

My mind filtered through everything I knew. "Derek's a Marine. He's also a daddy and soon to be a husband."

"Derek's always been different from me."

"So I'm a weakness." Pressing my lips together, I wouldn't argue with him any more. I was mad.

I swam back to the shore and climbed out of the water. It was warm and delicious running down my legs, but I scooped up my bikini bottoms and stepped into them, quickly pulling them over my hips. Next was the loose-knit top I'd worn. It was over my head in a quick swipe.

"What are you doing?" Stuart's voice was level, but I could sense a change.

Looking back at him, my braid flipped over my shoulder. "More than one of us can leave."

With that, I set off toward the cabin. We'd strolled here at a leisurely pace, but I took a fast, determined stride. Minutes later, I was back, pushing through the door and grabbing my bag. When Stuart made me drive over in the truck, I'd been sad because I'd wanted to ride with him again. I wanted my back pressed against his chest, his strong arms around my waist, our hands clasped. We were at the start of this mini-escape, and my brain was full of romantic dreams.

Today, I realized my head was just as hard as his, and I was glad I had a truck to drive back to the ranch. I almost wished I had a plane ticket as well. All of my things were quickly shoved into the duffel I'd brought, and I reached for the door when it opened on its own.

Stuart stood in my way, water dripping from his hair, eyes blazing. "You're not leaving."

As angry as I was, my breath still caught at the site of him, towering over me, seeming twice his normal size.

"Yes, I am." My voice was annoyingly small.

He surveyed me a moment before stepping into the cabin and pulling the door closed behind him with a slam. I was trapped. "Why?"

My brow lined. All the reasons I should go and never look back crowded together in my mind fighting each other to get out. The result was me stuttering. "You... Are you? Seriously...?"

In one quick move, Stuart caught me, pulling my face to his.

"Stop!" I cried out, slapping his hand off my cheeks.

I was angry. He was angry. I pushed at him, trying to get past, and he caught my arm, jerking it behind my back.

"Ow!" I shouted, twisting to get free. "Let me go!"

"No." His eyes were dark, and something wicked, low in my stomach tingled in response.

I pushed and fought harder. He blocked every blow, holding my wrists, turning them away, lifting me off the ground, pulling me closer to him. We were both breathing hard, our chests moving together.

My voice was low and angry. "What do you want, Stuart?"

In that moment, I saw the break in his eyes. "You."

Two blinks passed between us before our mouths crashed together. His large hands were on me, tearing my sweater, grasping my breasts. I whimpered, desperately holding on, chasing his kisses with mine, trying to hold him as his mouth moved over me. It was rough and painful, and my insides throbbed for him.

He lifted me in his arms, and we crashed against the sofa on the way to the bed, lips reconnecting. I grasped at his hair, his neck. His mouth moved to my chin and he lowered me then jerked my bikini bottoms off. I made a little noise, but he didn't stop. His shorts were off just as fast, and he gripped my waist, turning me on my stomach and pushing into me from behind.

"Oh, god!" We both groaned as he filled me. Rocking the bed, he lifted me off my feet with the force of his thrusting. Pain mixed with pleasure, and I tried to hold on, I tried to keep up as he fought this battle with himself.

His body flexed and then arched over my shoulder, sending him deeper than he'd ever been. I moaned louder, and a matching groan rumbled from his throat.

"Stuart," I gasped. In this position, my clit was pressed and rubbed against the mattress. It sent shockwaves tingling and shooting down my legs matching the force of him stretching and invading me from behind. The sensation was overwhelming.

Every muscle below my waist tightened with each move. My orgasm snaked up my legs, and my eyes squeezed shut at the building release.

He jerked into me harder and then *Smack!* A hard slap stung across my ass. Threading his fingers into my braid, he pulled my head against his shoulder.

"Oh!" I whimpered, reeling from the conflicting sensations.

"You're not leaving." His beard scuffed against the sensitive spot on my neck, and electricity shattered through my core.

My eyes squeezed shut as my orgasm, wicked and intense, blazed through my legs. "Stuart," I cried.

He pulled my hair again, biting at my neck. "Say it." It was a hoarse command coupled with a deep thrust.

His intense possessiveness, his grip, his words… all of it combined with the sensations racking my body to make my head swim. *What was he doing to me?*

"Say it." He demanded.

My thighs shook. Each push took him deeper, and he kept scrubbing my clit against the mattress. I'd gone from mind-numbing orgasm to pleasure that was now painful.

"I'm not leaving," I gasped, needing him to stop.

He didn't stop. He gave me three more swift thrusts before holding himself deep inside me, leaning over my shoulder as he groaned through his orgasm. He pulsed, filling me, then growing still. My heart beat so hard, and I couldn't move. My bones were liquid as I lay on the bed.

Two more breaths, and he climbed onto the mattress, pulling me with him. I couldn't resist if I wanted to as he wrapped me in his arms, holding me against his chest. His face was at my shoulder, buried in my hair, and he breathed deeply. We were both panting. Holding him, I could feel his pulse at my temple.

"Stuart," I whispered.

"You're mine." He rumbled against my skin. "You don't leave me."

My jaw clenched. I was still recovering from that blazing fuck, and I hated how shockingly true his words were. I'd need the strength of Hercules to walk away from him. At the same time, I knew I had to stay strong.

"But you can leave me?"

He didn't answer. He only held me firm against his chest. Our breath swirled in and out, mixing and mingling, and I wondered if he'd ever let me go. I wondered if I ever wanted him to. After a few moments, he did relax. He reached down and pulled the Indian blanket over me. Kissing my shoulder, he went to the bathroom and closed the door.

I pulled the blanket tight around me trying to calm my swirling emotions.

CHAPTER 10: CHANGE OF PLANS

Stuart

Mariska was asleep on the bed as I pulled on my jeans and canvass jacket. My eyes didn't leave her as I stepped into my boots. They traveled from her loose chestnut waves spread over the pillow to her lips, red and a little swollen. I'd been too rough with her. I couldn't help it. Shaking my head, I grabbed my hat and pushed through the door.

Freckles was quickly saddled, and we set off across the plain at a fast gallop in the direction of the falls. The sky was wide open. We were coming to the end of the Chinook, the reprieve from the harsh, bitter cold that would blanket this area for months. It seemed fitting for the mood I was in—facing the end. Only the end of what? I couldn't seem to answer that question.

The noise of galloping hooves formed a monotonous soundtrack as my thoughts wandered far into the horizon. My life had always been overseas. I graduated school and left, never planning to come back—at least not to stay. Yet doing what I was born to do had changed everything. My injury forced me to leave the only life I ever wanted. I was born to serve and protect, and they'd sent me home to join the faceless millions.

Derek said to find something new to serve and protect. Pulling Freckles to a stop, I slid out of the saddle to the ground. Releasing the reins, I started walking, pushing my legs through the brown grasses, heading for nowhere in particular. My stomach hurt. It wasn't a cramp. It was the sensation of air leaving my body in a rush. The truth hit me so hard, it knocked the wind out of me. Something new to serve and protect. *Mariska*.

The day I saw her in the gym, she was like a mythical creature. Something sailors encountered on long voyages. But was she singing me to safety or pulling me away from my proper course?

A small, rocky outcrop provided a seat. I leaned against it, resting my arms on my knees. She did so many things to me. She eased my pain. She made me relax. She made me laugh. She made me happy. She was mine.

Pushing my head in my hands, my hat slid back. My vision filled with scenes of me in the desert. Fearless, carefree, I went wherever the mission led. I didn't look back or worry about who was at home. I didn't write letters. If something needed to be done, I did it because it was why I was there. I'd always been that way. I was one of the best in the Corps as a result. Until the injury.

I was the same in private security. I was at the top of the pecking order, and I commanded the highest salary. Everyone did what I said, followed my orders. It was an acceptable substitute for where I really wanted to be. Until the drugs started, and I discovered people followed my orders in everything. They would do whatever it took to keep me working, even if it meant crippling me. I started out with one wound and came home with two, the second one invisible.

Which led me to this place. To this beautiful girl, who healed both my wounds. My leg was better than it had ever been drug-free, and the emptiness in my chest was gone. Now I tried to picture myself going back to the way I used to be. Going out with the guys, taking home whatever woman caught my eye. My jaw clenched. The notion of sleeping with someone not Mariska filled my stomach with disgust.

I could only see her long, brown waves, her small breasts and golden eyes blinking up at me as she came... Pushing to my feet, I started back in for the cabin. I didn't believe I could change, but I needed to see her again. I needed to hear her voice and know what she was thinking. If anything, it would give me something to go on, a starting point for figuring out what happened next.

* * *

Mariska

My entire body was sore when I opened my eyes in the quiet cabin. I was warm under the Indian blanket and my thoughts traveled back over the day. We were at the lake. I held him, loving him, and he pushed me away. He wanted to be alone.

I'd give him alone.

I collected my remaining clothes, my torn sweater, and shoved them in my bag. His gray Henley lay across the couch, so I pulled it over my head before stepping into my jeans and boots. I was out the door, throwing my bag in the truck bed and not looking back.

Freckles was gone. Pulling his shirt over my nose, I took a deep breath of Stuart scent. My eyes closed and I imagined him somewhere riding her. He'd be angry when he came back and found me gone, but I had to do this. I had to force him to see what we had. I pulled down the visor and caught the silver keys. I loved him. It was that simple. I'd come here wanting him then I'd given him everything, and the more time we spent together, the deeper I loved him. Even if that meant I had to fight him.

His reaction to the idea of me leaving was definitely encouraging, if a little painful. A shiver moved through my body. It was also smoking hot. He was right... I did like it rough. With him at least.

All these thoughts swirled in my head as I pulled into the yard and saw a new car at the house. A steel-grey Cadillac was parked conspicuously in the middle of Bill's old Ford and Patrick's rented Chevy.

I pulled the classic Silverado I drove just below it and hopped out, lifting my bag from the bed. Elaine walked out onto the porch as I approached, and her face lit.

"Mariska!" She hopped down the steps and flew to my side, but her face immediately crinkled. "Where's Stuart?"

A knot tightened in my throat and for the first time all day, I thought I might cry. "I left him." It was as much as I could say.

"What happened?"

Shaking my head, I looked down. I couldn't get into the whole thing with her here. We were on the porch, and Elaine stood in front of me. She held my shoulders, studying my expression.

"I was so happy when I saw your text. It was like everything made sense—you coming here, the crazy-protective way he's been acting, all of it."

She left her sentence hanging, and I knew she wanted me to fill in the rest. Clearing my throat, I grabbed hold of my emotions. "He says he's leaving, and he wants to be alone."

Elaine's green eyes narrowed. "Horse shit."

My mouth dropped open, and then we both started to laugh. A tear rolled down my cheek, and she pulled me into a hug laughing more. It was very possible I was losing it because I didn't think I could stop laughing.

With a sniff, my new bestie straightened up. She smoothed my hair back from my face and leaned closer, speaking low. "You're completely under his skin, and as much as Captain Asshat likes to act so tough, I'm betting money he's running scared."

"Maybe. But even if that's the truth, I have to walk away or he'll never see it."

"You're absolutely right." Her arm was back around my shoulder as she led me into the house. "The fact that you know him so well just proves you're meant to be together."

Animated voices rang out from the kitchen area, and I glanced at Elaine. "Who's here?"

"Oh!" She took off toward the noise, dragging me behind her. "Their mom Sylvia got here last night! Patrick told her to come and spend Thanksgiving with us."

The date hit me. "Oh my god. It's today!"

"You haven't missed a thing. We're being very casual this year, since everything's been thrown in the air. Patrick's old secretary Nikki flew in with her."

My brow lined. "Is that weird?"

"Well, she's not really his old secretary. She's the office manager in Princeton. She knows Stuart, too."

Rounding the corner, Bill and Patrick sat at the table across from a lovely older woman with sandy brown hair and sparkling green eyes. Beside her was a younger woman with white-blonde hair and blue eyes wearing a very tight wrap-dress.

"Elaine! Who is this?" The older woman stood and rounded the table. Her shoulder-length hair was swept back, and she wore beige slacks with a studded belt and boots. Her white ruffled shirt was open to reveal a large dark-blue Cabochon necklace.

"Sylvia, I want you to meet Mariska."

"Ahh." Mrs. Knight stopped to inspect my appearance, and I was acutely aware that I was in her son's shirt, no bra, and my hair was completely bedhead.

"You were at the cabin with Stuart? *His* cabin?" Her green eyes narrowed.

"I... well, yes." My cheeks blazed, but Sylvia caught me around the shoulders.

"That's fantastic! Stuart has always been my problem child when it came to settling down. Whatever did you do to him?"

"She put a spell on him!" Elaine hopped over to wrap her arms around Patrick, who pulled one to his mouth and kissed it. "Mariska's a gypsy."

"No shit! You never told me that!" Patrick laughed, and for a split second, I wished his older brother had a little more of the younger Knight in him. Patrick was a blast.

"Language, please." His mother shook her head, and I would've laughed if not for the daggers being shot at me from Blondie's eyes.

"Aw, shit, Mom. I'm sorry."

Sylvia slapped her son's shoulder, but I heard Nikki speak under her breath. "Gypsy." Her tone was definitely annoyed.

"So what can you do?" Patrick had pulled Elaine around, and she was now on his lap.

"Don't be an ass!" She pinched him, and he laughed. "She's not a trained monkey!"

"You've been holding out on us! Can you tell my fortune?"

How I ended up in this conversation, I couldn't fathom. "My grandmother taught me to read coffee grounds... but it's really just for fun." I didn't mention everything she taught me—interpreting dreams, sensing auras.

"Please ignore him." Sylvia stepped back to me and caught my hand. "We completely ambushed you. Why don't you freshen up, and we can visit more when you're ready."

"Thanks." I smiled up at her, grateful for the escape.

I walked down the hall to my room and dropped my bag on the bed. My skin was tight from the mineral spring, and I hadn't showered since Stuart manhandled me. Unzipping the black case, I pulled out my toiletries bag and grabbed the green silk robe Elaine loaned me when we got here. She'd insisted it was fine — she brought three. Going into the hall bathroom, I didn't bother to turn the lock. I was the only one on this wing who used it, since Patrick and Elaine had a suite.

The large, jetted tub filled slowly, and I sat on the stone edge, holding my hand under the warm water. The bathroom was rustic, with natural wood and stone décor. Very manly and cowboy like everything here.

With a sigh, I pulled my knee up and rested my chin on it as I tied up my hair. Of course Stuart dominated my thoughts, just like he dominated all of me. I wondered what he'd do when he got back and found me gone. I remembered his anger. I remembered that break in his eyes when he'd said he wanted me. A pulse of warmth moved through my chest. Another silly tear rolled down my cheek. Things between us could be so easy. Why did he have to make it so hard?

Elaine had also loaned me a jar of bath salts that smelled divine. I unscrewed the lid and took a whiff of Cactus Flower before pouring it into my bath. The entire room filled with the aroma. I let the robe slide down my back and stepped in, relaxing completely in the warm-hot water. I wasn't tired, since I'd napped earlier, but sitting with my back against the jet released all the tension of fighting with the one I loved.

I was a prune when my eyes opened again. My hair needed to be washed, but I'd deal with it later. For now it looked like a trendy updo.

Wrapped in only the silk robe as I walked to my bedroom, I couldn't miss the loud *SLAM!* of the front door. It made me jump in my tracks.

Next came Sylvia's loud greeting. "Stuart! I wondered how long it would take for you to appear."

"Not now, Mother." His voice was a low growl, and I couldn't mistake the thump of boots headed in my direction.

I ran for my bedroom, making it inside and pushing the door closed before it pushed right back open. My heart hammered against my chest. Stuart stood there gorgeous and fuming. He slammed the door behind him never taking his eyes off me.

For a moment, his stern expression slipped. His eyes skimmed my body wrapped only in green silk, and my skin caught fire with every lusty thought I saw reflected in them.

Finally, they returned to hold my gaze. "I told you not to leave."

"I needed to come back here." I couldn't believe how calm my voice sounded.

"Why?" The muscle in his jaw moved, and I felt my resistance slipping.

Fight, Mariska. I answered him with all the frustration he'd put in me. "You know why."

"You wouldn't leave here without telling Elaine. You took a fucking half-hour to write her a damn note, but you left me without a word."

My jaw dropped, but I recovered fast. "First, that's a total exaggeration. Second, I did tell you. I told you at the lake."

He crossed the room, catching my arm. My breath sped up. "We discussed that. You said you'd stay."

"We didn't discuss anything. You fucked me and made me say that." Jerking my arm back, I caught my robe that had slipped open.

His eyes darkened at the glimpse of skin I'd accidentally revealed. I wasn't trying to seduce him now, as heavenly as the prospect was. I needed him to come to me on his own, without sexual coercion.

"Are you trying to provoke me, Mariska? Because if you are, it's working. I can't remember the last time I've been this angry."

"Why are you angry? Because I won't play your games? Because I'm not going to sit around and wait for you to walk out?"

His eyes blazed, and he caught me by the forearms. "It's not that simple."

"Yes it is!" I pushed his hands away, and my damn robe fell open.

Rough hands immediately went around my waist pulling me against his body. His mouth was at my cheek. "You know it's not."

"Let me go, Stuart." My voice was stern, but he only held me closer. His hands scratched across my bare back, and the fabric of his shirt was rough against my sensitive nipples. Heat flared between my legs.

"All of this... it's a lot to take in." He kissed my temple, making his way down my cheek.

He had me. The warmth of his embrace, the intense pressure of him refusing to let me go was winning, but I pushed his arms. This time he relented, and I jammed the robe back around my naked body, tying the sash tight. Being silk, it was already slipping open again.

I turned so he couldn't see me struggle. Closing my eyes, I exhaled slowly, finding control again. What I'd said to Kenny was in my mind. I couldn't fight his battle. We'd reached the point where nothing I said or did mattered anymore. I had to be strong. He wouldn't respect me otherwise.

It hurt. It hurt badly. It ripped my insides in two, but I said it. "Please stay away from me until you know what you want. I need you to stay away from me."

Silence filled the room. I struggled to breathe as I died inside. If he fought me, I'd give in. It would be a mistake, but I wouldn't be able to stop myself.

I heard the noise of his arms cross followed by a deep exhale. "That's what you want?"

Nodding, I managed to answer him. "I'm headed back to Bayville. I'm trying to get a flight out Sunday."

More silence. I was afraid to turn around. Finally he spoke. "It isn't what I want, but if you need space—"

"I do. Thank you."

His arms dropped. I waited until he'd left the room and closed the door to collapse on the bed, burying my face in my pillow. I thought of everything he'd said, and everything he didn't say. As much as I loved him, I couldn't be a casualty of his war. He'd said he wouldn't put me in danger, but he didn't say he'd never hurt me. All I could do now was pick up my heart and keep moving forward, holding onto the hope that one day he'd see what I already knew.

CHAPTER 11: HOUSE GUESTS

Mariska

After our confrontation, I thought Stuart would go back to the cabin, but he didn't. He joined the rest of the family, including our new houseguests, for Thanksgiving dinner that evening.

I'd managed not to cry, so I didn't look like hell at the table. My stomach cramped, but somehow I felt strangely empowered by our showdown in my bedroom. I had to believe if the reason I'd flown all the way out here was true, if we were meant to be together, he'd see it and come around. If not...

Well, I hadn't gotten that far.

"How lovely is this?" Sylvia exclaimed, smiling and wrapping her arm around her oldest son's waist. "When I got here, I was afraid you'd stay out at that damn cabin the whole time, and I'd have to make Patrick drag you to the house."

"I didn't know you were coming." Stuart's voice was quiet. I wouldn't look at him. It hurt like blazing hot knives tearing my insides.

"I'm glad you didn't! I might've missed everything." She was either oblivious to the tension between us, or she chose to ignore it.

Stuart's uncle entered the room looking freshly scrubbed and quite handsome, and she walked over to him. "Why haven't we been doing this every year, Bill? The ranch is lovely."

He lightly touched her back. "I have no idea. It sure brightens the place having all these beautiful ladies around."

She laughed, and Patrick and Elaine emerged from our wing straightening their clothes. I was pretty sure they'd just had sex. I suppressed a little growl, wishing it didn't make me want Stuart.

"Is it time to eat?" Patrick crossed the room to kiss his mother's cheek.

Her eyes sparkled as she squeezed his face. "You are always hungry! How is it possible you're not fat?"

"Good genes."

Elaine skipped up behind him. "He's so full of crap. Derek's been busting his butt for a couple of years now." She squeezed his bicep. "I have zero complaints."

Sylvia caught her hand, and the two walked to the table. "Where is Derek?" she asked. "I would love to see him again."

"He was here last week, but you know he's got a little son now—"

"I didn't!"

The two went on catching up, and I was left standing behind a potted ficus tree, doing my best to avoid Stuart while trying to act like it wasn't killing me. The only other person in my boat it seemed was Nikki, but she made a beeline for Patrick's side. The two of them chatted like old friends. Of course, Patrick chatted with everyone like old friends.

I was about to give up when Uncle Bill appeared at my elbow. "I can't decide if I'm glad you're back or not." A mischievous twinkle was in his eye. "You seem to be giving one of my nephews a run for his money."

My body was still tense, but I managed to smile as I took his arm. "I hope you're glad I'm back."

His rough hand covered mine. "I told you the first night, you're always welcome here. I hadn't realized how ugly Ron was until all the pretty ladies showed up."

That made me laugh. Bill had the same easy personality as Patrick. "Where's your pretty lady? You're not such a bad-looking old cow poke."

He shook his head, his thick brows lowering over his brown eyes. "That ship sailed a long time ago, I'm afraid."

The way he said it hinted at a story, and I was curious to hear more. At that moment, however, Winona called us all to table. It was time to give thanks.

* * *

We were full of smoked turkey, stuffing, potato salad, and green bean casserole when we finally took our places in front of the fire. I'd managed to sit as far from Stuart at the table as possible, and now he lingered on the fringe of the room. His eyes were on me, I could feel them, but I'd also had a few glasses of wine. My stomach had finally relaxed, and I basked in an unmerited sense of power.

Bill, Patrick, and Elaine dominated the after-dinner conversation as always, and Sylvia joined them with matching energy. Nikki sat back and sipped her wine, answering whenever Patrick pulled her into whatever playful debate they were having. Apparently, Nikki and Patrick had become close the year he'd worked in Princeton, but she'd carried a torch for his brother the entire time. *Great.*

Finally, I decided to go to bed. Stuart still brooded in the background, and I was exhausted from not looking at him. When I got up and said goodnight, Nikki hopped up to join me. She was a new addition to our wing of the house, of course. I couldn't believe I hadn't thought of it earlier. Sylvia took a bedroom on the wing where Stuart and Bill stayed.

We said goodnight, and she followed me up the dim hall. "I'm sorry, I couldn't help overhearing your discussion earlier. In your room."

Her eyes said she might not be so sorry.

I tried to play it off. "It's not your fault. I wasn't thinking about where you were staying."

"It sounded like you didn't have time to think about much of anything."

I didn't have an answer for that, so I simply nodded. We were at my door, and I stopped, ready to say goodnight. Nikki wasn't ready.

"Just between us, I've known Stuart a *long* time." I didn't care for the way she emphasized *long*. "He's always been a... love 'em and leave 'em type."

My eyes narrowed. "You're speaking from personal experience?"

"Well, I don't like to kiss and tell." She blinked her stupid blue cow-eyes at me.

"Thanks for the heads up." I couldn't resist a little jab. "I think Stuart's dealing more with knowing he wants to stay."

She laughed. "If that's what you want to believe. I'm just warning you."

Suddenly, I didn't like Nikki at all. Still, I decided the wise thing would be for me to go to bed. "I'm tired. If you don't mind..."

"Oh, sure. Goodnight, Mariska."

She turned and swished her stupid hips in her too-tight dress down the hall in the direction of her bedroom. It took all the self-control I possessed not to slam my door in her wake.

* * *

Not approaching Mariska at dinner was almost more than I could take. The image of her naked in her bedroom with that green robe over her shoulders burned in my memory. I was starting to think I was obsessed, and dinner was nearly impossible with her so close. She refused to look at me.

Why the fuck was I doing this to myself? If I stepped back from what was going on, I'd see she was right. She was giving me an out. I wanted to go back to the desert. She opened the door for me to leave. Now I was the ass who wouldn't walk through it.

I passed a restless night in my old bed. My thoughts continuously drifted to our night in the cabin and pulling her into my arms, her soft body in my hands, sliding deep between her thighs. I'd tasted what I could have, and now being without it was torture.

This morning, I came to the barn to brush down the horses and clear my head. I knew Mom would want to ride, and Nikki... *Shit.* I hadn't even ventured into that problem. What the hell was she doing here? Talk about nuking my Fortress of Solitude.

Patrick at least took care of her. Those two were like a pair of chicks. They'd become *besties* or whatever when I was away. She was constantly hanging on his arm and whispering who knew what and giggling. I had no idea why Elaine put up with that shit. Strike that. I knew exactly why Elaine put up with it. My little brother was wrapped so tightly around her little finger she'd be blind not to see it.

Not that I could blame him. Elaine was cool. She wasn't my Mariska, but Patrick could've done a lot worse.

"You're up early, cowboy." My stomach clenched at her voice. Nikki. "You make those boots look damn sexy."

177

Straightening, I patted Scout as I made my way toward the stall door where she stood. "How's it going, Nik."

"Not bad." Her blue eyes traveled over my body like always. And like always, I ignored it. "I confess, I was really happy when your mom asked me to join her on this trip."

"I didn't know you and Mom were close."

"She seemed to think me coming here might be good for you."

Scheming women. Mom had been throwing barbs about Mariska and me all night. I was one more smart remark from going to the cabin. Only a pair of hazel eyes kept me from leaving.

Nikki reached up and stood on the stall door. The top she wore was low cut, and she leaned down giving me a shot of her breasts. "Patrick said there's a nice loft over the stables."

I exhaled through my lips and walked back to Scout trying to understand this one. I'd slept with Nikki once. Three years ago. I never made any promises to her. We were both pretty drunk at the time. I couldn't believe she was still holding on to that.

"Sounds like something he'd know."

"Want to show it to me, Cowboy?"

Clearing my throat, I was about to make some excuse when my little brother interrupted. "Going for a ride, Nikki?"

"I wish." She slanted her eyes at me.

"Well, stop wishing. I can give you the tour."

She stepped off the stable door with a sigh and leaned against it. "What's Elaine up to?"

"Driving Mariska into town. She needs a special kettle for Turkish coffee."

"Right." An ugly tone entered her voice. "The gypsy thing. Cute."

Patrick pushed his cowboy hat back and grinned. "Your eyes are sort of bluish-green aren't they?"

"Shut up, Patrick." She walked away from Scout's stall, and for the first time in my life, I was thankful for my little brother. Then she stopped. "On second thought, yes. I'd like the tour."

"Mom's coming with us."

They left the barn, and I rested my arm on the Palomino thinking of Mariska. The mention of her name sent my mind in pursuit of her image. Fuck coffee, she liked to paint. I wondered if I could somehow plant that seed in my future sister-in-law's mind. I wanted to see her art. I wanted to see her.

"Dammit." With a growl, I pushed through the stall door. Bill was standing outside the tack room holding a bridle and a rope.

Thankful for the distraction, I walked over. "What's going on?"

"Working with that colt." He started for the paddock, and I followed. "It's been years since I've broke a horse. Just trying to remember the best approach leading up to the saddle."

"How far along is he?"

"I've been working him with the lunge line about a week."

Stepping into the medium-sized, fenced yard, I watched the little brown colt running, shaking his head. My uncle let out a low whistle, and he stilled, hesitated, then started toward us. Bill lifted his hand, and the little guy ran past us.

"He's got spirit," my uncle mused. "I need to be more consistent in his training. He likes to run."

"What did you use to say? Teach him you'll let him run, but he needs a safe place to stop?"

My uncle grinned at me. "Good memory."

"I liked working with you back then."

"You've always been good with the animals. They like a quiet touch."

He handed me the bridle. "Why don't you take the morning shift? Get him use to this. I'll pick up after lunch."

It was exactly the kind of work I wanted. "Sure thing."

* * *

Mariska

Driving into Great Falls, I was able to see everything I missed that first night, hiding in the tiny backseat of Patrick's rented truck and freaking out about being caught in my lie. The terrain was beautiful, with rocky outcroppings and trees. It was cold, but the waterfalls were unfrozen, and Elaine took the long way around to the downtown area, passing a huge former train station with a massive brick tower and Ryan Dam.

Of course, we didn't find the type of coffee pot I needed for Turkish coffee, so after wandering along Central Avenue looking in gift shops and buying fudge, we walked five blocks west to the Sip-n-Dip Lounge for lunch.

"Patrick's going to be pissed we came here without him," she laughed, pulling me into an ancient tiki bar attached to a motor inn.

"What is this?" I blinked as my eyes adjusted to the dark.

Two curvy bars dominated the interior. One was blonde wood with brown barstools. The other was bright sea green with brass accents and garish sea-green seats. A few wooden tables with teal vinyl chairs and mustard-yellow booths were scattered around as well.

"There's a swimming pool behind the bar!" I couldn't help shouting, even though we were two of a handful of people having lunch.

Elaine laughed. "Isn't it great? They usually have mermaids swimming in it. The place is totally famous. It's even been in *GQ* magazine."

"You're kidding." My brow lined and she nodded. "Check out the carpet."

We walked under a wooden "Welcome to Paradise" sign on neon bubbles scattered over a field of black carpet. The ceiling was bamboo and sea grass, and the entire place looked like something out of *Beach Blanket Bingo* or *South Pacific*.

"A tiki lounge in Montana." I couldn't believe it.

My friend ordered each of us a blue cocktail and grabbed a menu. "We're probably supposed to eat at Clark and Lewie's, but I couldn't miss this."

Taking a sip of the super-fruity beverage, I winked. "I bet you'll be back with Patrick before you leave."

"We have to come back at night when Piano Pat is playing." She took a sip of hers. "I'd better not finish this. Somebody's got to drive us back to the ranch."

I giggled. The drinks were sweet, but the burn of alcohol lurked in the background. "Who's Piano Pat?"

"She's supposed to be fantastic." Elaine took another sip. "She's been here since... Forever, and she plays any song you want. It's a blast."

"Now I want to come back!"

From the pub menu, we ordered sandwiches with fries. They were in front of us in less than ten minutes.

"Good." Elaine took a big bite. "I need this to soak up the alcohol."

Nodding, I took a big bite as well. I was already feeling light-headed. "I'm kind of a lightweight, I guess."

"Not like the guys." She picked up a fry and watched my response.

I held my expression neutral.

"That does it." She tossed the fry back on her plate. "I've been waiting a day to get this story. Spill it. I covered for you, after all."

Exhaling loudly, I dropped my forehead on my hand, wishing a mermaid would swim past. "Look a shell lamp!"

"Mariska!" A light kick hit my shin, and I started to laugh.

"I don't know what to say! He's fantastic and wonderful and exactly how I expected, and he flat out told me he was leaving. Alone."

Elaine's brow lined. "Where's he going?"

"Back to the desert. Back to Saudi, I guess." I pulled the giant fishbowl drink toward me and took another long pull from the straw. The idea that I might end up drunk tickled at the back of my head, but I almost didn't care.

"So he's going back. I wonder if he's mentioned that to Derek. I know Patrick has no idea."

Blinking back at her, I shook my head. "Just keep that between us. The last thing I want is for him to think I'm discussing him with everybody."

My friend took a deep breath. "So you got to know each other pretty well, I take it."

I took another bite of sandwich, and cut my eyes at her.

"Right. All the way." Elaine leaned back in her sea-green barstool and was quiet a moment. I put the sandwich down and stirred at my basket of fries. "I've got to say," she finally continued. "I honestly don't know what to tell you."

"He's got to decide what he wants." My voice was quiet now. "That's why I'm leaving Sunday."

Elaine's head flicked around. "No! You can't leave. Stay until Sylvia and Nikki go home."

I took my last pull of blue drink. "When is that?"

"Tuesday, I think."

"You're not going back?"

She shook her head. "Hired a sub for the two weeks leading up to Christmas." I watched as she took out her wallet. Instantly, I fished mine out to help. "No, no—it's totally my treat." She pushed my hand back.

"You can't buy me lunch!"

"I dragged you out here looking for a special coffee pot and then made you eat with the mermaids." She waved her hand. "I'll treat."

I laughed. "It sounds like a mafia hit."

"Come on."

We left the bar, squinting in the afternoon sunlight, and took off toward where we left the truck. Walking made me realize how wobbly I was after too much fruity cocktail.

"I might have to go home and take a nap," I sighed.

"Hmm... I'm thinking I'll find Patrick and inspect the loft."

Frowning, I caught her arm. "Don't rub it in. I miss my cowboy."

"From where I sat, it looked like you could have him back any time you wanted."

"No." I shook my head. "That would undo all the progress I've made."

Elaine's voice grew wistful. "If you love someone, set him free."

"If he doesn't come back, hunt him down and kill him."

We both started to laugh, and I held her arm to keep my balance. She unlocked my door and helped me in the truck. "Nap on the way back, silly girl."

* * *

When I opened my eyes again, I was in my bed. The sun was still up, but a quick glance at my clock told me it was four. I sat up slowly, waiting for the headache. Instead I was just really thirsty.

Winona was in the kitchen alone when I took a bottle of water from the refrigerator. She smiled and nodded.

"Where is everybody?" I asked softly. I'd never spoken to the kindly cook, and I wasn't sure if she knew English.

"Mister Bill is in the side paddock." Her voice had an accent I couldn't quite place. Perhaps she was Indian? "The rest are off playing."

"Thanks." I smiled and headed out towards the small pen on the side of the barn.

The wind was dying down, and I knew that meant the cold weather would come barreling in soon. Walking around the side of the weathered-wood barn, I saw Stuart's uncle holding the reins for the new colt. I'd heard he was breaking him in, but I'd never watched him work.

He spoke low to the young horse, clucking and making sounds with his mouth. Occasionally the colt would try to pull away, but for the most part, he seemed comfortable with the leather and metal contraption holding his head. They walked around in a half-circle, when Bill glanced up and saw me watching. He led the animal over to where I stood on the fence.

"Hey, there," Bill smiled up at me. "Last I saw you, Patrick had you over his shoulder."

Glancing down, I felt my cheeks warming up. "Sorry. I didn't realize how strong that drink was."

He laughed. "No worries. The Sip-n-Dip is pretty famous for strong drinks."

"And mermaids."

"Right." He reached out and petted the horse's nose.

"It looks like you're almost done breaking him in."

He nodded, reaching up and sliding the bridle off the colt's head. The young horse instantly dropped the bit and turned. Bill made a low noise, and he shook his head, making me laugh.

"He's getting there," Bill said with a smile. "Still got a lot of fight in him, but he's a good horse. I expect he'll give me quite a ride the first time I mount him."

I watched as the horse took off, loping around the pen. "What do you mean?"

"After all the time I've spent working with him, when he sees me on his back for the first time, it'll spook him." He exhaled a laugh, shaking his head. "And if he throws me, it'll spook him more."

We were quiet a minute watching him.

"How long does it take to break a colt?"

"Depends on the animal. Not all of them are as strong-willed as this guy."

The horse shook his head and trotted a bit, then shook his head again.

"I think he's fighting the feel of that bridle."

Bill nodded. "Strong-willed animals are valuable. I don't want to break his spirit. Just teach him a better way."

Every word he said touched me deeply. I couldn't help seeing the parallel to Stuart and me. "What would happen if you didn't train him?"

185

"Wild horses are prone to injury. Loners have shorter lives." He rubbed his thick grey mustache. "Broken, they have safety, shelter. They live longer."

Quiet settled over us. I pictured Stuart like one of those wild horses, running free, refusing to take shelter, being injured...

Bill pushed away from the fence and turned to me. "I've been watching this phenomenon for years. It takes patience, a gentle hand, and a lot of love."

I squinted up at him. "Patience is the hardest part."

"Yep." He looked past me at the horizon. "But I think you've got what it takes."

I looked out at the horizon, too, hoping with all the feelings swirling in my chest that this wise old cowboy was right.

CHAPTER 12: WORST CASE SCENARIO

Stuart

The sun dipped low on the horizon as I headed across the yard to check on Bill and the colt. I'd just gotten clear when I saw Mariska standing on the fence watching them. Instead of interrupting, I took a quick turn into the barn and walked up the alley to the paddock door.

From there, I was hidden from their sight, but I could see and hear them. Bill explained the process of breaking the colt, and she watched, the wind pushing her long brown waves off her face, her strapless dress swirling in an arc behind her. The sun was in her face, and it glinted off the necklace she wore. Mariska always wore several necklaces and a few rings. I'd meant to ask her about them. Her long, slender hand moved over her face, and I leaned to the side. A slight twinge. Perhaps I needed more massage therapy...

"Spying are we?" Nikki's voice pulled me out of my thoughts.

I cleared my throat and backed away from the door. "Just checking on the colt's progress."

She walked to the paddock door and leaned over it, looking into the yard and then waving at Bill.

"So that's it." She turned those blue eyes on me, and I could see the irritation in them. "You're out here fucking that child."

"Take it easy, Nikki, she's not a child. She's twenty-six." I didn't want to be angry with her. I didn't want to fight. I wanted her to shut the fuck up and go home.

"Stuart." She was quiet a moment, studying me. I was about to tip my hat and go back to the house when she spoke again. This time her voice was placating. "I'm worried about you. You haven't been yourself since you got back."

"You're right." I nodded. "I wasn't myself when I got back. But I'm better now. You don't have to worry."

"I can't help it." She reached out and touched my arm. "I'd hoped we could pick up where we left off. I waited for you."

Moving my arm and sliding my hand in my pocket, I took a step back. "I didn't ask you to wait."

Her eyes moved from my face down my torso, lingering near my belt. Another blink and her eyes were back on mine, her voice soft. "I know about the drugs. I found the empty bottle you took from my apartment at Derek's."

That stopped me. "I'm sorry about that night. I was wrong—"

"You don't have to apologize." She stepped closer again. "I didn't tell anyone. I threw the bottle away. To protect you."

"You didn't have to do that."

"I wanted to!" Her hand was on me again. "I want to protect you now. I'm afraid you can't see what's happening here."

I studied her face. "What are you talking about?"

She shook her blonde head. "You can't see it, but it's not your fault. She's taking advantage of your weakness."

"Wait. You mean Mariska—"

"She's not friends with Elaine. She lied to you."

My brow lined.

"She came here uninvited. I overheard Patrick and Elaine talking last night in their bedroom. He thinks it's

188

hilarious. Elaine thinks it's romantic. That's why they covered for her."

Anger twisted in my chest. My scalp tightened, and I wanted to grab Nikki by the throat. Instead I took another step back.

"I'm sorry, baby," Nikki's voice cracked. "I'm not trying to hurt you. I'm trying to help you. She's playing you. I don't know if she's after your money or what, but she is a gypsy, after all. They're notorious con artists and thieves."

My forearms ached, and I realized I was clenching my fists. "This is bullshit." My voice was tight. "Mariska's innocent. She was a virgin for Chrissake."

"A twenty-six year old virgin?" Nikki laughed. "Never in a million years would I have expected you to fall for something like this." She turned and glanced out the paddock door again. "I guess she is a sexy little thing. She knows massage therapy? What a coincidence, since that's exactly what you needed."

I didn't want to hear more. Turning on my boot heel, I stormed out of the barn toward the house. Rage burned in my stomach, and Nikki's words echoed like a witch's cackle in my brain. *What. The. Fuck.*

I was halfway to the house when Patrick stopped me. "Hey, bro. You look like you're out for blood. What's up?"

"Got any whiskey?" The words came out in a growl.

My little brother paused for a moment to scan my expression. "I got a bottle of Jack in the back of the truck."

I turned and headed for his rented Silverado. He was right with me. "Want to talk about it?"

"No."

Reaching in the bed, I pushed aside a blanket thrown over a cooler. Unzipping it, I pulled out a bottle of caramel liquid. It was about three-quarters full. It would do. Heading for the house, Patrick called after me.

"Sure, you can have my Jack. You don't even have to ask."

"Thanks." I snarled over my shoulder. I'd deal with him later.

"Derek called. He's taking the red-eye. Should be here in the morning."

A houseguest I didn't mind visiting. The thought only glanced off the wall of anger building in my mind. Nikki's words clicked together like pieces to a puzzle, and I had my answer.

* * *

Six hours later it was dark and I was wasted. I'd holed up in my bedroom with the bottle of Jack and proceeded to drown my anger in booze. Yes. It was anger I was drowning. Nothing else. So why the fuck did I still feel like a knife was stuck in my chest?

She saw me that day at the gym when I was at my worst and decided I was an easy mark, a well-dressed drug-addict who only needed a little coaxing to fall into her clutches—or between her thighs. Nikki was right. She'd conned the pants off me, and like a first-class sucker, I fell for it hook line and pussy.

I could still see her innocent act, all dewy eyes and trembling hands. A virgin, my ass. No virgin gave a blowjob like that. She'd rubbed those expert hands all over my body, seduced me, and now she was waiting for me to cave. She'd never have to worry about being alone or her future again. I couldn't believe how close I'd come to pissing away all my plans for her.

Glancing at the clock, I saw it was after eleven. My uncle had gone to his room an hour ago followed shortly by my mother. I knew they were all probably asleep.

Except maybe my brother and Elaine. Those two were fucking rabbits.

Staggering to my feet, I threw the bottle across the room and headed for the door. I was getting to the bottom of this bullshit, and I was doing it now.

Mariska's room was dark. Her door wasn't even locked when I turned the knob and walked in. Standing, I waited a moment, listening to her breathe. That fucking familiar sound twisted the knife a little harder in my chest. She stirred and made a noise, and the knife ripped from my chest to my stomach. The emotions pissed me off. I'd seriously fallen for her.

"Stuart?" She switched on the lamp beside the bed and sat up.

Her brown hair fell in a gentle wave across her face, and she wore only a thin white cami. I could see her nipples through the fabric, and my dick stirred. *Dammit.*

"What are you doing?" She looked at her clock. "It's almost midnight."

"I need to talk to you." My voice was like sandpaper.

Her expression changed. Her brow relaxed, and her eyes warmed. I was pretty sure she wasn't expecting what I had to say.

She stood and her fucking beautiful legs were exposed all the way to the white lace panties she wore. "You weren't at dinner. Do you feel bad? Is it your back?"

"I'm feeling like I'm ready for the truth."

Her thin brows clutched together. "The truth about what?"

"Why you came here."

Silence filled the room. Her hazel eyes went round, and I saw it then. She knew that I knew. That fucking knife twisted again. Nikki had told me the truth.

"Elaine invited me —"

"Cut the bullshit." My voice was louder. "You didn't even know Elaine before you met her at the airport."

Her bottom lip pulled under her teeth, and she blinked fast like she might cry. It wasn't going to work.

"I don't like to repeat myself." Narrowing my eyes, I watched as she clasped her hands in front of her small body, twisting them together.

"Stuart…" Her voice trembled. "I'm sorry I lied to you about that."

The frail little creature act nearly pushed me over the edge. I knew she was tougher than that. I'd seen it. Crossing the room, I grabbed both her arms and gave her a hard shake.

"What do you want from me?" My voice was loud.

Two tears splashed on her cheeks, but she wasn't sobbing. She was fighting for control. That was more like it.

"Nothing." She shook her head. "I don't want anything from you."

"Bullshit." Releasing her, I pushed her back against the bed. "Try again."

She crawled onto it, pulling her knees under her. "It's true. I didn't know Elaine… but I came here for you."

"Why? For my money? Are you some kind of stalker?"

"No!" She adjusted her position. "It wasn't like that."

Crossing my arms, I exhaled. It sounded like a growl.

"I'd never take advantage of you, Stuart. I've cared about you since that day in the gym when I first saw you!"

"That day in the gym you saw an easy mark. You've been playing me for a fool."

Her cheeks flooded with color and tears were back in her eyes. "Oh my god! That is *not* true!"

"You made a joke of me in front of Patrick." That thought had me seeing red.

"Quite a coincidence you happened to know massage therapy."

Putting both hands on her face, she shook her head. "I took classes back at the gym! Rook—my boss—he's always pressuring us to add new services. I thought I'd like it, but it wasn't really my thing!"

"It wasn't your thing until me?"

"Yes!" Her hands slapped the bed. "I wanted to touch you! I've only ever wanted to touch you since the day you walked into my life. Don't you remember?"

"Why were you on the pill?"

Her expression turned confused. "W-What?"

"If you were a virgin, why were you on the pill?" That angry question had waltzed into my brain on whiskey Number Fifteen.

"I-I use them to control my periods." Her eyes blinked fast. "I've taken them since I was twelve. If I don't, I bleed too much." She shook her head, and her brow lined. "You thought I lied to you about being my first?"

Her voice cracked and more tears filled her eyes. They fucking burned my chest like a bucket of salt being poured on that stupid knife wound. My gut twisted between wanting to hold her and wanting to hit her. I couldn't sit here and let her rip me apart anymore.

"I've heard enough." I reached for the door.

"Stop!" She was across the room before I opened it. "I'll tell you the truth. Just... wait."

My lips tightened and I turned on her. Her head was just at my shoulder. "Now I get the truth? Which version?"

Her eyes still glistened with unshed tears, and my insides churned with anger and heartbreak. The anger was winning.

"Only two people know about this..." She dropped her chin, but I caught it, snapping her head up.

"Look me in the eyes when you're talking." I wasn't falling for another act.

She sniffed and blinked a few times. "It's going to make me sound crazy, but it's the truth."

I released her face and put my hand on my hip. "Go."

"After that day in the gym, I started having dreams." She started to turn away, but I stopped her.

Pointing to my face. "Eyes here."

She squared her shoulders and stared into my eyes. "They were nightmares. I dreamed about fires and explosions. Everything was beige and smoky, and I was paralyzed. Hands grabbed my arms and started pulling me away, against my will... away from something I'd sworn to protect."

With every word my insides clenched and twisted. She continued speaking, but I leaned against the door. I was having trouble breathing.

She sniffed, and I realized she was crying again. "I didn't understand why I kept seeing those things, but every time I woke up, I saw your face. All I saw was you, and I knew whatever it was, I had to come find you to make it stop."

It was impossible. What she was saying was Not. Possible.

"Stuart?" Her voice was shaky.

"How do you know those things?"

"I don't know."

My eyes went from her slim body to her sunset eyes full of concern. She reached for me, but I pushed her away. There was no way in hell she could know what she just described to me. Was she spying on me? How long had this been going on?

"You're lying."

Her cheeks paled. "No..."

She started for me again, but I jerked the door open and left the room, heading for my side of the house. I didn't know what the hell was going on, how she had gotten that story or from whom, but I needed to get to the cabin. The fucking whiskey clouded my brain. I needed to get away from here and figure this out. Nobody fucked with me.

* * *

Mariska

I couldn't stop crying. I wasn't sobbing or curled in the fetal position — outside of my mind — but the tears wouldn't stop streaming down my cheeks. The last thing I expected was Stuart in my bedroom, but his words, everything he said, destroyed me.

I'd told him everything. I'd told him the truth, and he called me a liar. He pushed me away. Anger burned in his eyes like nothing I'd ever seen, and I knew I couldn't go after him. My worst-case scenario, the thing I feared most when I came here, that he'd find out and run, had come true. I had to leave.

Throwing all my stuff in my bag, I grabbed my phone and called for cab service to the airport. They promised to be here in twenty minutes. All I could do was wait. Picking up my suitcase, I quietly went to the hall. I didn't want to wake anyone. I just wanted to go home, crawl in my own bed, and cry.

Everything was silent as I crept through the dim house. Small lights were scattered about illuminating my way through the living room to the door. Finally, I was outside on the porch alone, freezing. Noises came from the barn. Someone was with the horses, but I didn't want to see anyone or explain what I was doing. I was humiliated enough. Whoever it was didn't come into the yard. I heard the faint noise of hoof beats headed away across the plain.

Looking after them, I saw two tiny lights far down the lonely road. The cab. I just had to hang on a little longer, get back to Bayville, then I'd break down.

CHAPTER 13: AFTERMATH

Stuart

Derek stood over me frowning. "I thought you were getting better when I left."

Sitting up, I held my hand up to block the blaze of sunlight streaming through the window over the sink. It was fucking freezing.

"Chinook ended." My voice still sounded like sandpaper.

"No shit." My partner went to the fireplace and started loading wood. "I flew in expecting to find you on your feet." He pushed the empty bottle of Jack with his boot. "I thought Johnnie Walker was your brand."

"Are you alone?" Squinting around the wrecked cabin, the last thing I wanted to see was…

"Patrick's with me."

My brother stood in the kitchen, leaning against the sink.

"What the fuck do you want?" I stood then, but my head felt like it'd been hit with a sledgehammer.

"Good morning to you, too, fuckhead."

"This is no time to fuck with me, Patrick." I pulled down a glass and went to the sink thinking he'd better move his ass.

He slid down. "What happened yesterday?"

Taking a sip of water, I glanced at his relaxed face. How could anyone be so goddamn happy all the goddamn time?

Slamming the glass by the sink, I stepped toward him. "Why the fuck did you come out here?"

His hazel eyes burned, and he straightened. His nose almost came to mine. "Bill's my uncle too, asshole. I'm visiting my family."

"You're aiding and abetting, and I'm going to kick your ass."

Derek was at the sink in two steps. Only one person outweighed and outranked me in this room, and his hand gripped the front of my shirt.

"I'm going to kick both your asses if you don't settle the fuck down." His deep shout filled the small space.

Patrick took a step back and went over to sit on the couch. "If you weren't such a dick, you'd see what was right in front of you."

"I'd see you laughing behind my back." The idea of him and Elaine gossiping about me like a couple fucking teenage girls almost sent me into another rage.

Derek cut through the tension. "I don't know what either of you are talking about." He looked at me. "I came back to check on you, and you're fucking back in this cabin looking like shit."

I rubbed my face with both hands, taking a breath. The whiskey was gone, my head felt like a hammer, and my guts were shredded. Fucking women.

"I don't need you here." My voice was low, controlled. I wanted to be alone to get over this. Just like I wanted to be alone to get over the drugs. "I can handle this."

Patrick exhaled a jab. "Still proud."

My eyes flashed, but Derek stepped between our line of sight. "You saved my life, bro. I'm not leaving you out here alone."

"Well, I sure as hell don't need his ass here."

"Dude, can you ever stop being such a fucking pussy?" Patrick spoke from the couch, and I took a step forward.

Derek stepped forward as well. "You really want to us to go? Would that help you?"

Going back to the sink, I turned to the square window. Snow would blow in soon, covering everything feet deep, isolating this entire region. It could happen tonight. I rubbed a hand over my eyes.

"I don't know." Looking down, I just said it. "I survived one battle only to find myself caught in another."

The cabin was quiet. Thankfully, neither of them spoke. I didn't want to hear what they thought I should do, with their fucking charmed lives. I wasn't like either of them. Love wasn't on my To-Do list. It was on my To-Don't list, and then when it fucking appeared (unwelcomed), it kicked me in the balls.

"I need to get back to the desert."

Derek's voice was calm. "Okay." He watched the fire a moment. "Your mom leaves day after tomorrow. Come back to the ranch, and we can see what's available."

I knew he was trying to get me from this remote location. I knew it wasn't safe for me to be here alone with the weather looming. Still, the idea of seeing Mariska again was just... No.

"I don't want to go back."

Patrick's voice cut in fast. "She's gone if that's what's worrying you."

Frowning, I looked over my shoulder. "What?"

"Mariska left last night. We woke up this morning, and she was gone. No note or anything. I had to call Kenny to find out she'd asked her to pick her up at the airport."

"She left? I told her not to go." The last part was under my breath.

Why her leaving tore at my already-shredded insides was anybody's guess. I didn't care what she did. I wanted her to go. She played me.

Staring out the window, I focused on a place far in the distance. That was where my peace was—as far away from me as it could possibly get.

I didn't know if I'd ever get it back, because as much as I wanted to hate her. As much as I wanted to take her by the arms and shake her until her teeth rattled, just that much I wanted to hold her against my chest. I wanted to take a deep breath of jasmine and chase her kisses. I wanted her to chase mine with the force I knew was in her.

God, fucking Mariska. What have you done to me?

* * *

Mariska

Bayville was as uninspiring as ever, and for the first time in my life, I couldn't be happier. Kenny met me at the airport alone. Little, pale, and thin, she wore a black sleeveless top, and with her asymmetrical purple hair, black skinny jeans, and stilettos, she was every bit the badass I wished I were. I was just a crazy, impulsive girl who'd ruined the best thing in her life before it even began.

I struggled not to cry. "Thanks for meeting me."

"What happened?" She caught me by the arms. "I had to leave Lane alone with Slayde, and that makes him nervous."

"Slayde's back?" I sniffed. Despite my misery, I couldn't believe it. Looking closer, I saw her eyes shining with joy.

"He came back on Thanksgiving. He... he's a hero."

"What? What happened? I mean... I'm so happy for you! Tell me—"

Our fingers clasped as we walked to baggage claim. "I'll tell you everything, but not now. Now you're going to tell me why you dragged me out of bed at this ridiculous hour. What happened?"

We were at the carousel waiting for my black suitcase to appear, and I had the most distinct case of *déjà vu*—I was arriving in Great Falls and panicking over the crazy thing I'd done. I knew it would end like this. Yaya had told me to trust my premonitions, but I never did.

Checking my watch, I saw it was seven. "I remember a time when you'd be up before now beating the shit out of that body bag at the gym."

"That was P.S." Her ice-blue eyes winked. "Pre-Slayde."

In spite of my misery, I managed a smile. "I'm sorry. You're the best friend ever, and I owe you big time."

"Yes you do." My bag appeared, and she skipped forward on needle-thin heels to drag it off the carousel.

"I know I've said this before, but you amaze me with your sense of balance. And strength."

Clicking out the handle, she pulled my rolling case behind her. "Thanks. Now spill."

I sighed, taking her arm. My brown hair was swept over one shoulder. All I could think about was Stuart's face buried in it. His beautiful body in my arms. That luscious mouth kissing me roughly, taking me hard. "I don't know if I'll survive this one."

Her slim arm went around my waist, and she pulled me close. "You will. You've got me." Another squeeze. "You held onto me when all the shit went down with Slayde. Don't think I've forgotten it."

Tears burned in my eyes. "I just need to be home for a little while. I need to be alone."

We went through the sliding doors to the parking garage. She let me go and nodded back. "Trust me. I know that feeling well."

* * *

Two days hiding in my bed, and I had to get back to work. I'd only put in for a week off, and I was on a week and a half now. Rook was cool, but his patience only went so far. Also we were in those critical weeks leading up to Christmas. The club was jammed with members either trying to fit into holiday clothes or hold on to their figures through the holiday eating and drinking.

I was curled under my covers when I heard the door open and the sound of a little boy's voice. "Mommy! Elephant!" It was Lane.

"Don't touch that, baby." The thud of tennis shoes coming down my hall made me peek my head out from under the thick duvet. Kenny hopped up on my bed and crawled to where I was balled up like a baby kangaroo. I felt the smaller thump of Lane falling against the bedside.

"I know you want to be alone, but two days is a long time."

I blinked up at her. "What time is it?"

She was dressed in gym clothes, and her purple hair was up in a ponytail. "Ten. You have plenty of time to get dressed and ride with us to the gym."

Taking a deep breath, I looked up at the ceiling. "I don't know if I can do it today."

She stretched down beside me. "I know. The first day is the hardest. But you keep doing it, and eventually you realize…"

I was pretty sure both our thoughts had drifted to how she was when she and Slayde were apart. "How much you never stop missing him?"

More silence. The two of us lay on the bed with our heads together while Lane sat on the floor playing with his truck and making motor sounds with his little mouth.

"Want to tell me now? Why you came back so suddenly?"

Instantly, tears heated my eyes. I took a shaky breath. "He thought I was there to trick him. He thought I was after his money."

The shock and outrage I anticipated never came. She didn't answer, and I twisted around to look at her. "That doesn't surprise you?"

"I mean, it makes sense. He's probably got more money than fu... freakin Derek."

"How do you know that?"

"How do you *not* know that? First, their family has money. Patrick's loaded. Second, he's thirty-six, single, no debt, worked in overseas security. He was active duty so long, he never paid taxes... He's gotta be at least a millionaire."

Now it was my turn to be quiet. "I never thought about it."

My friend rolled onto her stomach and smoothed back my hair. "What did you think about?"

I remembered the day he walked into the gym. "He was hurt. He was wounded, and he needed me."

"He's also hot as hell!"

A hint of a smile tickled my lips. "Okay, I thought of that, too."

"Good in bed?"

"Ugh!" The duvet was over my head again.

"Seems like I remember saying he would be."

I didn't come out. "He's the greatest lover."

"Yeah he is, slut. You gave him your cherry!"

Lane's little engine noises stopped. "Cherries!"

"Oops!" She laughed. "Sorry, baby. They have cherries behind the juice bar at the gym."

I slapped the duvet down. "Is that a veiled reference?" Kenny's round eyes met mine. We both burst into giggles. After a few moments, I took a deep breath. The pain only receded for a moment before it washed in again full-force.

"I miss him so much." My voice cracked.

Kenny pulled at the shirt I wore. "What's this?"

"I stole his shirt."

She leaned forward and gave me a big sniff. "Mmm…. Stuart Knight smells sexy."

My chest clenched, and I finally said the words that had been tearing at my insides. "It's my fault. I was impulsive and reckless and I moved everything way too fast. Stuart doesn't do fast. I knew he doesn't do fast going in."

"What other choice did you have?" A tear slid down my cheek. Her arms went around me, and she gave me a tight squeeze. "What about the dreams?"

"They stopped."

"That's significant, right?"

"I don't know." My voice was a whimper. "I don't know about any of this anymore."

She sighed, thinking. "Well, I know I love you. Lane? Do you love Aunt Mare-Mare?"

"Yes!" A little blond head popped up at the foot of my bed. He looked so much like Patrick, which in turn meant he looked a lot like…

"Hop on Aunt Mare-Mare!"

His little body plowed up the mattress and in another blink the three of us were in a ball of hugs. We stayed that way a few seconds, until Kenny pulled him up.

"Get dressed, and we'll drive you to the gym."

She wasn't backing down. I'd have to go with her and start the process whether I wanted to or not. With a sigh, I pushed the covers down and staggered to my bathroom. It was going to be a horrible day.

* * *

Stuart

Derek had driven Bill's Ford out to the cabin, so Patrick rode back on Ranger. I wasn't in a particular hurry to collect the few things I'd carried out here with me. Besides another fifth of Jack, I only had one change of clothes.

"Traveling light these days?" He watched from the kitchen as I shoved everything into a small duffel.

"Just the essentials."

"Jack Daniels?"

I shrugged and carried the empty bottle to the trash in the kitchen. He picked up his phone. "Patrick said Elaine brought a friend with her. Said you two spent some time together."

"She wasn't Elaine's friend." I scooped up my duffel.

"Patrick said they were friends."

"More like... partners in crime."

Derek went out, and I pulled the door shut then we both climbed into the Ford. The wind was now blowing cold, and I wished I'd remembered my canvass jacket. It took a few minutes before the truck was warm enough to be comfortable.

"What crime did they commit?"

I exhaled through clenched lips. "I don't know. It wasn't a real crime. They just sucker punched me."

We rode for a ways in silence. "Mariska was the girl from the gym. She told us you were out here."

"She works with Kenny."

"Right. She's pretty."

A knot twisted in my throat. She was more than pretty. "She was just something to fill the craving left over by the drugs. If I'd been stronger..." I wasn't sure of my next words.

Derek rode for a minute, turning over what I'd said. "What if you've got it backwards? What if the craving you tried to fill with drugs was for Mariska?"

No fucking way I was going there with him. I looked out the passenger-side window at the grasses bending in the breeze. The wind would occasionally shake the truck, and occasionally, a small flurry would drift past.

"I hope Mom's able to fly out before the snow comes."

"We checked the weather. She should make her flight. I'm thinking about leaving when she does. If you're serious about the desert, you should, too. Otherwise, you'll be stuck here for the duration."

I nodded, thinking about time and how it would go. He was right. "I'll get online when we get back to the house."

"You can stay with us in Wilmington until you leave."

My elbow was bent on the door, and I rubbed my aching head. "Thanks. I'll probably go to Chicago."

We were back at the ranch, and pulling up beside the house, I saw my little brother and Elaine hugged up on the porch. I couldn't stop a frown. Leaning for the door handle, I was just getting out when Derek stopped me.

"Hey, don't fight with Patrick. He's strong as I am these days."

Squinting back at him. "Are you suggesting he could kick my ass?"

He cracked a smile. "I'm saying you've had a tough year. That wouldn't make it any better."

I just shook my head and got out of the truck, grabbed my duffel, and slammed the door before heading up the porch. I wasn't planning to stop, but Elaine called out to me.

"Stuart!" I didn't stop, but the fast clip-clop of her boots told me I couldn't escape her. "Wait."

We were just inside the house when I stopped. She almost ran into me, but didn't. Instead she stood in front of me a second before shoving her golden hair behind both ears.

"I wanted to tell you..." She paused as if trying to find the right words. "Blaming Mariska for what happened is a big mistake."

"I don't want to talk about it." I started to go, but she caught my arm and pulled. I was surprised at how strong she was.

"If you're going to be my brother, you can't think the worst of me." Green eyes held mine, and I couldn't miss the worry reflected there. "She wanted to leave. That first night, she totally panicked. I think she realized how crazy it was coming here."

"She panicked because she lied."

"She panicked because she's young and impulsive, and she really cares about you. I made her stay because I thought it was romantic."

"You should've trusted her gut."

"She wasn't trying to hurt you."

My body was still sick from last night, and my insides were twisted and painful. Her words only wound the frustration and anger I felt tighter, and I still hadn't had time to think.

207

"Doesn't matter. I'm heading out as soon as I can line something up." Elaine's shoulders dropped and she looked like I'd kicked her favorite puppy. I reached out and patted her arm. "I won't hold it against you. Don't do it again."

Her lips tightened like she might try to argue with me, but I walked fast toward my side of the house. I had work to do online.

CHAPTER 14: CLOSURE

Mariska

Pete leaned over the bar to peek at the sketch I'd returned to in my recipe book. "I didn't know you did portraits."

Snatching the book back, I flipped a few pages over my drawing. "I don't."

"Who was that?"

"Nobody. It was... a homework assignment. We were supposed to see how well we could draw from memory."

His brow lined, and I could tell he didn't believe me. It didn't matter. I wasn't interested in explaining Stuart or discussing any of it with him.

"Did you need something?"

He stretched his hands out on the bar, and I knew it was to make his muscles flex. Everything Pete did was to show off his physique to me. In the past, I'd tried to get onboard with all his flirtations. Now they just fell flat.

"Kenny tried to make my cinnamon bun protein shake while you were gone and it tasted like ass."

"Kenny doesn't follow recipes." Flipping through my notebook, I found the drink in question. "You want one now?"

"Please. And be sure to dip that little finger in it." Frowning up at him, he winked. "To make it sweet."

"Oh, good lord." I shook my head, and he laughed, going back to the weight room to spot his client.

I was doing well. I was on Day Two of being back at work, and I only wanted to crawl under the counter and cry once every fifteen minutes instead of once every five.

Watching Kenny and Slayde together did not help. They were so blissed out by their reunion, they hardly ever stopped touching each other. It was heart wrenching. Kenny said it should be encouraging, since none of us believed they'd ever make it back to love. I was truly happy for her, and I couldn't look at them.

Rook was very understanding about my prolonged absence. He made some comment about that was what he got hiring overly dramatic college kids. I noted I was in graduate school. His response: Same difference.

Returning to the sketch in my recipe book, I used the crappy No. 2 pencil behind the bar to add some shading along Stuart's jawline. His beautiful eyes watched me, brows lowered over them, of course, as I finished his straight nose in a perfect point. Top lip a little fuller than the bottom one, and that light shadow on his jaw. A shiver moved across my shoulders. I'd added a dark cowboy hat, even though I loved threading my fingers in his brown hair. Defying all logic, sketching him made me feel better.

"You're blushing."

I jumped and made a little squeal. Slayde's clear blue eyes narrowed at me, teasing. I slammed the book closed and pushed it under the phone book.

"What do you want?"

"Wow. I thought we were friends!"

Shaking my head, I rubbed the daydream away. "I'm sorry. You startled me. Did you want a shake?"

"I was going to ask if you'd like to have dinner with us. I'm making steaks. Kenny's making salad. Bring your coffee pot."

"My coffee pot?"

"I need another reading. I'm thinking about asking Rook for a raise."

That made me laugh. "I think we'd do better slipping him a special smoothie before you meet with him."

"You're saying I'm not worth it?"

"I'm saying our boss is a tightwad, and he's planning to add a nursery to keep that new Y from stealing all our young mothers."

"Fucking YMCA."

His tone was totally teasing, and I smiled. "It's fun to stay there."

That got me a rare Slayde laugh. "See you tonight."

"Hey," I reached for his arm. "I'm really glad you're back. Kenny was a wreck without you."

"Thanks. I was worse."

* * *

Lane was on my hip twirling his baby fingers in my hair, and I was doing my best not to imagine him as Stuart's and mine.

"Mare-Mare pretty."

His little blue eyes blinked at me, and I kissed his nose. "Laney is my sweet boy."

Shaking his head hard, he pointed a fat finger toward the patio where Kenny and Slayde were watching the steaks grill and talking.

"Lainey is Mommy."

Whoops! "Right! Lane has two mommies."

Kenny slid the glass door back at that moment, and he started to wiggle. A huge smile broke across her face, and she ran over to scoop him from me. "Who's my baby?"

He wiggled again, shaking that towhead in the most hilarious way. "Not a baby!"

Kenny only buried her face in his neck and kissed him. "Right. You're mommy's big boy."

"Lainey?" His big blue eyes held Kenny's, and hers instantly filled with concern.

"Do you miss Lainey?"

His head dropped on her shoulder, and her eyes flew to mine. I recognized that look of panic.

"It was my fault, I called him Laney." Her lips pressed into a little frown, and I was afraid I might cry. "I'm sorry!"

"It's only been a week, but of course he misses her." She gave him a little bounce. "Want to call Lainey?"

He nodded, and she carried him to the MacBook Patrick had bought her. "What if we Facetime? Then you can show her your turkey tummy."

That brightened his expression. He patted his stomach. "Turkey tummy."

She sat down at the computer and started clicking, kissing the side of his neck. "Lane ate all the turkey."

They laughed, and in a few moments, Elaine's face appeared on the computer screen. The entire room burst into shrieks and *I love yous* and *I miss yous*. I hung back, but I couldn't help peeking around Kenny's shoulder, wondering if I might catch a glimpse of anyone else at the house so far away.

Patrick's head soon joined Elaine's, and the conversation got even more animated. They talked about the weather and flights back and forth. I decided to slip out to the patio where Slayde was finishing dinner.

He stood by the balcony railing, looking out at the stars. "I love how this place is far enough from the city we can see the stars. It reminds me of being on the ship."

I walked over and stood beside him, remembering a night under a star-filled sky, making a wish on a shooting one. I'd wished we would always be together.

"That must've been an amazing experience."

"I was pretty miserable the whole time." He glanced at me. "I'm sorry things didn't work out for you. I know how that feels."

"It's okay," I shrugged. "I didn't listen to my instincts. It was great while it lasted, but it was doomed from the start."

"Not forever."

"That's the part I don't know."

I leaned against the balcony wall and thought about the week of time I'd stolen with Stuart. Even if I'd known it would end like this, I had to confess, I wouldn't change a thing. From the ride back after he pulled me out of the lake to the massage to the nights in the cabin, all of it was so worth the risk I'd taken.

"Hey." Slayde bumped my shoulder, and I glanced up. "You're a beautiful girl. You went out there because you wanted him. Trust me. From a guy's perspective, that's fucking huge. He'll come around."

My chin dropped. "If he can ever not think of me as a crazy, gold-digging stalker."

"I've been around you long enough. You probably acted crazy, because that's just you. The gold-digging stalker part? He'll realize that's bullshit. Or he's not a very smart guy, in which case you're better off without him."

I blinked up and smiled. "You're pretty awesome, you know that?"

"Just making up for my mistakes."

* * *

Stuart

Patrick and Elaine were on the computer talking to Kenny and Lane. I'd ventured from my wing of the house because it was dinnertime, but now this was happening. Even my mother and Bill were getting in on the action. Nikki had left the day I disappeared, so it was just the

213

family and Derek now, although Derek was family. He was like a brother to me—and Patrick.

Naturally, my thoughts drifted to Mariska. Patrick trusted Kenny to keep Lane while he and Elaine were here having a vacation or whatever they were doing. Kenny and Mariska were best friends—from what I understood. Would Kenny be best friends with someone who'd con me? My younger brother wasn't known for his good judgment. Who knew Kenny wasn't the same. I stared at the fire as I turned these conflicting thoughts over in my head.

"It's hard being away from him." I looked up to see Patrick standing beside me.

Dropping my leg, I straightened my shoulders. "I wouldn't know."

"I wanted to talk to you about something." His expression was serious.

"Okay."

"It's two things, really." This time he put his boot up on the hearth. "Elaine and I were thinking about getting married here. At Christmas."

My eyebrows shot up. "Is that enough time—"

"It's quick, I know, but we've made great memories here. We love it." He rubbed a hand across his chin. "I know you're wanting to head out pretty quick. Think you might be able to come back? Or stick around a few extra weeks?"

The idea of prolonging my stay for a wedding was not the most appealing suggestion I could imagine. Patrick seemed to read my mind.

"I know we've never been tight, and I know you're sort of ticked at us over how things went down with Mariska... I guess, just think about it."

I nodded. "What was the other thing?"

He glanced over his shoulder towards Elaine still talking to Kenny and his son. Mom and Bill were standing behind them smiling, and I noticed my uncle's hand on her lower back.

"You ever picked up on that?"

I blinked a few times, and it was like a curtain sliding back. "No."

"Me either, but I guess it's been brewing for a while."

Mom and Bill? Flipping through the pages of history, these past days, the months after Dad died, how much Bill had stayed around. Then he left with no explanation, came out here to the ranch and kept his distance. Yet at the same time, he was always there whenever Patrick or I needed anything.

"I felt like an idiot when I realized it," he whispered looking back at the fire.

"You are an idiot." I couldn't resist, and he socked my arm. I mentally noted the strength Derek had warned me about. "What you got on your mind?"

"Bill was always more of a father to us than Dad. He kept us every summer, spent time with us, listened to our problems. Maybe they're worried we'll be angry. Maybe they need our permission."

"Maybe we should keep our noses out of their business." I was still smarting from my little brother's "help" with my love life.

"Either way, if you get the chance, be ready to greenlight the hell out of that shit."

"Mom's a grown woman. She can do what she wants."

He turned back to the fire and watched the blue flames licking over the black logs. "I'll be glad when you get your head out of your ass."

"What the fuck?"

"Time passes, situations change. Mom never expected Dad to be killed, but it happened. Now she's looking at a new path." His hazel eyes cut to mine. "You've got to see when it's time to change paths, start something new."

Stepping back, I patted his shoulder. "I'll keep that in mind."

"Stuart!" Mom was headed in our direction.

I considered our conversation. She was still a beautiful woman with years of life ahead of her. Why shouldn't she spend them with Bill?

"Derek said you're heading back to Chicago on Tuesday with me." She stopped between my brother and me at the fire. "Does this mean I'll have my son back under my roof for a few weeks?"

"No." I shook my head. "I'll find a place."

"What! You're only going to be in town a short time. Am I right?" Her eyes were flashing, and I remembered how hard it was to argue with her.

"Yes."

"Then why not?"

"Because I'm a grown man."

"So you'll spend countless hours finding a place to rent for only a few weeks, for which you'll probably spend a fortune, rather than stay with your own mother?"

Shit. "Yes."

Her lips pressed into a thin line, and I could almost see little curls of smoke rising from her ears. "I swear sometimes you are exactly like your father."

Patrick snickered, but I didn't like the comparison. "I'm not just like him."

"Stubborn as a mule. Proud." Her arms crossed, and I could read that body language a mile away. She was hurt. *Dammit.*

All I'd been trying to do for the last two weeks was find a place where I could be alone for a little while, to think. The closest I'd gotten were those first nights with Derek, and I'd been so cramped up and suffering, I hadn't been able to enjoy them.

The muscles in my stomach were tight, but I caved. "I'll stay with you, Mom."

Instantly her eyes lightened. She reached out and squeezed my arm. "I'm so glad."

That was how I ended up in her place in Chicago my final nights before leaving the States.

* * *

I hadn't been in a Chicago winter for at least six years. It was cold as fuck, and when the wind blew across the lake, only wool could face down that onslaught. I had on wool slacks and a thick wool topcoat over my button-down shirt and tweed blazer.

Tonight after dinner, I'd said I needed a walk. Mom said I needed my head examined, but I took off before she had a chance to finish her lecture on catching pneumonia. Now I was thinking she was right, although I'd keep that to myself. Patrick learned gloating at his mother's knee.

Her condo was on the Lakefront, so I headed east of Michigan Avenue down Grand. My thoughts were miles away, and when I looked up, I was facing Navy Pier. It was such a tourist trap, I had no idea why I'd walked out here.

The night was dark, and snow flurries were already drifting down. The place was deserted at this time of night, the Ferris wheel wasn't running. I walked all the way to the end and stood looking out across Lake Michigan. I wanted to be near the water. Something about the waves made me feel closer.

Everything came together easily when I arrived back in town. I made a few phone calls, put it out there I was back, and the next thing I knew job offers came rolling in. I had my pick of the best. I should've been pleased.

Derek asked me to stay. He made the hard sell of expanding Alexander-Knight to include whatever type of business interested me. He suggested I move to Wilmington. He suggested I stop running.

Those weren't his exact words, but he touched on that idea of something new to serve and protect. My thoughts went to Mariska, and I couldn't say yes. The nagging pain still twisted in my chest every time I thought of her. If I stayed, I'd never get over her. I had to get over her.

A bell rang on one of the buoys far out in the darkness. I looked towards it, straining to see the light. Why the hell did she have such a hold on me? I barely knew the girl. We'd only been together a week, and the first half I'd spent trying to avoid her. Yes, the last half had been pretty fucking fantastic, but the way it ended...

Maybe that was my problem. It hadn't ended. I'd walked away. She'd run away. We never said goodbye. The door of possibility was still cracked, and it had me thinking crazy thoughts. Thoughts like she let me be myself. She touched me and the pain went away. She helped me sleep. She made me laugh. For the first time outside of being in the military, I was happy. Also, she had my body responding stupidly. My chest would tighten when I smelled jasmine or caught a glimpse of chestnut hair.

Something final, a conclusion would fix this. Then I could leave behind dreams of her hands on my ass, her soft lips touching mine, her moans... *Shit.* Pulling out my phone, I touched the digits Elaine had given me.

* * *

The ocean breeze was frigid in the winter. I wrapped my fleece jacket tightly around me before heading out to the shore. I missed Yaya. I wanted to feel close to her, and for whatever reason, sitting in front of rolling waves under the full moon helped with that.

Two achingly long weeks had passed, and the hole in my chest was gaping as ever. I'd tried so hard to tell myself to let him go. It didn't matter if he never came back. I was young. I had my whole life ahead of me. Not only that, I was lucky. I had a beautiful memory of my first time with an incredibly sexy man...

It didn't work.

I parked near the wooden pier by Slayde's old place. He'd moved in with Kenny, and now those apartments were set for demolition. The last of the old beach shacks would soon be gone, and in their place would be high-rise condos. Huge blocks of concrete.

Turning away from that, I watched the water lap against the pier posts. Closing my eyes, I indulged in memories I'd tried to stop having. I saw his smoky hazel eyes, his beautiful smile. I felt his strong arms pulling me against him, his rough kisses, his gentle touch. I remembered sliding my hands down his back, tracing the lines of his muscles, his ass... Before I realized, I was sniffing.

"Oh, Yaya," I lifted blurry eyes to the black sky. A million stars filled the space, and all I could think of was making love in an Indian blanket by a crackling campfire. "I really screwed up this time."

A lone tear streamed down my cheek, and the pain of heartbreak burned in my chest. I missed him. I missed being happy. I missed being able to take a deep breath without pain.

Resting my head against the post, I thought of my grandmother now in heaven. She'd told me so many times to control my gift, to listen to my instincts. I'd shot it all to hell in what was possibly the most important moment of my life. I'd wanted him so much, I'd forgotten everything she taught me.

Pulling my knees under my chin, I hugged them. "I wish you were here. I wish you could tell me I'd be okay, tell me I'll make it through this."

A buzz from my phone cut through my misery. I'd forgotten it was in my pocket, and fishing it out, I expected to see Kenny's picture smiling at me. Instead it was an unknown number. I almost dismissed it, but the tiniest pull in my stomach made me slide my finger across the face.

"Hello?" I hoped I didn't sound like I'd been crying.

"Mariska?" His voice was like a jolt of electricity to my heart.

"Stuart?"

For a moment, neither of us spoke. I heard his breath on the line, and I felt the stream of tears on my cheeks. My chest rose and fell with my rapid breathing. *He called me! What did this mean?*

"I got your number from Elaine."

His tone was terse as always. I didn't care. I closed my eyes and saw his strong jaw. I thought of the time I'd run my tongue up it.

"Okay." I held my tone neutral. "How are you?"

"I took a job with AI."

"I-I don't know what that is."

"It's a private security company." He paused. "I'm going back to the desert."

Pain twisted in my chest. He called to tell me goodbye. "When?" I could only manage one word.

"Three days."

The stream of tears running down my cheeks grew thicker. I couldn't speak.

Finally, he continued. "I don't write letters."

I covered the phone and took a shaky breath then I asked, "Why did you call?"

"Why did you fly to Montana?"

We were back to that question. I tried to answer as truthfully as I had the first time. "I needed to see you. I felt like you needed me." Taking a chance, I added, "I wanted to be near you."

More silence. The winter wind blew my hair back and the waves lapped against the pier posts. I closed my eyes holding my phone as if it were his face against mine. Oh, how much I wanted to hold him this way.

"You said you had a dream." His voice was rough.

"That's right."

"Why?"

I wasn't sure if he were asking why I said it or why I dreamed it, so I went with the latter. "I've always had vivid dreams, but it was the first time they weren't about me."

He didn't speak, and I waited. I didn't know what difference it made, but I'd determined to be completely honest with him going forward if I ever got the chance again.

"Okay." A note of finality was in his voice. "Take care of yourself."

My hand flew to my mouth, and I clutched my lips, fighting for control. Taking a quick swallow, I blinked and more tears fell. Even I could hear the tremble in my response this time. "You too."

The line went dead.

Chapter 15: Fire in the Desert

Mariska

Kenny sat beside me in the White Lotus tattoo parlor. She worked quickly on the sketch pad in front of her, covering it with carbon and quickly tracing out the S-shaped pattern of little stars.

"You want this to start at your hip and curl up your ribs?" Her dark brows pulled together.

"Yes."

She picked up the sponge and dampened my skin before applying the stencil to my side. Once it was in place, she took the tattoo gun and screwed the black ink into the base.

"It shouldn't hurt too much," she said. "I try to have a light touch."

"I trust you." It was the first time I'd ever gotten a tattoo, and all I could think of was the night we'd sat under the stars and talked. The night Stuart told me his dreams, and I hinted at mine.

The first touch was a stinging pain, but not unbearable. Kenny's blue eyes flickered to my face, gauging my response. I blinked back at her and smiled.

"It's okay."

She continued working. "It won't take long since you don't want color." She was already on the second little star. "What made you choose stars?"

"A few reasons." My chin rested on my hand as I leaned forward. "Yaya is with the stars, and I feel close to her when I look at them."

She didn't answer right away, and when she did, her voice told me she was concentrating. "Want me to fill in a few of these? To make it more of a design?"

"You're the artist."

"You're an artist, too." She winked. "You should paint. It'll take your mind off things."

"I've been planning something." My voice was quiet.

The stinging grew worse as she filled in a few black stars. "Any other reason you chose this?"

Stuart's face in the firelight, the way he held me against his chest. Wishing on that star. "A dream. It's far away now, but maybe this will make it feel closer."

We didn't talk as she finished, and before long she was straightening up. "You're all set. Want to see?"

I walked with her to the full-length mirror in the back and examined the small constellation curving up my side. Only the slightest pink tinge was around the edges, making it stand out more. "It's perfect!"

Kenny laughed. "Another satisfied customer."

I traced my fingers lightly over the scattering of stars. They were so confident, almost magical. "I don't know why, but it gives me hope."

My friend wrapped her arms over my shoulders and leaned her head against mine. "I know it's going to work out," she whispered. "It has to."

* * *

I'd started a new painting. Pete kept asking me to go out with him, but I couldn't imagine anything less appealing than spending time with another guy when I only wanted one man. So I stretched a large canvass and gathered my oil paints.

Starting out, I experimented with a Georgia O'Keefe style—bold colors and oversized images examined in anatomical detail. My mind was in the desert, and as I painted the image transformed. I closed my eyes and revisited my nightmare. Fiery yellows and oranges flowed from the brush. It was a volcano, rising in an inverted *V* and wrapping all the emotions we'd shared in a sheath of red and purple. I didn't know how long I worked, pouring all the feelings I'd had since the beginning of my journey with him into the lines and shades of the canvas. When I stopped, it was dark outside and my eyes were heavy.

Dropping the brush in a jar of turp, I left it for now. I'd look at it in the morning and decide if it was worth a damn. For now I needed to sleep. Paint was on my fingers and in the tips of my hair, even though I'd tied it up in a high ponytail.

I washed my hands in the sink and brushed my teeth. Not worrying about the bits in my hair, I pulled off my tunic top and leggings and tossed them on my hamper. Sliding between the sheets in only my panties, I was asleep the moment my head touched the pillow.

A burst of white melted into screams of missiles flying overhead. Another noise. Another explosion. Looking down, I wore a long, beige robe that billowed and flowed around my legs. My head was covered in a beige scarf.

It was different, yet the same. I was in this place, but I was in my own body. Instead of fleeing the destruction, I ran toward it. Something was pulling me further. I needed to keep going. Then I saw him lying there. Fear seized in my chest, but he moved. He was alive! He was alive and he needed me.

I ran faster towards him, hard as I could. A cramp stabbed my ribs, but I didn't stop until I was at his side. I stretched out my hand and touched his cheek. His skin was so hot, I moved my hand down to his neck. He turned his head and looked up. Our eyes met...

With a gasp, I sat straight up in my bed. My chest rose and fell like a bellows as I tried to calm my breathing. My whole body shook, and light sweat covered my skin.

It was the first time I'd had the nightmare since Montana, but it had changed. Instead of looking through his eyes, I was there, seeing him with mine.

Was it prophetic? Was it a dream of the past? I reached for my dream journal and wrote down everything I could remember — the colors, the sounds, the feeling of desperation. I lay back on my bed and closed my eyes, trying to see it all again. A little tremor of fear moved through me, and I said a silent prayer.

Please be okay, my love.

* * *

Stuart

I was on fire. The burning in my legs was overwhelming. My skin was frying off my muscles, leaving me bleeding and exposed. Excruciating pain tore through me, and I couldn't even scream. I was back in the paralyzed state, lying on the sand under the blazing-white sun.

Where was Derek? Had I lost him? Had the hands that dragged me away gone back for him or had they presumed he was dead? I had to get up from here. My heart beat too hard with all the adrenaline surging in my veins.

Again burning flayed my senses. Fuck! It hurt like hell! I couldn't make it stop. I tried to pull away, but my body was useless. I was going to die here in torment, twisting in the fires of hell. Pain scattered my thoughts until something changed.

A cool hand touched my forehead. I groaned in response to the small taste of relief. It moved to my cheek and smoothed back the sweat dripping from my brow. A small thumb pulled at my bottom lip, and I opened my jaw in response. Cool water touched my tongue. Cool water… The memory of a kiss.

It was so good, my bones revived. My eyes that had been squinted shut in agony relaxed, and I blinked away the stinging drops of sweat. Searching for the source of comfort, I strained my neck. I hadn't been able to make my body respond since the explosion. It didn't matter.

The cool hand touched my cheek again. It was such a loving touch, so full of comfort. Feather-light locks of hair tickled my cheek. She leaned down and the scent of jasmine flooded my senses. Opening my eyes, I looked up to see…

Sunset.

The dream replayed in my mind like a movie on repeat as I walked through the concourse. I couldn't shake it no matter what I tried to focus on.

Heading back usually hyped me up. It was the only time I felt truly happy.

Until now.

It was all fucked up.

For almost twenty years, I'd gone to airports like this one, handed over my ID and bag, and waited for the long flight to the other side of the globe. I didn't overthink it. It was my plan. It was exactly what I wanted to do. I went after the action. I lived to be in the zone. It was what I was made for.

Until now.

God dammit.

Metal benches lined the interior of the ticketing area. I stopped and sat on one, placing my pack between my feet. Again the dream replayed in my head, again I felt my body's visceral reaction to her touch. The intense longing when I saw her eyes that jolted me awake and left me reaching for her in the darkness.

Placing my head in my hands, I rubbed my forehead. Everything had changed, and it was time I got my head out of my ass.

* * *

Mariska

The Jungle Gym was only open a few hours on Sunday, and for the first time, I was so glad. Usually, I enjoyed spending the afternoon visiting with the gang, trying new smoothie recipes. None of it made me happy anymore.

Patrick and Elaine had decided to get married in Montana. They wanted to have their wedding at the ranch house and the reception at the Sip-n-Dip. Patrick had sent plane tickets for all of us.

Kenny was working on vacation times and travel arrangements for Slayde to leave the state. I was working on my excuses.

Elaine insisted I be one of her bridesmaids, but I couldn't do it. Even though I knew Stuart had left the country, I couldn't go back there for a wedding. The pain of my last night with him still throbbed in my chest like ice water hitting a sore tooth.

"She's planning the whole thing Boho Ranch." Kenny was inside the bar with me leaning against the counter. "She wants you to be there as creative consultant."

"You're just as creative as I am." My friend had been lobbying for this since the day Patrick's email about plane tickets arrived.

"We've never taken a girls' trip. We might never get this chance again!"

"Don't be such a pessimist. I might win the lottery."

Her eyes narrowed, but I wasn't feeling as happy as my tone suggested. I wanted to go home and paint.

The vibrant yellow, orange, and red abstract I'd made had turned out really well. I called it "Fire in the Desert," and I wanted to see what new feelings I might exorcize with a vigorous night of art-therapy. Last night I'd stretched a new canvass, and I was thinking of an impressionist version of the colt.

Bill's musings about gentling him and spending time with him, teaching him and still being thrown swirled in my head like a metaphor.

"Patrick's already reserved four tickets. You have one more week. Just think about it."

I was tired of arguing, so I only nodded. A quick glance at the clock told me it was three forty-five. The club closed in fifteen minutes. I'd already cleaned all the blenders and wiped down the counters.

"Would you mind covering for me? I'd really like to cut out early."

"Only if you promise to think about it." Kenny stepped forward and kissed my cheek.

"I promise," I sighed, rolling my eyes.

Sliding my lanyard into my cubby, I ducked under the counter and headed for the door.

* * *

Deep blues, olive greens and brown. Tonight I started with as much of the landscape as I could remember. A lot of it had been brown prairie grass, but when Elaine and I had driven to town, I'd seen more variety — silver spruce trees, red rock formations, soaring waterfalls. We were there in the winter, but I used my imagination to see what it might be like in the spring or summer.

A square butte west of the city formed a backdrop for

the brown of wild horses running across the prairie. It was all so open and vast under the sky. I had to capture the orange arc of clouds over the Chinook.

Again, my hair was up in a high ponytail, but tonight I wore the grey Henley I'd borrowed from Stuart. His scent was fading on it, and I wished I'd thought to snoop in his toiletries bag for whatever cologne this was. Sure it was torture, but I was an artist. Suffering was good for my art.

I decided to have a glass of wine. It was Sunday, technically a work night, but our hours at the gym allowed me to sleep in, and I'd had to work every day but Friday. I pulled out a bottle of Chardonnay and had just twisted off the cap when someone knocked on my door.

My heart flew into a panic. I'd left my phone in the other room, and Kenny always texted before she came over. She knew I didn't like opening the door at night when I wasn't expecting visitors.

I crept through my living area, which really was getting too crowded with books. I needed to get an eReader, but I still liked to hold them and smell them.

The knock came again, and I jumped. Carefully, I rose on my tiptoes to look through the peep hole, and my heart stopped working.

His back was turned as he seemed to scan the parking lot, but I easily recognized those broad shoulders. The canvass jacket I knew as well as the short, dark hair that I loved to slide my fingers through. He turned back, and the sight of his eyes was like warm honey poured through my veins.

Stuart Knight stood outside my door. He wasn't overseas.

As much as I wanted to throw it open, I quickly assessed my wardrobe. My hair was up in a ponytail, and of course, I had flecks of blue paint in the tips. I seemed to remember touching my cheek with the brush at some point, so I knew there was a streak of green there. You'd think I was freaking Jackson Pollock the way I threw paint all over myself.

Another loud knock, and I let out a little shriek when I jumped.

"Mariska?" His low voice clutched my insides through the wooden barrier.

There was no hiding now. I'd have to see him looking like this. I didn't have time to change or clean up.

Turning the lock, I slowly opened the door, wishing all this had come ten minutes from now. After I'd had that glass of wine. Our last telephone conversation wasn't the most confidence inspiring.

Our eyes met, and his gleamed with something. I remembered the night I'd seen a break in his wall. The night he'd said he wanted me. Those few glorious days I'd been His Mariska.

"I'm sorry I didn't call first." His eyes flickered quickly over my body and the change I saw in them scorched my insides. I hadn't worn a bra under his Henley, and other than that, I only wore black footless leggings.

"You came back." My voice was breathless. *God, how I still loved this man.*

"I never left. Are you busy?"

"I-I was just painting."

Again his expression changed. His obvious lust was replaced with something like cautious optimism. "I've wanted to see your art. Would you show it to me?"

Several obvious questions—*What are you doing here? Why aren't you in Saudi? What do you want from me?*—were forgotten for the moment. I stepped back to let him in, and like a gentleman (a good Marine?) he slipped off his boots.

"It's back here," I said, pushing the door closed and turning the deadbolt behind him.

His canvass jacket slipped down his arms, and I took it, tossing it on the sofa. He followed me through the crammed living room, the sparse kitchen where I hadn't cooked in weeks, back to the guest room I'd converted into a studio. It was always too small for a bedroom, and I never had overnight guests.

"Fire in the Desert" was leaning against the wall drying, and "Chasing the Dawn" was up on my easel. It looked better than I thought when I left it minutes ago.

"You do abstracts." His voice was quiet as he squatted in front of the blaze of orange, yellow, and red on the floor. His eyes lifted to mine, and the mixture of approval and desire made my legs weak.

"I've never been much of a portrait artist." My hands were fluttery, but I gestured to the unfinished work on the easel. "I got the idea for this one talking to your uncle about the colt."

He straightened and stepped toward it, toward me. He scanned the canvass, and I scanned him, broad shoulders under a navy tee. His dark jeans hugged his ass in the most pleasing way, but they were loose down his legs. I swooned from his handsomeness like I had since that very first day.

"What did he say?" It was as if he needed my answer before he could go on.

"I asked him how long it took to break a horse, and he said it depended on the animal." I tried to remember his exact words. "He said after all the work he'd done, brushing and gentling him, the colt would still get spooked when he saw him on his back. And he said if the colt threw him, that would spook him, too."

Stuart's body seemed to tense at my words. It was time to get back to those obvious questions.

Reaching out, I carefully touched his arm. "I thought you were in Saudi."

"You're wearing my shirt."

"It smells like you."

Before I could blink, he'd grabbed me. Emotion pulsed fiercely in my chest as he held me against the wall. His arms were under mine, and my head was in his hands. Our noses just touched, our lips a whisper apart as he spoke.

"I couldn't get on the plane." His breath came as fast as mine, and my lips throbbed for his kiss. "I thought my dream was in the desert, but it's not. It's here with you."

I held his shirt, gripping the cloth. "Stuart..." It was all I could say.

His voice was unyielding as always. "You saved me from going back to a life that was killing me. How?"

It was a valid question. All of this was useful discussion, but I wanted to kiss him. Leaning forward, the smell of cedar and Stuart filled my senses. His strong arms supported me, and my lips grazed his as I answered.

"I told you. It was a dream."

His mouth covered mine, demanding as always. He kissed me like I was a country to be liberated, and he was the Marine for the job. Tongues collided, another small noise ached from my throat. Fire sizzled under my skin.

Leaning back, he breathed in my hair, his lips grazed my ear. The scruff of his beard sent sparks down my limbs as he spoke. "I'm so sorry I didn't trust you. I'm so sorry I thought you lied."

Tears burned in my eyes. I clutched at his biceps, his strong shoulders. I wanted to feel his skin. "I should have told you everything."

His lips pulled at mine again. Hungry kisses moved my mouth over and over as he desperately quelled the pain that had nearly torn me apart. I was against the wall, and he was between my legs.

"I never gave you the chance." He kissed a line to my ear, pulling my earlobe between his teeth, giving me a little nip.

I felt his erection against my thighs, massaging between my legs. I wanted to lose the leggings, lose all our clothes and make crazy love.

"I'm covered in paint," I gasped.

He lowered me and looked around the small room. "We should give you a shower."

That white-hot memory flashed in my mind. My voice was trembling and eager when I answered him. "Okay." I was on my feet and following him across the hall to my bathroom.

"Lift your arms." He was giving orders again, and I followed gladly. I reached up, and he swept his grey Henley over my head and off.

His breath hissed when he saw me topless. Rough hands rose to cup my breasts, thumbs circled my nipples, and ecstatic desire roared through my body. How I had longed for this moment.

Lowering his caress, he touched the line of stars covering my left side. "This is new." He leaned down and lightly kissed it, tracing a sizzling trail up my hips.

"I got it for our night under the stars." He leaned up, eyes full of longing. "The night I made the wish."

"You never told me what you wished for."

"I'm still hoping it's coming true."

Cupping my cheeks, he kissed me softly this time, pulling first my top lip then my bottom between his. "I love it."

I could barely take the anticipation. "Now you." Lifting the navy shirt he wore, I smoothed it off, running my hands up and over his broad shoulders. I rested my nose against his skin, breathing deeply. "You smell so good."

Strong arms gathered me up, and once again our bodies were skin to skin. A part-groan, part-sigh rose from both of us.

He leaned down to find my mouth with his, and we were lost in a deep kiss. I could only follow along wherever he planned to take me. This reunion was so unexpected and sweet and incredibly welcome, it ached in my bones.

Releasing me, he stepped back to turn on the shower. Water roared against the back wall. I was still clutched against his firm torso, and his light sprinkling of chest hair teased my nipples. I was so wet. I dropped my face against his shoulder, pressing my lips to his skin, touching it with my tongue.

We had to talk about what happened, what brought him here, but for now I didn't want to look my gift horse in the mouth. I wanted to hold him, love him, let him surround me, take away all the pain. *I'm feeling no pain now.* I smiled remembering his words.

"What?" His eyes were back on me.

"I was thinking of our last shower. We got dirty while getting clean."

"I'd like to get dirtier."

Passion bubbled in my veins in the most pleasing way as he led me into the small, rectangular space. He was behind me under the steaming hot water, and his hands slipped up my torso. Strong hands cupped my breasts while long fingers pinched the tight tips.

Dropping my head back on his shoulder, I let out a moan. His erection was at my back now, and I wanted him inside me. In one fluid motion he turned us. "Put your hands on the wall."

I did as he said, and he spread my legs apart with his knee. Before I could think, he was inside me. "Oh, yes!" I panted, my thighs humming with the intensity.

He had me around the waist as he started to rock. Slowly at first, he filled me, stretching me, massaging every place that had missed him so much. His hand traveled around my thigh to my clit. Two fingers circled slowly, tantalizing me. It wouldn't take much. The anticipation and surprise combined with his steamy kisses and caresses had already peaked my orgasm to the edge.

As his thrusting became more violent, sparks flushed through my torso. My insides quaked and exploded with so much pleasure, my elbows bent. I would have collapsed if he hadn't scooped me around the waist.

"Mariska." His voice was a ragged groan at my neck as he leaned us forward on his forearms, pounding into me from behind. Four more quick thrusts, and he held me clutched in his arms, my back against his chest. I could feel his body tremble as his cock pulsed inside me. He finished with another low groan.

Sliding out, he turned me slowly so that I was facing him again, my back against the cool tiles. Large hands smoothed my hair from my face as his lips trailed kisses from my brow down to my temple. The softness of his touch followed by the scuff of his jaw teased my fading orgasm. At last our mouths reunited, and he kissed me as if taking a slow drink of water.

Leaving me with my head back against the wall, he looked deep in my eyes. "I can't live without you. Please say you'll forgive me for hurting you."

My body was weak with pleasure and relief, but I reached for his face. "If you'll forgive me for not being completely honest with you."

He kissed me again, and my insides tightened with intense joy. We were back, he was back, and we were in that magical place I never wanted to leave.

"Those weeks apart, you never left my mind." He kissed my cheek holding me against his body. "You changed me. I can't leave you."

The time I threatened to leave him crossed my mind. "We've closed the circle then." His brow lined, and I continued. "I can't leave you."

"Come on." He reached back and shut off the water. "I don't know that we got very clean, but it's the thought that counts."

"All my thoughts were very dirty."

"I hope you'll tell me every one."

I took the fluffy towel he held out, rubbing it over my hypersensitive body. The tips of my hair were now damp and not covered in blue.

"Hang on," he said, eyes sparkling. I waited as he took the damp rag and rubbed it over my cheek. "Got a little green there."

"I'm as much of a paint slinger as an artist, I guess."

He scooped me into his arms again. "You're an amazing artist." A light kiss on my lips and he released me. "I love your work."

Every word sent healing pulses of joy through my heart. This was heaven, and I never wanted to leave. "You have to tell me what happened to bring you here, but are you hungry? I could order takeout."

His hands were on my waist again, thumbs circling against my skin. "Just as long as it can be delivered."

* * *

We were surrounded by Thai food boxes, and the bottle of Chardonnay sat empty on my coffee table between two half-full glasses. He only wore his jeans, so his gorgeous lined torso was on full display. The sprinkling of light hair across the top of his chest made my mouth water, and his dark hair was messy bedhead. Every time his smoky hazel eyes met mine, a little surge of electricity moved under my skin.

I was dressed only in his Henley and my panties, but I'd taken my hair out of the high ponytail and fixed it in a low braid over my shoulder. Yes, I'd done it on purpose.

"You're going to have to tell me at some point." I took a sip of wine, and my eyes danced over the rim of the glass. Again, he looked as if I'd hit him with a sledgehammer.

"Have I ever told you what your eyes do to me?" His voice was controlled, level.

A little thrill surged low in my belly. "No, please do."

He leaned forward and pulled me onto his lap in a straddle. I put my wine glass on the table.

"They're the color of sunset in Montana." My hands rested on his broad shoulders as I listened. "They remind me of the one place I can find peace. They make me believe you're my peace."

Moving my hands to his neck, I held him as I feathered kisses across his brow. "I want to be."

With a groan he pulled me closer, burying his face in my chest. I wrapped my arms around his shoulders and held on.

He turned his head to the side and his voice was husky. "It happened to me."

I was touching him, smoothing my hands over every part of his skin I could find. "What, baby?"

Lifting his chin, he looked up at me with troubled eyes. "I've had stress-dreams since the attack that sent me home. Explosions, fire, everything you described to me. Things you couldn't have known."

My eyes heated with tears, and I placed my palms on his cheeks. "My nightmares?"

His head dropped, and he ground out a reply. "I'm sorry I didn't believe you."

I kissed his temple, then I turned and placed my cheek on it. "What made you believe me? What did you dream?"

"The dream changed. It was similar, but little things were different." He moved, and I leaned back so our eyes could meet. "The pain was worse. I was in agony..."

Images of my own dream flooded my mind. The burning, him lying on the sand.

"Just when I thought I'd die there, something cool touched my cheek. Small hands held my lips and gave me water. It was you."

I didn't know what to say. I'd never had this experience before, so I'd never talked about it with my grandmother. Clearly it was significant, but why? I didn't know if we were being sent a message or if it was a sign. I wasn't sure I cared.

Tracing my finger down his arm, I felt a tinge of insecurity. "Nothing like this has ever happened to me."

"I can safely say it's never happened to me."

Not meeting his eyes, I had to ask. "What do you want to do about it?"

A finger hooked under my chin, lifting my gaze to his. "I want to make love to you. Then I want to take you back to Montana. I've heard a wedding's happening there. Two people we both know and love. After that, I'm going to take you to the cabin, and we're going to spend more time getting to know everything about each other."

The smile that started at the words "make love to you" grew bigger, spreading across my face more with every word. "I love that plan."

His eyes grew serious. "I love you, Mariska Renee Heron." A light kiss. "You loved me when I wasn't strong enough to love myself, let alone you."

"I had no choice," I smiled, kissing him back. "I saw you and my soul came to life inside me. All the reasons no one was ever good enough made sense. They weren't you."

We held each other. I was still on his lap, facing him in a straddle, the promise of lovemaking hung in the air. Leaning into his ear, I whispered. "Does your back hurt?"

"It's a little tense. I'd like a massage if you feel like it."

Standing I held my hand down. He took it and stood without putting any pressure on me. I led him to my bedroom, and he shrugged out of the jeans he wore. Nothing was underneath. My eyes ached at the site of his beautiful body.

"Lie across the bed," I said.

He swept the duvet back and lay on his stomach across my double bed. It was just like the first time, me drooling over his perfect ass, tight with those palm-sized indentions on each side. I climbed up and sat beside him, and when I placed my palm to his skin, we both exhaled. We'd been here before, and I'd dreamed of being here again so many times.

Pressing my hands against his muscles, I kneaded with my thumbs until the tension released. Working my way down, I applied pressure, loving his skin, the relaxation of his muscles.

I slid tentative fingers lightly down the arch of his back, up over the rise of his ass. Leaning forward, I feathered a kiss against the side of his derriere. His breath hitched louder, and I kissed a trail up to the top. I skipped over to the other side, and followed another trail across the other perfect cheek.

My braid slid across my shoulder and fell across his back, and he groaned. It was a deep, rumbling sound, and satisfaction unfurled in my tummy. Parting my lips, I took a little bite of that luscious bum, and before I could blink, large hands gripped my arms, moving me up to his body.

"That's enough." I was under him and his strong mouth claimed mine. He was rough and demanding, but now so was I.

I threaded my fingers in his hair and pulled, claiming his in return, biting his lip. He groaned and tightened his hold on my arms. He grew rougher, and the excitement in me grew as well.

"Roll over," he ordered.

I turned onto my stomach, and he spread my legs. "Ass up."

Arching my back, I tingled with the thought he could see all of me until with one swift plunge, he was deep inside.

"Oh!" My voice was muffled in the pillows. He caught my arms and held them crossed over my back, using them for leverage as he slammed into me harder.

My knees slid apart until my clit was pressed between the mattress and his relentless thrusting. It was primitive and erotic, and I could feel the orgasm tightening every muscle in my core. He kept going, and I could sense he was barely holding on.

"Come on, baby." The groan in his voice sent shudders through my thighs, and with two more hard scrubs the tingling friction assaulting my clit exploded in a blinding orgasm radiating down through both my legs. I cried out his name as my body shook with the force of it, and at once he let go, pulsing his own release as I trembled through the aftershocks.

Lying beside me, he gathered my limp body against his chest. "You are the most amazing woman." He kissed my eyes, my brow, my nose, my lips. "I plan to spend the rest of my life exploring your beautiful body..." (another kiss) "your soul..." (another kiss) "your gifts..." (another kiss) "and every other part of you."

I couldn't help a laugh. "I love you Stuart William Knight."

He paused, smoothing his palm back over my forehead. "Mariska." So much emotion filled his voice, it ached joy in my chest. "Be sure to thank your soul for wanting my broken one."

"You weren't broken. You only needed a safe place to run free."

"To serve and protect." A sly twinkle sparked his eye. "Can I rock your gypsy soul?"

Our lips combined, mixing all the wonder of what we had in a breathless kiss. "You already have."

The end.

EPILOGUE: A WEDDING

Elaine

Sheer black lace stretched over my breasts, fastened by a little tie behind my neck. It was the top half of a one-piece lingerie set. The bottom was a thong that had high legs and a sheer-lace front. I stepped out of the bathroom into our master suite, and a little thrill moved through my stomach as Patrick's eyes immediately widened.

"Damn," he groaned, pushing himself up straighter against the headboard.

I could've said the same. My fiancé was stripped down to his boxer briefs, putting his toned chest, broad shoulders, and ripped arms on full display. Patrick had a gorgeous body.

Instead I gave him a sassy smile and a wink. "You like this, cowboy?" I turned, stopping so my back was to him, and looked over my shoulder. My blonde hair swept to the front, giving him the full view.

"Shit, yeah." The predatory tone in his voice tightened every muscle in my body, and I had to stay focused or I'd give in to the growing wetness between my thighs.

"It's only the beginning." I quickly dashed into the bathroom and closed the door, slipping off the black one-piece. Up next was my favorite.

A cream-satin strapless bra that tied in a bow at the back. I pulled it tight so it pushed my breasts up into nice rounds at the top. The bottom was lace-overlying cream satin with little ties on each side. Two pulls and it was gone.

I stepped out, and laughed as another low groan met my ears. "You're killing me, babe. Can I please fuck you now?"

I pranced over to the chair where his pale-straw cowboy hat was tossed. Picking it up, I put it on my head then I leaned forward on the bed, pressing my arms against each side of the bra so my breasts nearly spilled over.

"You're not enjoying the show?" I made a little pout and instantly strong arms went around my waist, dragging me against his chest to the headboard.

"I love it," he growled, burying his face in the side of my hair and kissing my neck.

"Patrick! Wait! I've got one more!"

His arms relaxed, and I slipped of his lap, giving his erection a little stroke in the process.

"Why are you torturing me like this?" He was grinning, but that bad boy sparkle was in his eye. I was torturing myself a little, truth be told, but it was so sweet.

"One of these will be under my dress Saturday." I did a little swish as I returned to the bathroom. "You can be wondering which one while we say our vows."

"Shortest service in the history of weddings."

I jumped into the bathroom giggling. This last one was just for fun. Black lace boyshorts, zero bra. I stepped into my high-heeled cowboy boots and walked out, one arm draped over my breasts.

His eyes darkened, and I knew this was as far as we'd go. Turning my back, I leaned forward to poke the fire, arching my back and wagging my ass. "I'll just make sure this doesn't go out."

"Hmm..." His low rumble met my ears, and when I looked over my shoulders, the boxers were gone. His erection rose in his hand, and he made slow passes up and over it.

Heat flooded my core, and I stood, walking slowly toward him, watching the motion of his hand working his cock. It was absolutely erotic.

My black satin robe was at the foot of the bed, and I took the belt, sliding it out of the loops. It was a long, black sash in my hand. "I can imagine several uses for this."

I was beside him now, and his low voice sizzled under my skin. "I can think of several uses for your beautiful mouth."

The sash slipped to the floor, and I crawled up between his legs, allowing the tips of my nipples to brush his thighs. The light hairs tingled them and made me shiver. Kissing his hand, I peeled back his fingers, replacing them with my tongue. His head dropped back as I took the mushroom tip in my mouth, giving him a hard suck.

"Fuck." He groaned, and I caught the base with my hand and pumped it up and down.

Another hard suck, and I let him pop out, sliding my tongue around the tip. I could taste that he was close. Dipping my head, I pressed my lips to his scrotum and sucked. His hips jerked, and I had to glance up to see if he'd finished. Our eyes met, and he motioned for me to come up.

"I can't hold on much longer." He took my arm. "Lie on your back."

Rolling over, I sighed as he gripped the sides of my panties. I still had my boots on, so they wouldn't go down.

"I'll get you a new pair." It was the last thing I heard before the stinging rip of fabric tore across my ass.

"Oh, shit!" I cried out.

245

My own orgasm sparkled just below the surface, and his sudden roughness amped it up even more. I was a goner when he caught my hips and pulled me to his mouth. "Give me that pussy."

"Patrick! Oh!" Electricity roared through my legs as his tongue followed a slow, insistent trail around my clit and down to my wet opening, taking a dip then heading back up to complete the circle. My back arched, and I moaned as he gave me a forceful suck, driving two fingers deep inside me.

I was trembling on the edge, and he rose to position his tip at my entrance. Gripping the headboard, he drove in with a forceful thrust that left me screaming his name. A large hand covered my mouth, and he dropped to his elbows beside my face still rocking me.

"Shh," he laugh-groaned, kissing my ear. "You don't want to wake my mother."

"Ahh!" I couldn't stop jerking my hips. His cock massaged my clit, stretching every part of me in the most delicious way.

"She's on the other side of the house," I gasped.

He caught my earlobe between his teeth, and I jerked again. "You're wailing like a banshee." His voice was thick, and he pushed harder into me.

Eyes squinted shut, my entire body shook as waves of pleasure exploded through my midsection. "Oh, god!" I cried out again, and I felt him coming with me.

His voice grew ragged, and his thrusting more frantic. Two more hard pushes, and he stilled, pulsing inside me, making low noises as he gasped. We held each other a moment longer, then he rolled onto his back, staring at the ceiling as his chest rapidly rose and fell. I curled to him, and strong arms hugged my shoulders.

"God, you're amazing." My ear tickled with the vibration of his voice, and I smiled, kissing his salty skin.

"I don't think I'll ever get enough of you."

"So you liked my little fashion show?"

He rolled me onto my back, hovering over my face. "I loved it. Sorry about that last pair of panties."

Holding his cheeks, I rose up to kiss him deeply, shoving my tongue into his mouth and chasing his. He leaned into it, pressing my head into the pillow and devouring me.

We broke apart and his lips moved to my cheek, then to my ear. "I'm looking forward to using that belt."

A little thrill skated across my stomach. "I've been practicing my knots."

"I've been thinking about blindfolds." His gorgeous hazel eyes twinkled at mine, and I couldn't resist.

Wrapping my arms around his neck, I hugged him as tightly as I could. "I can't wait to be Mrs. Patrick Knight."

He kissed my shoulder. "I've been trying to make it happen since the day Lane was born. What finally won you over?"

"All of it." His brow lined. "Having Lane, how things have gone with Kenny, being here, seeing your mom and Bill…"

"Mom and Bill?"

"They're clearly in love, and yet they're still apart. It made me see I don't want to waste any more time starting our life together."

"I agree." His lips trailed across my jaw, and I traced my fingers along the lines of his back.

"Plus I love your mom. I'm ready to join the family."

His head rose, and those naughty eyes caught mine. "You're saying these things, but I know you better. It was all the cowboy sex. Admit it."

Laughter burst from my throat, and I hugged him again. "It's true! That day in the loft when I rode you like a bronco. It was the moment I knew. This was the place."

247

"Damn, that was hot." I felt him stirring against my thigh. "You ready to ride me again? Your boots are still on."

"Maybe I'll rope you first."

He was up and moving down my body, pausing at my breasts to pull a nipple into his mouth. A hard pull and a little bite, and I moaned. Heat rose between my legs. His mouth continued lower to my ribs, lightly tickling me, sending sparkles shimmering under my skin.

"I'm going to tie you like a calf and fuck you senseless." He flipped me onto my stomach and I squealed. "Please do!"

He held my ankles, spreading my thighs and dragging me onto his cock from behind. It was rough and demanding, and I pushed against the mattress. He dropped beside me on the bed kissing a line up the middle of my back. It sent excruciating waves of pleasure all the way up my scalp. Then he rolled us to the side, his chest at my back, and grabbed my thigh, lifting me open.

"Patrick!" In this position he was so deep, pumping fast and hard. His mouth moved from my shoulder up my neck.

"Think I can make you sore tomorrow?"

"Oh! Yes, don't stop!" I moaned as he hit deeper, bucking me with all his force.

I wailed and he spoke in my ear, "Come on." Hard thrusting, his fingers circled my clit fast. Sparks of light broke out behind my closed eyes. "Come for me."

Two more pushes, and my orgasm shot me to the moon. I jerked and arched, doing everything I could to move even though he had me pinned against his body by the strong arm across my breasts.

"Yes, yes..." My voice was ragged as the trembling continued in my thighs. He kept pumping, still going strong. I was limp like a rag doll as he finished with a shout, pulsing into me.

Still inside, he held me spooned against his chest. My eyes were squeezed closed as the afterglow washed over us like warm water. Our breathing descended together, back to this planet, and his hand spread over my stomach.

"Nope. Never enough."

A satisfied smile curled my lips and I laced our fingers together. He kissed my shoulder softly, and I drifted to sleep wrapped up in the man I loved.

* * *

The first person in my arms when the Yukon XL pulled up to the ranch was Lane. "Mommy!" I laughed and kissed his neck, his ear, his head, every spot I could get to as his little body wiggled in my arms.

Kenny and Slayde were next out of the truck, followed by...

"Mariska!" I jumped and released my wiggly little boy, dashing forward to catch Kenny and her in a big hug. "You came! Kenny said you wouldn't!"

Her pretty cheeks flushed, and she looked down. "Yeah, I wasn't going to, but..."

My mouth dropped open when Stuart opened the driver's side door and stepped out.

"Hey, sis." His low voice carried a note of something new... Happiness.

I let out a little squeal and ran to hug him. "I'm so glad you're here! You didn't leave!" I couldn't help a sigh. "Everything's perfect now."

"So after two years of putting him off, you decided to marry my little brother in two weeks?" He smiled, putting an arm around Mariska's waist. She flushed, and it was such a handsome sight.

"It's all this freezing fresh air, I guess." Stepping toward the vehicle, I grabbed Lane's bags. "Get these inside before we turn into icicles!"

Mariska picked up her duffel, but Stuart took it from her. "I can get this. Head inside with the girls."

She blinked up at him, and just like that, he leaned forward and kissed her. Another sigh pushed through my chest, and I twirled on my heel, the biggest grin splitting my cheeks as I hustled inside.

Kenny and Slayde had beat us in with our little boy. Patrick had Lane up on his shoulders and was running around the living room as his son squealed and laughed. Sylvia chased them waving her hands and looking frantic.

"Patrick!" She cried. "You're going to hit his head! Oh! You're going to drop him!"

I rushed over to save her from a heart attack. "Give him to me."

His daddy stopped, and Lane slid down complaining into my arms. Kenny emerged from the hall where we were staying. Slayde followed, hands in his pockets, hanging back.

"Do we just pick a room that's empty?" She asked, and Lane kicked out of my arms. I put him down, and he scampered into hers.

"Mommy, Daddy a bronco!"

My eyes cut to Patrick's, and his were dancing. Kenny didn't miss a bit of it.

"I don't even want to know how that got started."

"That goes double for me!" Sylvia cried going to her. "Hand me my grandson."

He went meekly into his grandmother's arms, and I answered Kenny in the affirmative. Mariska stood behind the sofa where Patrick flopped, and the sounds of Stuart banging in the door interrupted everything.

"Shit!" Patrick jumped up. "I can help with that."

His mother's lips pursed, but I shook my head. "We thought you two could stay on the wing with us and Lane."

"We'll alternate who he sleeps with each night."

"Right!" I nodded. "Mariska, you and Stuart can stay on that wing with Derek, Melissa, and Dex."

Stuart stepped up behind her and rested his hands on her shoulders. "Sounds like a good setup. When are they getting in?"

"Thursday."

"Even better."

Mariska blushed, but I couldn't resist. "That gives you two nights to have all the loud monkey sex you want."

"Lainey!" Mariska gasped, but I jumped forward catching her hand.

"Please. Sylvia's thrilled you finally tamed her lost boy. The only thing missing is Amy." The youngest member of the Knight clan was in Europe, but she'd made it known loud and clear she was pissed I was marrying her favorite brother without her being here. "Well, and my dad and older brothers..."

My impulsive optimism dimmed, but Patrick smoothed his hands over my waist. "They'll be all right. We can reenact it for them."

Spinning around, I kissed his cheek, giving him a tight squeeze for restoring my joy. Then I pulled Mariska up. "We have to get busy. I've made three pin boards of wedding ideas. I want the whole thing to be Western Boho, and if anyone can help me with that, it's you!"

A quick glance back at Stuart was all she managed before the three of us were crammed around Bill's iMac going through dresses.

"It's going to be way too cold for these," Kenny complained, examining the photos of light-rayon, assorted-color gypsy dresses. "They're all spaghetti straps and thigh high."

"Mine's asymmetrical." I pinched her leg, garnering a squeal.

"They're really beautiful." Mariska gave me a worried look. "Kenny's right, though. It's fourteen degrees outside."

"We'll just stay inside then, and Bill can make a huge fire in the hearth."

"Whatever you want." Kenny shrugged, leaning back and propping her black Doc Marten on my chair. "It's your big day. What will the guys wear?"

"Cowboy boots and hats, of course, with jeans, button-downs or Henleys…"

"I love it!" Mariska, sighed.

"You're going to have to trade in the stilettos for boots," I winked at Kenny. "But they can be high heel boots."

"I've always wanted a pair of those."

"Good, because I have a pair coming overnight delivery."

"Show me!"

We spent the rest of the evening making calls and express-ordering hair scarves, silk flowers, and pastel woolen knee-highs for us to wear with our boots and short dresses. Despite the season, or because of it, we got guaranteed delivery by Saturday, when the fairytale would come true.

* * *

Two Chinook winds so close together in the same year never happened. As in *never*, Bill said. Sylvia blamed

Global Climate Change, but I knew it was my wish on a shooting star come true.

The day dawned frigid then everything changed. A strong wind blew in from the west, and in an hour the snow was gone. Temperatures had risen into the fifties, and we moved everything outside to the barn.

Bill secured a local minister, who was on stand-by in case we got a heavy overnight snowstorm, in which case we'd planned to have the ceremony, and make it official the next time we could make it to town.

The Impossible Chinook changed everything.

Waiting in the living room for the minutes to count down, Sylvia stepped forward. "Elaine," she said, catching my hand. "This is for you."

From her pocket, she produced a delicate silver bangle with a dark-blue Cabochon like the necklace she'd worn her first night here.

"Oh!" I gasped as she slipped it onto my wrist. It accented the ivory chiffon dress I wore perfectly. "It's so beautiful!"

"Patrick's grandmother gave it to me on my wedding day, so I'm passing it down to you." She smiled, smoothing my hair over my shoulder. It extended just to the top of my eyelet bodice. "Now you have something old and blue."

"I loaned her my favorite elephant ring!" Mariska stepped forward, and I hugged her, imagining the day when we'd be sisters.

"And here's the new." Kenny handed me a Tiffany-blue box tied with a white-satin bow.

"Kenny!" My eyes went round. "How?"

"Don't worry about that part." Melissa stepped forward, holding her shoulders and smiling. "It's part wedding gift, part thank you gift for being such an amazing mom to my little boy."

I slid the white ribbon away and lifted the lid. Inside was a silver necklace with two heart pendants. The word "Mom" was printed on one. My eyes flooded, and we hugged each other.

"It's been a long road," I whispered, squeezing her.

"You ladies ready?" Bill stuck his head in the door, and I straightened. He wore brown slacks and a cream-colored button down with a brown tie. His thick grey hair was combed back, and when he saw Sylvia, he passed a hand over his mouth under his mustache. Stuart was behind him, wearing dark jeans, a light-green button down, and a maroon tie.

Kenny whistled loudly, Mariska cleared her throat, and my tears gave way to laughter. "You guys sure clean up good!"

Melissa stepped forward touching away the tears under my eyes with a handkerchief. "You look amazing." As my maid of honor, she handed me a bouquet of wild flowers. "Ready?"

I nodded and moved to the back of the line where Bill took my arm. "Derek and Slayde are on their way."

He was still speaking when the door opened and Derek walked in, stunning as usual in grey slacks and a light-blue button down with a navy tie. His dark hair was away from his face, just grazing the top of his collar, and his blue eyes went straight to Melissa. They stayed on her until he was at her side, and I was pretty sure I saw my best friend shiver.

Slayde was with Kenny, dressed in a brown shirt open at the neck, Wranglers, and boots. Kenny caught his shirtfront and kissed him hard. It was perfect.

"Mom?" Stuart held his arm for her.

She caught it and rubbed his bicep. "So glad you're here with us."

He squeezed her hand, and glanced at Mariska. "I'll be back for you."

She smiled as if he were a wonderful dream. "Okay."

Bill and I exchanged a knowing glance. He leaned into my ear. "Wedding number two, coming right up."

I squeezed his arm, and it seemed like no time passed before his nephew was back for her, leading us from the house to the barn.

The flower-entwined arbor we'd planned for the living room was arranged at the end of the alley, and Patrick stood near the minister, waiting. Holding his hand, Lane wore jeans and cowboy boots, a plaid-flannel shirt with a little vest, and the cutest cowboy hat.

He called out, "Mommy!" when he saw me, and everyone laughed.

Patrick captured my attention, though. He was gorgeous in dark jeans and a tan button down. His collar was open as well, and his hazel eyes glowed with love. My breath caught, and tears filled my eyes. Bill stopped and as we faced each other, my heart beat so hard, I didn't even hear Bill present me to him.

Patrick reached for me, and I took his arm, scooting into his side, unable to take my eyes off him.

"I've guessed which ones," he whispered.

My brow lined for a moment, until I knew what he meant. My underwear! I started to laugh, but the minister was waiting on me.

Stammering "I do!" I looked up at him.

He smiled kindly. "We're not quite at that part yet. It's time for the vows."

Everyone laughed as I blushed bright red, and Patrick turned to face me, clearing his throat. We'd written our own.

"Elaine Rose Merritt, I have to start by thanking God for bringing you into my life, even if I almost ruined everything by being an ass before I met you."

Soft laughter crossed the barn, and he continued.

"You are the sexiest, most beautiful woman, and you don't just make me happy, you complete me. You've made all my dreams come true. You're an amazing mother, an unbelievable lover, and I can't think of anyone I'd rather spend my life with. I promise to spend every day loving you, taking care of you, and looking for new ways to make you make that little sound you make…"

His eyes twinkled, and I felt the heat rising in my cheeks.

"You know the one? When you—"

"Patrick." I cut him off, and everyone laughed again.

He stepped forward and said low against my cheek. "I'm ready to kiss you now."

The minister cleared his throat. "Miss Merritt?"

My lips pressed into a smile, and it was my turn to go.

"Patrick James Knight…" I took a deep breath to recollect my thoughts as his eyes burned my clothes off. "The first time I saw you in Arizona, I knew you were something special. Only, I thought it would just be a week-long special."

A little hoot from the audience made me grin. "I'm so glad you proved me wrong. I'm so glad I couldn't live without you. You make me laugh, you've made me cry…" His brow lined, but I pushed on. "You make me swoon, and you are truly my dream guy. Thanks for making my life exciting and fun. I promise to do all I can to keep you smiling, to love you, and to take care of you until the day I die."

Patrick's expression turned serious, and as the minister finished our vows, it was like the two of us were lost in our own special place of the declarations we'd made and the promises we'd given. After what felt like an eternity, we heard the words we'd been waiting for: You may kiss the bride.

I was in his arms before the sentence was through, and for a moment, he touched my cheek. "My wife." I held his shoulders, and his lips covered mine, pushing them apart, finding my tongue. I held his neck as he lifted me, still lip-locked. Applause broke through our haze followed by Lane's little exasperated voice.

"Mommy, Daddy kissing again."

Our kiss broke with our laugh, and we turned to face our friends and witnesses as we were declared Mr. and Mrs. Patrick Knight. Guitar music began, and everyone headed toward the back of the barn where tables were filled with finger foods and casseroles. Beer and wine were on hand, and a photographer moved through the group snapping photos. Later this evening, Bill and Sylvia had offered to stay home with Lane and Dex while the rest of us continued the celebration at the Sip-N-Dip in town.

Dex wore a matching little cowboy outfit like Lane's, complete with boots and a tiny hat, and he was adorable riding around on Derek's arm.

"The wedding was gorgeous," Melissa said, hugging me tightly. "I can't wait for spring."

"Yours will be just as beautiful." I kissed her head and looked around as our loved ones laughed and celebrated with us.

"I'm only making one change," she said, leaning her head against mine. Derek had wandered over to where Stuart stood with Mariska, and Lane dragged Patrick to where they stood with Kenny and Slayde embracing beside them.

"What?" I asked absently, thinking what a great-looking group.

"I'm insisting all the guys be in uniform."

"Oh my god." I clutched her arm, my eyes round. "Hot."

"I know, right?" We laughed and she pulled me. Derek motioned for us to come there, and we ran over to them. Patrick's arm was around my waist, and it was exactly what I'd wished for. A Christmas miracle.

* * *

A Little Later...

Patrick

My hands slid up Elaine's dress, smoothing her narrow thighs. "I've been counting the minutes until I could do this."

She held my shoulders, dropping her head forward to kiss me. I was on my knees in front of her, and silky blonde hair spilled around us like a curtain. Two pulls, and her cream-satin panties were gone.

"I love these underwear," I groaned, as her bare pussy was unveiled before me.

"You don't have to tear them—" she started, but it was cut off by a gasp as I sunk my tongue between her luscious folds. "Patrick..." she moaned.

I held her soft ass as I circled her clit, feeling the change in her muscles. Her breathing picked up, and my fly grew tight. We were in the loft in the back of the barn as our friends and family continued to celebrate below. The first glimpse I got of an opening, I'd dragged her away and up here.

Her thighs began to quiver, and I knew she was getting close. Sliding two fingers inside, my semi went to solid hard-on.

"You're so wet," I murmured, kissing the crease of her leg. She whimpered, and I made short work of getting my pants open and down so she could drop onto me.

Her dress was bunched around her waist, but it had little buttons on the front. She quickly unfastened them, and I used my nose to push her strapless bra down. Her ass was in my hands, and I was moving her up and down my shaft. It was fucking heaven.

"You are so sexy, Mrs. Knight." I leaned forward to take a hard pull on her tight nipple, and she cried out.

Her thighs tensed, and she started riding me faster. God, I loved it when she got off on me. She gripped my shoulders and set her pace, bucking on my hips and scrubbing her clit against my pelvis.

"Oh, God, Patrick!" She was coming, and her inside muscles flexing around me were getting me off just as fast.

"Fuck," I groaned, gripping her hard. She moaned again, and I moved her faster, slamming into her until she let out a broken wail and shuddered in my arms. My stomach tightened, everything went tight.

Her blonde hair covered me, the scent of flowers surrounded us, and my orgasm shot off, temporarily blinding me. I groaned against her neck, and she held me, breathing hard, her soft breasts rising and falling like beautiful pillows under my chin. I lowered my face to kiss each of them once more, and she made a little whimper.

"I love being married to you already," she sighed as I kissed her mouth, smiling.

"You just wait. That was only a quickie. It gets better."

She giggled, tracing her fingers over my cheeks. "I'm one lucky lady, Mister Knight."

"Not as lucky as I am, Mrs. Knight."

Another long kiss, and we had to get back to our wedding reception.

* * *

Derek leaned beside me against the sea-green bar that wound its way through the Sip-N-Dip Lounge. He held a scotch, and I had a vodka, smiling as we watched Melissa, Elaine, and Kenny sing along with Piano Pat. Slayde sat in a nearby booth talking to Mariska, while Stuart quietly watched. A scotch was untouched on the table in front of him, and he kept touching the beautiful girl at his side, seeming overwhelmed by her.

"Looks like the Marines lost another lifer," I laughed, taking a hit of vodka.

"Damn, that's a great setup," Derek agreed, tilting his scotch side to side. "Mariska seems good for him. He did not need to go back to Saudi."

"I couldn't agree more." My eyes traveled to my beautiful bride, smiling and singing and glowing bright gold.

Today's miracle Chinook had blown out as fast as it had blown in, dropping the temperatures back to single digits. The girls were all wrapped in heavy coats over those sexy, filmy dresses they'd worn for the ceremony. Damn, if my wife didn't know how to turn me on.

I caught Melissa blowing Derek a kiss and laughed. "Looks like you're up next."

He frowned for a moment then understood what I meant. "Oh. Yeah."

I had to give him a double take. "What the hell? I know you're not having second thoughts."

He turned back to the bar, bending his elbows as he looked into his drink. "Melissa wants us all in full dress uniform for the wedding."

"She also wants us to be on the beach. I guess we can break a few regulations for her."

"It's not like I haven't broken a lot more."

He said it under his breath, but I knew where his mind was. "Come on, man. You're not thinking about that old thing again, are you?"

"I have to tell her everything before she marries me. I have to give her the chance to walk away." He winced and took another sip. "If that's what she wants to do."

This burden had been weighing on him for a year. I'd talked myself blue in the face trying to get him to let it go. I couldn't give him the same speech again, but I also couldn't let him think the worst.

"You know what I think."

He quickly interjected. "I have to tell her. She deserves to know."

"If that's what you need to do." I took a deep inhale. "But you'd better do it now if you're going to. Don't wait until the night before the wedding."

"I won't." His voice was solemn. "If she tells me to go... I don't know if I can live without her, Patrick."

"Won't happen." I could say that with absolute certainty. "Stop borrowing that trouble, and let's celebrate. I've got a fucking kick-ass wife. And damn is she sexy."

That cut the tension. He laughed and nodded. "Good work."

I patted his shoulder and started to where the girls had joined the others in the booth near the piano. Derek was behind me, and Melissa hopped up and ran to him as we got closer.

"Have I told you how sexy you are?" She purred, kissing his lips. He held her tightly, kissing her back, and I nodded.

"That's right."

Derek took that moment to put a hand on Slayde's shoulder. The younger man tensed, his ice-blue eyes cutting to my partner. My chest tightened. Slayde had been a killer boxer during his career, and I didn't know what my partner was about to do. These guys had a beef the size of Texas between them.

"I saw the article in *USA Today* about your recognition," Derek said. "You saved the lives of every man on that freighter."

Slayde's body visibly relaxed. Kenny walked over from where she'd been with Piano Pat, and I knew she was worried. She'd seen their exchange.

"I only did what needed to be done," Slayde said.

"It was heroic," Derek continued. "I'm proud to know you. I'm sorry I attacked you the way I did."

I had to wonder if Derek's apology was prompted by our conversation at the bar.

"No hard feelings," Slayde nodded. "Thanks."

Kenny sat on his lap, wrapping her arms around his neck. He held her like a lifeline.

Elaine was on my arm, and as I surveyed the group, it was difficult to imagine any problem we couldn't solve together now that I had my Lainey by my side. Even my asshat older brother was smiling. I shook off Derek's dark mood and embraced my wife.

Life was good, and it was time to celebrate.

* * *

Curious about the secret Derek's keeping?
Keep turning for an Exclusive Sneak Peek of One to Protect*!*

Missed Patrick and Elaine's first meeting?
An Exclusive Sneak Peek of One to Keep *follows* **One to Protect!**

If you enjoyed this book by this author, please consider leaving a short, sweet review on Amazon, Barnes & Noble, and/or Goodreads!

Reviews help your favorite authors reach new readers, have advertising opportunities, and sell more books!

* * *

Don't miss a single SALE or NEW RELEASE by Tia Louise!

Get exclusive TEXT UPDATES straight to your phone or mobile device:

>> Text "TiaLouise" to 77948 Now! <<

(Max 6 messages per month; **HELP for help; STOP to cancel**; Text and Data rates may apply. Privacy policy available, allnightreads@gmail.com)

~ AND/OR ~

Sign up for the New Release Mailing list today! **(http://eepurl.com/Lcmv1)***

*Please add **allnightreads@gmail.com** to your contacts so it doesn't bounce to spam!

* * *

Bonus Content

-Hear some of the music that inspired *One to Leave* on Spotify!

-See the images that inspired *One to Leave* on Pinterest!

-Keep up with the guys on their Facebook Page: *The Alexander-Knight Files*! (**https://www.facebook.com/pages/Alexander-Knight-Files/1446875125542823**)

* * *

Thank you for reading!

Dear Reader,

I hope you enjoyed *One to Leave*! Stuart's character has lurked in the background of the One to Hold series since the first novel, and it was time for him to come out and meet everybody!

Originally, I had a different idea for how this love story would go, but when Mariska joined the series in *One to Love*, I knew she was the free spirit who could steal that wounded soldier's heart.

Up next, I'll be diving back into the problem hanging over Derek's head. He's been keeping secrets again, and Melissa might not be so ready to let him off the hook this time. We'll see if their love is strong enough to survive the bombshell and if Derek will have to go away for good. *One to Save* is due out Spring 2015!

I hope you'll let me know what you think of my books! Email me your thoughts, feedback, what you liked — even what you didn't like! I really like hearing from readers.

You can write to me at **allnightreads@gmail.com** or visit me on Facebook at **https://www.facebook.com/AuthorTiaLouise**!

Finally, if you enjoyed my books, I hope you'll leave a short, sweet review on Amazon, Goodreads, and/or wherever you purchased this book!

Reviews help authors so much, not only in reaching new readers, but also in helping secure advertising opportunities.

Thank you again for spending time with me. I hope to hear from you soon!

Stay sexy,
<3 Tia

BOOKS BY TIA LOUISE

NOTE: All are stand-alone novels. Adult Contemporary Romance: Due to strong language and sexual content, books are not intended for readers under the age of 18.

All books are available as eBooks on Amazon, iTunes, Google Play, AllRomanceEbooks, Barnes & Noble, and Kobo. Print copies are available on Amazon, CreateSpace, Book Depository, and Barnes & Noble. Audiobooks for One to Hold, One to Keep, and One to Protect are available on Amazon, Audible.com, and Tantor.com.

One to Hold
(Derek & Melissa)

Derek Alexander is a retired Marine, ex-cop, and the top investigator in his field. Melissa Jones is a small-town girl trying to escape her troubled past.

When the two intersect in a bar in Arizona, their sexual chemistry is off the charts. But what is revealed during their "one week stand" only complicates matters.

Because she'll do everything in her power to get away from the past, but he'll do everything he can to hold her.

* * *

One to Protect
(Derek & Melissa)

When Sloan Reynolds beats criminal charges, Melissa Jones stops believing her wealthy, connected ex-husband will ever pay for what he did to her.

Derek Alexander can't accept that — a tiny silver scar won't let him forget, and as a leader in the security business, he is determined to get the man who hurt his fiancée.

Then the body of a former call girl turns up dead. She's the breakthrough Derek's been waiting for, the link to Sloan's sordid past he needs. But as usual, legal paths to justice have been covered up or erased.

Derek's ready to do whatever it takes to protect his family when his partner Patrick Knight devises a plan that changes everything.

It's a plan that involves breaking rules and taking a walk on the dark side. It goes against everything on which Alexander-Knight, LLC, is based.

And it's a plan Derek's more than ready to follow.

* * *

One to Keep
(Patrick & Elaine)

There's a new guy in town...

"Patrick Knight, single, retired Guard-turned private investigator. I was a closer. A deal maker. I looked clients in the

eye and told them I'd get their shit done. And I did..."

Patrick doesn't do "nice."
At least, not anymore.

After his fiancée cheats, he follows up with a one-night stand and a disastrous office hook-up. His business partner (Derek Alexander) sends him to the desert to get his head straight--and clean up the mess.

While there, Patrick meets Elaine, and blistering sparks fly, but she's not looking for any guy. Or a long-distance relationship.

Patrick's ready to do anything to keep her, but just when it seems he's changed her mind, the skeletons from his past life start coming back.

* * *

One to Love
(Kenny + Slayde)

Tattoos, bad boys, love...
Boxing, fame, fortune...

Loss.

It's the one thing Kenny and Slayde have in common. Until the night Fate throws them together and everything changes.

It's a story about fighting. It's about falling in love. And it's about losing everything only to find it again in the least likely place.

***

One to Leave
(Stuart & Mariska)

Some demons can't be shaken off.
Some wounds won't heal.

Until a pair of hazel eyes knocks you on your ass, and you realize it's time to stop running.

***

One to Save
(Derek & Melissa)

Against his partner's advice to keep silent, Derek decides to come clean and tell Melissa the whole story of what happened to her abusive ex-husband Sloan.

Before he can do it, however, a new threat emerges, blackmailing Star and set on putting Derek Alexander away for life. Worse, when Melissa finds out her fiancé is once again keeping secrets, she isn't happy or understanding.

Devastated, he prepares to take whatever fate hands him, but no one in the Alexander-Knight family will let him go down without a fight.

Coming Spring 2015!

***

NOTE: All of my books are part of the "Kindle Matchbook" program. If you purchased the print copy of each book from Amazon, you can get the ebook version FREE! One copy for you, one for a friend. Please visit Amazon.com for more details.

ACKNOWLEDGMENTS

No book is an island, and authors get so much support from readers, family, and friends. It would be impossible to list them all.

For starters, I have to give enormous thanks to my dear husband, who I love so much and who helps me more than I could ever express. Thank you for reading, editing, brainstorming, and being the "ass model" for Stuart (*wink*).

To my two sweet daughters who never complain when Mommy has to spend way too much time at her computer because of crazy deadlines. I love you both more than I can say.

To my beta readers, Ilona Townsel and Candice Royer—you guys are my eagle eyes! Your enthusiasm and love for these characters is indispensible. To my "Keepers" for helping me spread the word and letting me vent, specifically Chrissy Fletcher, Jackie Wright, Kimberly Hulsey, Rebecca Bennett, Crystal Mullen, Melissa Jones, Lucinda Pilsbury, Angela Craney, Pam Brooks, Karrie Puskas, Christina Badder, Elizabeth Roberts, Heather Carver, Susan Storm, Jas Dela Cruz, Tamela Gibson, Lorraine Black, Jennifer Noe, Ali Hymer, and Kendall Barnett...

To Ilona (again!) for running the Alexander-Knight Files, and last but *never* least to my right arm, A.M. Jones, (best PA evah!)...

To Steven Novak for the amazing cover design, and to Natalie and Mary at Love Between the Sheets for your marketing services. To all the author-friends I've met and who I gladly support and who support me right back. To all the book bloggers who read, review, and help me spread the word...

Finally, to you, my readers. You allow me to live my dream every day.

Thank you. <3

ABOUT THE AUTHOR

Tia Louise is a former journalist, world-traveler, and collector of beautiful men (who inspire *all* of her stories. **wink**) — turned wife, mommy, and novelist.

She lives in the center of the U.S.A. with her lovely family and one grumpy cat. There, she dreams up stories she hopes are engaging, hot, and sexy, and that cause readers rethink common public locations.

It's possible she has a slight truffle addiction.

Books by Tia Louise:

One to Hold (Derek & Melissa), 2013
One to Protect (Derek & Melissa), 2014
One to Keep (Patrick & Elaine), 2014
One to Love (Kenny & Slayde), 2014
One to Leave (Stuart & Mariska), 2014
One to Save (Derek & Melissa), **coming Spring 2015**

Amazon Author Page: **http://amzn.to/1jm2F2b**

Connect with Tia:

Facebook
Instagram & Twitter (@AuthorTLouise)
Email
Pinterest
Goodreads
Tsu.com

Keep up with the guys on their Facebook Page: *The Alexander-Knight Files.*

One to Protect
(Derek & Melissa)
© TLM Productions, 2014

"Special Skills"
Derek

Only two hours have passed since I told Melissa goodbye, and already that tightness is creeping across my chest. It's a mixture of anger and needing her in my sight where I know she's safe.

She didn't press the subject, but all weekend I could tell she wanted to know what I was working on, what was "bothering me."

Damn Nikki. If I weren't so pleased by the luscious surprise of finding Mel waiting for me half-nude in my condo Friday night, I'd reprimand her for keeping tabs on me. I don't need an office manager who doubles as my mother, or who reports my behavior back to my aunt—or my fiancée.

Melissa stayed to this morning, Monday. She's so different than when we first met. Even back then she had that confidence, but she's happy now. She's also a little rounder, with our baby on the way. It's a killer combination. I love it, and every time I'd bury my face in a new curve, she'd shriek and complain loudly. I almost couldn't let her leave.

Smiling at my desk, I look out the window at the bare winter landscape of the courtyard, thinking of her. This morning as I watched her sleep, I couldn't help breathing a little prayer of thanks. I don't pray, but with that angel in my bed, how could I not? She was curled up facing me, her delicate hand under her chin and her dark hair spread behind her on the pillow.

It was like our own world, secure and full of love. She'd stirred, and meeting her beautiful blue eyes, another quiet *thank you* echoed through my mind, only this time my memories were on our first encounters. How incredibly sexy she was giving in to me, and how breathless I'd been waiting for her to push me away. She never did.

"How long have you been awake?" She'd touched my cheek then smoothed her fingers into my hair.

"Not long." I'd caught her hand and brought her palm to my lips.

She touched my brow, smoothing it back. "You're less tense than when I got here, and now I have to leave again."

"You forget, I'm trained for periods of separation." Even as I said it, I knew nothing would make telling her goodbye easier.

She pushed up into a sitting position and moved me onto my back. "So being a Marine means you don't miss me?" Her elbows were bent, and one cheek rested on her palm.

I couldn't help laughing at her eyes narrowed in disbelief. I wasn't fooling anyone. "I miss you like the worst pain in the world. Like the desert misses rain."

"That's a song." She kissed me lightly. "And something you have experience with."

Catching her neck, I pulled her forward for a better kiss, but she arched away before I could take it further. "I want to know more about your training. What are your special skills? Besides not missing me when we're apart, of course. Can you fly a plane?"

I shook my head with a chuckle. "Sorry, darling. No piloting for me, but I think Patrick did some flying—"

"I don't believe it. You know things. Tell me!"

Pressing my lips together, my eyes moved down to her chin then to her slim neck where my heart dangled on a thin, gold chain. *Yes, I know things.*

"You keep so many secrets from me," she sighed. "What are you thinking now?"

"The things I know aren't things you want to hear about." Reaching over, I slid my palm over the curve of her waist.

She caught my cheeks in her hands and drew my gaze back. "I want to know everything about you."

For a moment I hesitated. Then my eyes were drawn to the scar, that tiny silver line that starts at the top of her forehead, just above her temple, and disappears into her hairline. "I can kill a man with my bare hands."

Our eyes met again, and I could tell she knew where my thoughts had gone.

"Have you ever done it?"

When I answered her, my voice was quiet. "I've had to kill people."

She hugged herself close against my chest. "I'm sorry. I'm not trying to bring up painful memories. We don't have to talk about it."

Wrapping my arms around her, I pulled her up slightly so I could kiss her neck. "Have I told you how amazing you are?"

A laugh bubbled in her throat. "You always say that. I'm not so amazing."

Rolling us so she was on her back, I looked down into her beautiful face. "You're smart and beautiful. You're incredibly busy, but you make time to show up here—"

"When I know you need me." Leaning down, I kissed her jaw as she continued.

"You'd do the same for me. Besides, I can work from anywhere."

"Then work from here."

"You can work anywhere, too."

Our old argument. Neither of us chased it any further—not on our last morning together. We were counting down the hours before we'd be apart again, and instead, I focused on trailing my lips down to her collarbone, past the floating heart, lower to her breasts until we were lost in our special place once more.

Now, sitting at my desk remembering, the only thing strong enough to spoil the afterglow of our weekend is this new case... and her old scar. That damn silver line, a constant reminder of what that fucker did to her. Even worse, it reminds me he's still out there walking around free.

In my line of work, I know how those assholes are. They all have some fucked up notion their victims belong to them—only them. My fist is clenched on the desktop, and I focus on relaxing it.

Sloan will pay for what he did to Mel. I intend to make sure of it, but she's right. Letting him spoil our present gives him too much power. I'd rather put that aside, in my "To Do" file, and focus on my weekend with my little family—sheer red lingerie, loads of sex, and nonstop affection—hell, I should have a shitty week more often.

Shitty week...

I turn to my computer and stare at the report on the screen. As much as Mel wants to know, I can't bring myself to tell her what I'm investigating. It's not that I want to hide my work from her. She could probably help solve half the cases on my desk. I don't want her to be afraid, and I don't have a reason to make her worry yet.

Patrick's in Wilmington watching over her for me, being the guard he is when I'm not there, and I've got tabs on Sloan. We'll know if he leaves the city or makes any threatening moves. Privately, I wish he would. Nothing would make me happier than taking him out in an act of self-defense. With his record, not a jury in the world would convict.

Nikki snaps me out of my reflections. "I'm headed to the coffee shop. Can I get you anything?" She's standing at the door in one of her usual, too-tight wrap-dresses.

It takes me back to her first day here, assigned by my aunt Sue's temp agency. I was still grieving Allison. Three years had passed since my first wife died, but time didn't matter. I didn't want a replacement wife or a girlfriend or an outlet or *anything*, and the idea that my aunt might've selected this woman for any of those reasons got under my skin like nothing else. I didn't need help getting over my wife. I had no intention of getting over her ever, and Nikki's appearance pissed me off.

The reality is, despite her former, inappropriate assertions that I needed to "get laid," she never once made a pass at me. She'd actually seemed more interested in Stuart, my first partner and Patrick's older brother.

I suppose after all this time I should put the past behind us. It doesn't make sense anymore now that I have Melissa. Everything has changed.

She's waiting, and I exhale. "No. Thank you." The departure from my usual, impatient tone makes her pause, and I continue. "You're always thoughtful, Nikki. I appreciate it."

Her mouth drops open and then quickly closes. "I'm... um... well." She stops stammering, pokes her lips out duck-face style, then nods. "Okay, then. You're welcome."

Turning on a stiletto heel, she heads out of the office, and I grin. That may be the first time I've had Nikki at a loss for words.

Back to my computer, I pull up the file I've been studying for ten days—the one that's had me so distracted. I keep telling Patrick we don't do domestic work, yet I always end up being the one old friends or acquaintances call when they need help.

That's how it started—a runaway case for a friend of a friend.

I was culling through mug shots of beat-up teens and file photos of dead girls. Patrick would say this is the worst part of our job, but truthfully, I don't mind it. I can see past the tragedy to my role here, giving people closure. I know what it's like to need it, and I don't mind helping people get it.

Then I saw *Jessica Black*. Dead.

The name was so familiar, but I couldn't place her at first. Staring at the photo, trying to think, I'd been struck by her appearance—fair complexion, petite frame, and long brunette waves. She looked a lot like Melissa—minus my fiancée's bright blue eyes.

I'd clicked on the thumbnail to read the report. Runaway. Missing five years. Arrested for prostitution several times. Found beaten once. Badly. Now deceased under mysterious circumstances.

Minutes passed as I stared at her photo. Why was she so familiar? She wasn't from Princeton. Her hometown was listed as Raleigh. Shaking my head and chalking it up to overprotectiveness spurred by her similarity to Mel, I closed the document and went back to searching for the runaway.

Nikki had interrupted me that day as well, stopping in with a BLT from the cafeteria.

"I know it's your favorite." She placed the thick sandwich in front of me with a smile. "You need to eat."

I only nodded. "Thanks."

She didn't leave. "Remember the last time I brought you lunch? It was the day Melissa showed up here so angry and unexpected. I was sure I'd never like her, but now she's the sweetest..."

Nikki continued talking, but I wasn't listening. Cold realization flashed in my brain like lightening striking a tree.

Jessica Black. It was the name on the email Melissa had put in front of me that day she visited our offices. The day she dropped a nuke on all my dreams of a life with her, when she revealed my former "mentor," her ex-husband Sloan Reynolds's secret double-life. He had high-end escorts all over the country, and Jessica Black was his first careless slip. Melissa had found it.

Nikki was still reminiscing as I spun around in my chair, shaking my computer awake. Fingers flying over the keys, I pulled up all the information I could find on the dead girl.

She'd been living in Baltimore for a year. I wondered if she followed him from wherever they'd hooked up the first time. *Why would she do that? Was it possible she was in love with him? Was it for the money? Had he promised her anything?*

It didn't matter. She'd disappeared off the police blotter from the time she arrived there until now, when she'd turned up dead.

Reasons scrolled across my brain of all the possible causes of death, but looking at her beaten face, all I could see was the photo Melissa had put in front of me all those months ago.

My instincts were on high alert. Sloan was getting antsy, and I knew what he wanted. Jessica Black might look like the real thing, but she wasn't it.

Substitutes would never fill the possession he felt. I'd followed enough of these twisted fucks to know. He was coming for Melissa, and it was just a matter of when.

All last week, I'd tracked down every misstep I could find on him, looking for anything that would stick, that would get him off the streets or at least keep him in Baltimore. I hoped to find a recent paper trail linking him to Jessica, but every lead came up cold. He was either too slick, or his people buried everything.

Even the guy I had watching Sloan in Baltimore had nothing. Jessica disappeared a week before I'd hired him, a month after Sloan had broken into Mel's beach cottage and then gotten off with a slap on the wrist. Apparently I'd moved too quickly when he waltzed into her home threatening to rape her. We had to wait until he actually committed the crime for his money and position not to matter.

The thought clenched my jaw. It was the one thing above all that caused the "stress" Nikki kept texting Melissa about. Only "stress" wasn't what I felt. What I felt was flat-out fucking rage.

The best part was when he threatened me in court with police brutality charges. I'd nearly brutalized him on the spot, but Melissa held me back. I'll never forget her face. She went still as a stone, as if it was the ending she always expected. It was like a heel-kick straight to my gut. I couldn't let her down that way.

Now all she'll say is she wants those memories left in the past. *Just let it go*, she tells me.

Fuck that. That asshole is a threat to my family, and it's clear he's dangerous. Priority 1 is devising a plan to bring him in, and it has to be something that won't ooze off his slimy back.

Snatching my phone off its base, I hit the speed-dial button.

Patrick answers, cocky as always. "Don't tell me. You've come to your senses and realized life at the beach is the only way to live."

"I need you to up the watch on Melissa."

I appreciate how his tone becomes immediately serious. "What's going on?"

"I have to finish a few details for our new Houston client, and then I'm headed your way, possibly for a while."

"This can only mean one thing. Or one asshole."

"I'm emailing a report and mug shots to you now. The name's Jessica Black." Fingers clicking on the keys, I shoot everything I've found to him. "I've exhausted all my sources here. See if you can do anything from there with it."

"Sure." He's silent for a moment, reading. "Jessica Black... Raleigh? That's just down the road. I'll rattle a few cages."

"If you do find anything, I need to know why she moved to Baltimore. What she was doing there. If she was seeing anybody and who."

"Did you tell Melissa about this?"

Pressing my lips together, I rock back in my chair. "No."

"Think that's a good idea?"

"Not really, but I'll tell her when the time is right. I don't want her to be afraid."

Sitting forward again, I pull up the report for our Houston client and read over what's still outstanding. A full system analysis is due Friday. I lost a significant portion of last week searching all the police databases for information on Miss Black.

"If I pull some extra hours, I can have Houston wrapped up and out of here by Wednesday." I start a log on my desktop of what's still outstanding, what jobs are lined up next, and what I can handle from Wilmington in case I can't get back right away.

Nikki's thank you gift can be a week off with pay, maybe a Spa Finder mini-holiday. In the middle of planning my getaway, I realize Patrick is still on the line.

"Sorry to keep you in a holding pattern."

"No worries. I can tell this is serious. Somehow. Even though you haven't told me any details."

Patrick can turn any situation into a joke, and I alternate between being pissed and being glad about it. At the moment, I'm too focused on closing the office and getting to Wilmington to lose time on it.

"I'll tell you everything when I get there. Just keep your eyes on Mel."

"She'll be as protected as the crown jewels."

It doesn't satisfy the tightness in my chest. "Maybe Elaine could invite her to stay in your guest room til Thursday."

"You're joking, right? You know Mel won't leave that cottage without a mandatory evacuation order."

Studying my notes, I wonder how many boxes I'd have to pack if I left for Wilmington today. No, I have to wrap up this damn Houston case here, where I can focus.

Frustrated, I push the laptop back on my desk. "We're professionals, dammit. Get creative."

He laughs. "What would work if you were Melissa? I'd say we invite her over for dinner and mix her drinks too strong, but she's pregnant. And even if she were still drinking, we couldn't keep the party going for three nights. Just tell her what's up."

"If I can be there on Wednesday, I will."

"Fine, but will you at least tell me what's going on? Who is Jessica Black? Or who *was*, I guess…"

"Jessica Black was a high-end hooker, an escort. She was also one of Sloan's regulars. A few years ago, she was beaten pretty badly, but she wouldn't report the guy. Then she moved to Baltimore. I don't have anything concrete, but my gut says she fell in love with him. How, I can't imagine. Now she's dead."

Silence meets my ear for several moments. When Patrick speaks again, his voice is sober, all joking gone. "And she looks a helluva lot like Melissa."

"Right."

"I know what to do."

In that one sentence I hear my partner lock into closer mode, and it's right where I want him. Patrick can be a royal fuck up when it comes to women, but he's damn good at his job. And to her credit, Elaine seems to have put an end to his screwing around.

"I've got an idea," he continues. "It's something I floated past you a while back, but now with this… Raleigh… I might have a connection to what you need."

"I didn't expect anything less. See you in a few days, and Patrick? Thanks. I owe you one."

"It's nothing more than you'd do for me."

"You know it."

* * *

Get *One to Protect* **Today!**

Amazon | **Barnes & Noble** | **iTunes** | **Google Play** | **Kobo** | **ARe**
Print copies on **Amazon** | **Createspace** | Book Depository | Barnes & Noble
Audiobooks on **Amazon** | **Tantor.com**

Exclusive Sneak Peek

One to Keep
(Patrick & Elaine)
© TLM Productions, 2014

In Scottsdale…

We sat with our bodies touching, and we sat apart, with her feet in my lap. But that never lasted long before we were back to bodies touching again. Finally, I looked around at the deserted patio and realized how late it was. I could see she was tired, and I stood, holding out my hand to help her up.

"I'll walk you back to the spa."

She nodded slowly. We didn't speak the entire way, and all I could think about were her lips and covering them with mine. I'd been thinking about it all night, but I wanted to handle this one differently — right for a change.

Stopping at the entrance, I paused, lightly cupping her cheeks. Her green eyes met mine, and she smiled. In a flash I kissed her, opening her mouth, finding her tongue for the first time. My arms moved to her waist, pulling her closer. Our bodies molded together and a little noise escaped her throat. The sound sent a blaze of desire racing through me, focusing directly below my belt. But I wasn't rushing that. Not this time.

"Goodnight." My words should have parted us, but I held her closer.

Her arms held me tightly as well, and I knew this was different from anything I'd experienced before. All of this was tectonically different.

Forcing myself to let her go, I stepped back. I couldn't look in her eyes or I'd never do what I had to do right now.

"I hope I'll see you tomorrow." An ache was in my throat.

"I'll call you." Her voice was quiet.

I turned away, and my heart, my soul, everything stayed behind as I took the first step and then the second back to the main hotel where I was staying. I'd only made it three feet when I heard her rushing up to me.

"Patrick?" It was a high whisper, and I immediately stopped, turning to face her.

She was gorgeous standing in the moonlight, the dry breeze pushing her silky hair off her shoulders. I wanted to cover those shoulders with kisses, wrap my fingers in that hair. She reached out, and I caught both her hands in mine.

"Yes?"

"I don't want you to leave me." She was breathless. "I know this is fast. It seems crazy, but... I want to spend the night in your arms."

Her delicate pink tongue touched her bottom lip, and she didn't have to ask me twice. Two steps was all it took to have her body secure against mine again. I caught her cheeks and lowered my mouth to cover her soft, beautiful lips.

Our kisses came fast, hungry, and she held my neck, my face, her hands quickly dropping to my waist, making their way under my shirt to the skin beneath. I loved her touching me. I kissed her jaw, and another noise came from her mouth. The sound killed any hesitation on my part. Breaking away, I looked around for somewhere close I could take her.

"Come with me," I said, holding her hand and leading her back the way we came. We weren't far from the smaller pool, and while it was dark and locked, I'd noticed a break in the bushes when we'd strolled past it the first time.

Leaning down, I carefully stepped through, and it took me right into the dark courtyard. Going back, Elaine was waiting and when our eyes met, she smiled. My chest rose at the sight of her, and all I could think of was sliding that dress off her body, tasting her, being inside her.

I pulled her into the small pool area and into my arms again. Our mouths collided, and I only broke contact to whip my shirt over my head. Pulling her back to me, I eased the top of her dress down, allowing her bare breasts to meet my skin, and we both sighed.

"Mmm," she breathed, moving her hands to my back and pulling me closer. The little noises coming from her with every breath had my cock straining against my zipper. I wanted to lift her against the tiled column and sink inside her right then, but I stepped back, guiding her to the cushioned lounge chair hidden in the back corner. She held the top of her dress, as if trying to pull it back up.

"No," I whispered, taking her hand away and replacing it with mine. Her breasts were heavy in my palms, and I circled my thumbs over her taut nipples. Her eyes closed and she lowered her forehead to my shoulder with a little moan. "I want these out," I said, kissing her jaw, her lips, leaning down to pull a nipple into my mouth.

Another little noise, and she kissed my neck. "What if someone sees us?"

I looked around quickly, making sure we were well hidden in the locked courtyard. "Don't worry, we're safe here."

Laying her back on the cushions, my hands slid down the smooth skin of her legs. I kissed the top of her foot, and she sighed. Traveling higher, I lifted the hem of her dress and my breath disappeared. No panties, and her skin was completely bare.

"Gorgeous," I murmured, leaning forward and kissing the inside of her thigh before sinking my tongue between her folds.

"Oh, god!" Her back arched and she cried out, clutching the sides of my head as I tasted her sweetness. I pulled her up to me, her ass in my hands, and I sucked, nipping her clit then plunging two fingers inside.

"Patrick!" she moaned as her thighs jumped. Her noises grew louder the more I kissed and sucked her. She was sweet and swollen, a juicy peach I slid my tongue through, circling as she gasped and whimpered my name. My tongue explored every opening and crease, teasing and tasting, until I felt her coming hard against me. Her hips bucked, and I lowered her fast, condom in place. One last kiss and I plunged inside.

"Fuck me," I groaned. She was hot and tight and so slippery.

Her arms wrapped around my neck as her hips continued to rock, and I thrust again, harder. Inner muscles tensed, pulling and massaging my dick so beautifully.

"Elaine," I breathed as I kissed her shoulder, holding her body, trying to slow my pace. I didn't want it to end too fast, but I was powerless against my desire for her. My stomach clenched as need took over and my thrusting grew faster.

Her body surrounded me, tightened on me, and had me shooting over the edge. My ass tensed with each push and the sound of her moans filled my senses. Everything had gone dark, and my sole focus was the mind-blowing pleasure of my cock shooting off deep between her thighs, over and over.

"Jesus," I groaned as my orgasm slowed. My lips were on her neck and her hips moved against me. Her insides spasmed, drawing me out as she held me close, bonding me to her. I couldn't imagine letting her go.

I kissed her neck, cupping her bottom in my hands. "You are so fucking amazing," I murmured, and she started to giggle.

I leaned up to cover her mouth, smiling as I kissed her, tasting her peppermint kisses as she sighed happily and giggled again.

"Stop laughing and kiss me," I murmured against her cheek.

"Oh, god, I can't help it," she gasped, a smile in her voice. "That was fucking incredible."

I kissed her again. "Have I told you it's very sexy when you swear?"

She leaned forward to kiss me hard, quickly curling her tongue with mine before moving her lips to my ear as she whispered, "As sexy as your groans when you come inside me?"

My cock was stiffening again. "Damn, woman," I said with a grin, and she hugged me, her breasts pressing against my chest. "Keep that up, and I'll have to fuck you again."

"Mmm," she purred. "Please do."

I leaned back to remove her dress completely, but she slipped to the side. I disposed of the condom, and she took my arm.

"I want you in the pool with me." Her lips grazed mine. "Now."

* * *

Get *One to Keep* **today!**

Amazon | **Barnes & Noble** | **iTunes** | **Kobo** | **ARe**
Print copies on **Amazon** | **Createspace** | Book Depository
| Barnes & Noble
Audiobooks on **Amazon** | **Tantor Media**

Made in the USA
Lexington, KY
15 January 2015